Married for a Month

"*Temptation Island* meets *Oprah* in [this] contemporary romp. . . . [T]his sweet story will delight as it provides food for thought."

—*Publishers Weekly*

"Compatibility, passion, and love are all on the line in this wonderful book. . . ."

—*Romantic Times*

Sweet Success

"The humor, warmth, and rich characterizations make this a must read."

—*Romantic Times*

"[A] sweet tale from beginning to end. . . . A delightful read."

—*Rendezvous*

"[An] exceptional book . . . filled with warmhearted laughter and wonderful relationships. . . . Delightful."

—*The Belles and Beaux of Romance*

"*Sweet Success* is a wonderfully fast-paced delight! . . . You can never go wrong with Ms. Mallery's fascinating storytelling!"

—*Romance Reviews Today*

"Witty dialogue, plenty of romantic tension, and delicious characters."

—*Publishers Weekly*

"A warm, reassuring romance."

—*Old Book Barn Gazette*

"*Sweet Success* is a treat. . . . The characters seem to jump off the page."

—*Romance Journal*

Also by Susan Mallery

Sweet Success
Married for a Month

And the *Marcelli Sisters* trilogy

The Sparkling One
The Sassy One
The Seductive One

SUSAN MALLERY

The SPARKLING ONE

POCKET STAR BOOKS
New York London Toronto Sydney Singapore

This book is a work of fiction. Names, characters, places and incidents are products of the author's imagination or are used fictitiously. Any resemblance to actual events or locales or persons, living or dead, is entirely coincidental.

An *Original* Publication of POCKET BOOKS

 A Pocket Star Book published by
POCKET BOOKS, a division of Simon & Schuster, Inc.
1230 Avenue of the Americas, New York, NY 10020

ISBN: 0-7434-4394-2

First Pocket Books printing September 2003

10 9 8 7 6 5 4 3 2 1

POCKET STAR BOOKS and colophon are registered trademarks of
Simon & Schuster, Inc.

For information regarding special discounts for bulk purchases,
please contact Simon & Schuster Special Sales at
1-800-456-6798 or business@simonandschuster.com

Designed by Melissa Isriprashad

Front cover illustration by Frank Accornero

Printed in the U.S.A.

The
SPARKLING
ONE

Prologue

ᗢ

"**Y**ou kiss it."

"No, you kiss it!"

Eight-year-old Katie Marcelli glanced from her seven-year-old twin sisters to the small green frog perched on a log in front of them. Summer sunlight shone through the trees, creating patterns on the grass and the log that made her think of fairies dancing in the breeze.

"Mommy said kissing a frog meant becoming a princess," Francesca said, sounding doubtful. "I don't want to be a princess *that* bad."

Brenna pushed back the cardboard tiara Katie had carefully cut out, then covered with glue and glitter. "Boys are stupid and so are frogs. And princes." She crossed her arms over her tattered lace-and-tulle dress-up costume and scowled.

Katie didn't like boys all that much, but princes were different. Princes rode white horses and carried girls off to beautiful castles, where they got to eat ice cream any time they wanted and never had to write thank-you notes.

But Francesca had a point. Was all that really worth kissing a frog?

"How do we know it's a magical frog?" she asked.

"In the book the frog had a little crown on its head. I don't think this one used to be a prince at all," Francesca told her.

Katie crouched down until she was eye level with the frog. It regarded her with big eyes, but didn't jump away.

Francesca was right—there wasn't any crown. No twinkling lights filled the air. But they'd never seen a frog here before—not in their special place.

She glanced around at the ring of trees and the soft, springy grass. Here she and her sisters pretended to be everything from elegant travelers taking a boat to a mysterious new land, to Cinderella, to mermaids. Sometimes their games were so elaborate they went on for days and Katie helped their Grammy M make special costumes. Today they were dressed to be fairy princesses. They'd just been deciding who was going to be kidnapped by the evil Dark Duke, when they'd spotted the frog.

"What if it's magic and it wants to be sure we believe?" Katie asked.

Brenna rolled her eyes. "Then kiss it and find out. If it's not magic, you'll get warts all over your face and have to stay in your room because you'll be so ugly."

Not a happy outcome, Katie thought. But she *really* wanted to find a handsome prince and fall in love. She wanted a big wedding, with lots of lace and flowers and a sky full of stars.

"I believe you're a prince in disguise," she whispered to the frog. "I'm going to kiss you and then wait every night for you to come find me. You'll be my one true love, and we'll live happily ever after."

She sucked in a deep breath for courage, leaned close, and pressed her lips against the frog's small face. It croaked and hopped away.

Brenna laughed while Francesca tried to hide a smile. Katie wasn't discouraged. When she'd kissed the frog, she felt . . . something. Like a tingle. Or a promise.

"You'll see," she told her sisters. "One day my prince is going to come for me. He's going to want only me, and you'll be sorry you didn't kiss the frog, too."

Francesca looked wistful, but Brenna shook her head. "You'll be waiting until you're old, because no prince is gonna show up."

"You're wrong. He will and I'll be right here."

Katie did wait. Every night for the next three years, she stood at her window and watched the sky, waiting for her prince to ride up on his white stallion and whisk her away.

In time she forgot about the frog, the kiss, and her beliefs, which was a good thing, because twenty years later there had been a lot more frogs, but not a single prince.

1

Katie Marcelli knew that with the right staff, she could organize the world. But as good help was hard to find, she contented herself with smaller projects, such as organizing closets, parties, and seminars. She owned her own business, made a decent living, and had a five-year business plan that would make a Fortune 500 CEO weep with envy. She was tough, confident, in charge.

On the outside.

On the inside her nerves were currently playing baseball in her stomach, and someone had just hit a foul ball down the third base line. She pressed a hand to her midsection and knew that fourth cup of coffee she'd gulped in her car was about to turn to acid. She was tense, wired, and pacing in high heels that might make her ankles look as slender as a gazelle's but also threatened her future ability to walk without a limp.

Oh, please, oh, please let me say just the right thing, she thought as she paused in front of a large window overlooking Century City and Beverly Hills. Opportunities like this didn't come along every day. She'd wanted to take her company to the next level, and this job was going to make it happen. All she had to do was be . . . sparkling.

The word made her smile. Ah, yes. She *was* "the Sparkling One." Bright, bubbly, like fine champagne that had—

"Ms. Marcelli? Mr. Stryker will see you now."

Katie turned toward a well-dressed fifty-something woman who held open a thick door and motioned for her to enter.

Katie stepped from the nicely carpeted hallway into sink-to-your-ankles plushness in an office the size of Rhode Island. A *corner* office, with floor-to-ceiling windows, sleek yet traditional furniture, a massive pair of leather sofas on the walls opposite the windows, and an elegantly dressed man good-looking enough to grace one of the billboards that lined Sunset Boulevard.

Zach Stryker, one of only three senior partners in the largest family law firm in the Los Angeles metropolitan area, and the youngest partner. He had a reputation for being tough, unflinching, and a hell of a negotiator. Oh, and he wasn't just a winner in the courtroom. Rumor had it he broke at least two female hearts a week.

The nerves in her stomach instantly abandoned their baseball game and began flying in a "man-alert" formation which warned her that caffeine overload was not all that far away. Perfect, she thought, because staying calm in a meeting was so overrated.

"Ms. Marcelli?" the man said, his voice low and sultry enough to make him a fortune in radio. "I'm Zach Stryker."

"Mr. Stryker. A pleasure."

She managed to cross the carpet without twisting her ankle. As he came around his pool-size desk, she transferred her briefcase from her right hand to her left, then shook with him.

Oh, great, sparks, she thought as sexual heat arced from her fingers to her chest and beyond. Wildly attractive, tall, dark, and blue-eyed. How L.A. How her luck. Wasn't she only supposed to care about the job?

A good question, she thought as she took the seat he offered in front of his desk.

Instead of circling back to his "I'm the man" leather chair, he settled next to her, then angled toward her and gave her the kind of engaging smile that could send an angry, gray-haired nun into cardiac arrest. Katie told herself she was made of sterner stuff.

"I guess we're going to throw a party together," he said.

Right. A party. The reason she was here. "Absolutely."

She opened her briefcase and pulled out a light blue folder. "Your assistant filled me in on the basics. Your law firm hosts an annual fund-raiser, with the proceeds going to several local family charities."

"Right. The event is generally coordinated by one of the partner's wives. John's wife volunteered, but then she discovered she was pregnant with twins. Her doctor didn't want her stressing herself with all the planning, so I stepped in and said I'd take care of things." He rested one ankle on his opposite knee. "Not having a wife, I needed to call in a professional. That's where you come in."

"I see." Which she did. Sort of. Yes, she'd planned parties before, but never one of this magnitude. It was black-tie, A-list, and exclusive. She would never personally have been invited, although she'd read about the fun and good times in *In Style* magazine.

No doubt he couldn't ask one of his women to do it. That would require him keeping her around for more than fifteen minutes. A circumstance that would no doubt cramp his style.

He pushed a stack of folders toward her. "Everything you need to know about the previous two parties, including the guest list. John's wife got as far as picking the hotel, so you're going to be starting from there."

Which meant practically starting from scratch. Easy enough. If she had six months and hired three or four more staff members, she could—

"The party's in May."

"Not a problem," she said, holding in a shriek. May? As in less than four months from now? As in ohmygod, now what?

He gave her the exact date, and she wrote it down on her pad.

"I know it's a lot to ask," he said.

"As you said, Mr. Stryker, I'm a professional. This is what I do."

"I'm sure you do it very well."

The intensity of his gaze unnerved her. Or maybe it was the heat he generated. She felt as if she were sitting too close to a furnace. Or maybe it was the drop in his voice, as if they were having an *intimate* conversation.

She glanced around at the impressive office, then studied his tailor-made suit, expensive shoes, and casually elegant good looks. Uh-huh. She knew the type. Zach Stryker was the kind of man used to getting what he wanted in business, and in life. Women lined up by the dozens just to throw themselves at his feet.

She might be experiencing a little attraction, but there was no way she would become one of a crowd. So she would keep her thoughts and her reactions to herself. Besides, this was business.

"If you're the kind of woman who enjoys a challenge, this is going to be exactly what you were looking for," he said.

"I do like a challenge," she admitted. "I'm not afraid to take risks or work hard. That's why I'm successful."

"I'm sure it is." He shrugged, and gave her another dazzling smile. "I'm a typical guy about party planning, so I'm not sure I'm going to be much help to you. Still, I'll do what I can." He shifted so that both feet were flat on the floor, then leaned toward her. "We'll have to work closely together."

She had the feeling they were talking about more than the party, but she wasn't going to let on.

"I appreciate your willingness to cooperate, but the bottom line is, Mr. Stryker, you're hiring me to make the party happen with a minimum of disruption to your already busy schedule."

"Call me Zach."

Call me anytime.

Fortunately she only thought the words, rather than saying them aloud. When she got home she was going to give her hormones a stern talking to. Over the years they'd quivered over any number of inappropriate men, but never one this far out of her league. Men like Zach chewed up and spit out women like her with their morning coffee.

She mentally winced at the awkward metaphor, then turned her attention back to business.

"I'll look over the plans from the previous fund-raisers," she said as she gathered the files. "I'll review the location and come up with three or four possible themes. I should be back in touch with you by the middle of next week."

"That sounds good. I've notified my assistant to get you in to see me as quickly as possible."

Talk about an invitation. "Great."

Katie snapped her briefcase closed and they both rose. Which meant they were standing close together. Too close.

Despite her potentially crippling high heels, she found herself several inches shorter than Zach. He smelled good—clean, sexy, powerful. His cobalt blue eyes crinkled slightly at the corners. She couldn't decide if they were his best feature or if she liked his mouth better.

The job, she reminded herself. His ability to pay her was by far his most appealing characteristic.

"This event is very important to my law firm, Katie," he told her. "I'm looking for a win."

Hardly a news flash. He wasn't the kind of man who looked for anything else. Still, she could reassure him.

"I don't believe in second place, either. You'll have your win."

He smiled. She felt her insides shift slightly. The sensation was nearly as disconcerting as the heat washing over her. If the man ever got tired of the law, he could make a fortune simply smiling at women.

She doubted any of his attentions were even personally directed at her. No doubt he knew he was God's gift to women and couldn't help sharing the bounty. She was smart enough not to take any of it personally.

"Thank you for your time," he said as he led the way to the door.

Katie followed, then paused when he opened it.

"I haven't done any work for your firm before," she said, because in addition to being efficient, she was wildly curious. The combination occasionally got her in trouble. "How did you find my company?"

"A recommendation." He held up his hand before she could speak. "I don't remember from whom. I have it somewhere. I'll get back to you."

"I'd appreciate that. Most of my business comes through referrals. I'd like to pass on a thank-you."

"Sure." He took a step back, then paused. "Make sure Dora has your number."

"Of course. Good-bye."

She nodded once and headed down the long corridor toward the bank of elevators by the reception desk. Dora must be his assistant. As she'd already given the woman her card, she knew Zach had her number. If he needed it. Not that he would. There was nothing more to say until she'd gotten up to speed on the fund-raiser.

Unless he wanted to call for some other reason. Seduction? The thought made her chuckle. Right. So likely to happen.

As the elevator doors opened, she stepped inside and pressed the button for the parking garage.

What very few people knew and what she took great pains to disguise was that under her expensive business suit beat the heart of a romantic. Men like Zach Stryker would never appreciate that. They wanted the new, the trendy, the easy. She had been told more than once she was anything *but* easy.

If he wanted a conquest, she wasn't his woman. She wanted hearts, flowers, and happily ever after. He wanted a cheap, sexual encounter.

As she walked out of the elevator, her hormones took great pains to remind her that it had been some time since the last emotionally significant relationship in her life and that a cheap, sexual encounter would go a long way toward smoothing some of her frazzled edges.

"Not my style," Katie said aloud and unlocked her car door.

Oh, but if it were, Zach Stryker would certainly be her man.

• • •

Katie drove out of the underground parking lot and headed west. While mid-February could be cool and rainy in Los Angeles, the past week had been perfect. California blue skies, balmy temperatures—no smog, no haze, and not an earthquake in sight. It was the kind of weather that drew tourists like flies to a pest strip, especially those suffering with snow and blizzards in their regular lives.

After crossing under the 405 freeway, Katie turned left, toward Santa Monica and her dollhouse-size bungalow. Traffic was lighter than it would be in an hour or so, as lawyers, accountants and financial types packed it in for the weekend.

Okay, yes, it was only two in the afternoon, and she really should still be working. But hey. She'd just landed a huge contract, been smiled at by one of the best-looking men in LaLa Land, and somewhere north of the city there was a cannoli with her name on it.

Inspired by the thought of dinner, she threaded her way through the growing congestion and made it home in about twenty minutes. After changing from her suit and high heels into a sleeveless dress and sandals, she grabbed a cardigan, the already-packed overnight bag, and headed for the bathroom. There she plucked pins from her hair until the shoulder-blade–length reddish-brown waves tumbled free. A scrunchy secured them at the nape of her neck. She paused long enough to slather sunscreen on every exposed inch. She might be half Italian, but she'd inherited her mother's Irish skin. Just thinking about the sun was enough to start her burning.

On her way to the front door Katie glanced at her answering machine. No flashing light announced the delight of a waiting message. Obviously Zach Stryker had manfully resisted the nearly overwhelming urge to call her and beg her to return to his office where they would make love on his designer leather sofa.

Once in the driveway she stowed her luggage in the trunk, then slipped into her Sebring. The convertible top opened, then folded neatly behind the backseat. An adjustment of her radio from NPR to a rock station completed her travel ritual. It was time to go home.

By three o'clock she'd crested the hill that marked the line between L.A. and the valley. The exit to the 101 freeway was on her right. Katie slipped into that lane, all the while singing along with a song about broken hearts and holding on.

Her car phone rang.

Katie hit a button on the console, muting her radio and activating her hands-free microphone.

"Hi," she said, speaking loudly to be heard over the wind and the sound of the other cars.

"Oh, good. You're in your car," her youngest sister, Mia, said, sounding delighted. "I was calling to make sure you're still coming home this weekend."

"I'm already on my way. How's school?"

"Good. I'm settling into my classes and getting ready for midterms."

Katie frowned as she followed the curving interchange. "Didn't you just start the quarter?"

Mia sighed dramatically. "Tell me about it. I love UCLA, but the quarter system is so tough. I barely figure out what the class is about and suddenly it's time for midterms."

"And despite the pressure, you dazzle us all with your straight A's."

"I try." Mia giggled. "Guess what? There's gonna be an announcement at dinner."

"Announcement?" Katie eased into the fast lane and

concentrated on the minivan in front of her. "Good or bad?"

The Marcelli family had a tradition of announcing news at large family gatherings. Once everyone was seated and the meal had been served, the pronouncements began. Confirmations of births, blights, and illness were made, along with surprises, some welcome, some not.

Katie quickly considered the possibility of damage to the vines, but it was only February. Everything was dormant.

"Good," Mia said with another giggle. "Very good."

"Want to give me a hint?"

"Not really. So how was your Valentine's Day?"

Katie remembered the quiet evening she'd spent in front of her tiny fireplace. She'd celebrated one of her favorite days with a bottle of champagne, Godiva chocolates, and a romance novel.

"It was perfect," she said honestly.

"Was there a man involved?"

"Nope. I'm currently blissfully single."

Mia sighed. "Katie, you know that means trouble. If you're not seeing anyone, the entire family is going to jump all over you this weekend."

"I know."

The Marcelli family might be incredibly close and loving, but they were also rabid about marriage and kids. At twenty-eight and still single, Katie wasn't just considered an old maid, she was thought to be unnatural and in need of serious therapy.

Which she didn't want to think about. "So how was your Valentine's Day?"

"Fabulous."

Katie pictured her sister's petite yet curvy figure, her

streaked blond hair and doe eyes. She grinned. "Let me guess. Forty-seven guys wrestled for the honor of buying you dinner."

"No. I just saw David."

"You've been seeing him for a while now, haven't you?" She vaguely recalled a good-looking kid breezing through at Christmas.

"Uh-huh. Since September. He's really special, Katie. We're in love."

"I'm happy for you," Katie said, speaking the truth. She was two parts thrilled and one part envious. When was the last time she'd been in love? Not her previous boyfriend, or the one before that. They'd been great guys, but not *the one*.

"I should let you concentrate on driving," Mia said. "See you in a couple of hours."

"I'll be there. Give my love to everyone."

"I will. Bye."

The connection clicked off. Katie pushed the button to restore her radio, but instead of joining in with the song, she shook her head. Mia in love? Was her baby sister really old enough to fall for a guy?

She laughed. Mia was eighteen. In the Marcelli family that was the perfect age for a short engagement, followed by a long marriage. Katie's other sisters, Francesca and Brenna, had both married at eighteen, although Francesca was now a young, beautiful widow. Katie herself had been engaged at eighteen, although the marriage had never taken place.

Whispers of the past threatened, but she wasn't interested in spoiling her drive, so she ignored them. Instead she cranked up the volume on the radio and fantasized about a certain lawyer she'd recently met. He might be fifteen kinds of bad for her, but he sure knew how to make her body burst into flames.

A wrought-iron arch announced the entrance to the Marcelli Winery. Hundreds of acres of vineyard stretched out on both sides of the two-lane drive amusingly named Pleasure Road. Come summer, the plants would be thick with leaves and budding fruit. In September, right before harvest, they would hang low with heavy, ripe grapes, but now, in February, they were simply gray and bare.

As Katie drove under the arch, she noticed that the winter pansies flourished. The dozen or so flower-filled half barrels surrounding the base of the arch were filled with colorful blossoms waving in the soft breeze. She could inhale the scent of flowers and earth, and the ocean in the distance.

The road to the main hacienda was nearly three quarters of a mile. Up ahead the three-story, pale yellow hacienda stood at the end of a long driveway. Wrought-iron balconies decorated the front of the structure. Katie didn't have all that much interest in growing grapes or making wine, but she considered herself a real fan of the Marcelli family home. So many happy memories lingered in the corners and crevices of the old place. So much history filled each of the rooms. Coming back always made her feel good.

She pulled up next to the large house, parking her car next to Mia's five-year-old Accord. A beat-up pickup sat on the other side, which meant Francesca had also come home for the weekend. Brenna would be arriving later. Katie smiled in anticipation. The four sisters hadn't been under the same roof since Christmas, nearly two months before.

She'd barely popped the trunk when a side door opened and Francesca strolled out.

"I figured you'd be the next to arrive," she said with a wave. "Brenna won't be here for a while. She had to take Jeff to the airport."

"He's not coming for the weekend?" Katie asked, more than a little disappointed. She, along with her sisters, adored Brenna's husband. He was funny, affectionate, the brother they'd never had.

"Nope. He had to go to some doctor convention."

"I can't believe he'd rather go there than hang out with us."

"I agree. I mean, we're charming *and* we have unlimited access to pasta. What's not to like?"

The two women laughed, then embraced. Katie hugged her sister hard, holding her close for a second. When they released each other, she tried not to notice how great Francesca looked in her white cropped T-shirt and pale blue skirt.

Francesca had always been the pretty sister . . . pretty and nearly physically perfect. She was perfectly tall (5 feet 9), perfectly slender, with that annoying combination of large breasts and nonexistent hips. Her perfect features—wide hazel eyes, a full mouth, and cheekbones that defied gravity—combined to create a face that could not only launch a thousand ships, it could heal several debilitating personality flaws. Long, thick brown hair tumbled down her back, while perfect, olive-colored skin seemed to radiate light.

All of this and a brain, too, Katie thought with a combination of love and pride, flavored with a touch of sibling rivalry. Katie had always been the smart sister, but Francesca's success in her Ph.D. program demonstrated there were fairly efficient brain cells firing behind those big eyes.

Katie grabbed her suitcase. "Poor Dad and Grandpa Lorenzo. They always look forward to Jeff's visits. He keeps them from feeling outnumbered by the women."

"They'll survive, but I'm not sure we will," Francesca said as they walked to the back door and stepped into the utility room. "You need to brace yourself. There's an estrogen fest going on in the kitchen. The Grands are on a roll and Mom is only making it worse. If you don't keep your distance, your ovaries may mutate."

Katie smiled as she dropped her suitcase and purse. She stepped into the kitchen and took a deep breath.

"Hi!"

Three women stood around the central island of the massive kitchen decorated with hand-painted tiles. Dozens of bowls, casseroles, and pots filled every inch of counter space that wasn't already holding fresh produce and homemade pasta.

Three heads turned, three pairs of eyes widened in delight, six arms reached for her. Katie found herself being engulfed in a hugging competition designed to snap at least two ribs, while making her feel she was the most important person on the planet.

"Katie, at last! We were so worried. The long drive. A young woman alone. Who knows what could happen?"

Her paternal grandmother pinched her cheek hard enough to leave a mark. Katie smiled, even as her eyes watered from the pain. "Grandma Tessa," she said warmly. "If you stopped worrying, what would the saints do with their time?"

Grandma Tessa, born and bred in Italy, dismissed the blasphemy. She was used to it from all her girls.

Katie's mother, petite and stylish in a designer suit, sans shoes, cupped her face. "You look thin. Katie, you're a beautiful young woman. You don't need to starve yourself. Are you dieting again?"

Katie kissed her soft, pale cheek. "I swear, I'm not dieting. In fact, I weigh exactly the same as I did the last time you saw me, and the time before that."

Colleen O'Shea Marcelli harrumphed, obviously unconvinced. "I think we should talk later. When your father and I were in San Francisco, we met the nicest young man. He's a sous chef in a restaurant up there."

Francesca stole a slice of cheese. "I thought all chefs were gay."

Grandma Tessa brought the cross on the rosary around her neck to her lips. "Francesca, God did not make you so lovely on the outside so that you could have such a dark heart. Katie needs a man. For that matter, you need a man."

Francesca looked at Katie. They both rolled their eyes.

Finally Katie turned to the tiny woman still holding her arm. "Grammy M," Katie said, her voice warm with affection. "How are you feeling?"

"I'm grand. The sun feels good on these old bones. I've no complaints a'tall."

"You're not so old," Katie reminded her. "Besides, I'm counting on you living forever."

Mary-Margaret O'Shea had been born in Ireland and married at seventeen to a young man she'd only met twice. Less than two weeks after the wedding he'd taken her away from home and family, bringing her across the ocean to a great new land. They'd eventually settled in California.

Grammy M squeezed her hand. "I'm plannin' on it, darlin'."

"So," Katie's mother said, expectantly. "If you're not interested in the sous chef, does that mean you have someone special in your life?"

Katie looked at Francesca, who stuck her finger down her throat and silently gagged.

Katie knew she had two choices. She could tell the truth—that she wasn't seeing anyone and that she was perfectly okay with that. Only no one would believe her. Instead her grandmothers and mother would fuss and chide and torture her for the entire weekend. They would bring up names of men who had never married (and once they reached forty without tying the knot, how *couldn't* there be something wrong with them?), men who were recently divorced, even men who were thinking about divorce. They would talk about her growing old alone, about the odds of finding a man after she turned thirty. They would try to love her into submitting to the family credo of "marry young and have many babies."

Or she could lie.

While she generally tried to tell the truth, desperate times and all that.

"I recently met the most amazing guy," she said.

The Grands did a second swooping thing, while her mother beamed.

"Tell us everything," she insisted. "What's he like?"

"His name is Zach Stryker and he's a very successful lawyer."

"Ooh, a man with a profession," her mother said happily. "So he has money."

Katie didn't have a clue, but unless Zach spent every weekend redecorating his house at the Neiman Marcus home store, he should have gobs. "Sure. He's gorgeous and charming and I think he's really special."

Francesca nearly choked on her cheese. Katie tucked her hand behind her back and crossed her fingers. "He hired me to handle a big fund-raiser for his firm. It's a huge job and it's going to put my company onto the 'A' list, but that's not nearly as exciting as meeting the right guy, you know?"

Francesca still stood behind the Grands. Now she chewed the last bit of cheese and wrapped her hands around her throat, as if strangling herself. Katie knew she was laying it on a bit thick, but she was on a roll.

She sighed heavily. "The man is a hunk."

Just then footsteps clattered on the dining room hardwood floor. Katie was almost disappointed by the interruption. She could have done another five minutes on the unlikely virtues of Zach.

Everyone turned toward the sound as Mia burst into the kitchen.

As usual, she was dressed in jeans and a cropped shirt. Her highlighted hair looked more blond than brown, although the roots were showing, the way Mia liked it. Heavy makeup emphasized her brown eyes. She looked like a makeover gone bad, and yet so lovely and full of life that Katie couldn't help smiling.

"You've got to start blending," Katie said, crossing to her youngest sister and hugging her. "That's why God invented Q-tips."

Mia puffed out her glossy lips, then gave an exaggerated sigh. "I'm still experimenting to find my style. We can't all be perfect like Francesca or together like you." Mia fingered Katie's cardigan. "I mean, you match, for God's sake."

Grandma Tessa fingered her rosary. "Mia Theresa Marcelli, your mouth shames the entire family."

Mia dropped her head in mock surrender. "Sorry, Grandma. I didn't mean to take the Lord's name in vain."

Never one to stay contrite for long, she quickly straightened. "Is Brenna here? I really, really want to tell everyone my news. Where are Dad and Grandpa Lorenzo?"

"They'll be back for dinner," Grandma Tessa said. "You'll have to wait."

Katie grinned. Telling Mia to wait when she wanted something was about as productive as attempting to change the Earth's axis. No matter the effort, not one thing shifted.

"Oh, sh—" Mia glanced at her paternal grandmother and quickly modified her word choice. "Oh, shimmy! I'll just tell you, and then we can tell everyone else when they get here." She frowned.

"Have you been working on your plan to rule the world?" Katie asked her youngest sister. "Remember, I'm only going to organize it. You're in charge of world domination."

"Not today." Mia drew in a deep breath, then spun around once. She clapped her hands together and grinned. "I've got the best news. I'm getting married!"

2

Their mother and both grandmothers swooped down on Mia like peregrine falcons diving for a hapless mouse. Katie laughed as her baby sister was alternately squeezed, kissed, cheek-pinched, and cooed over.

Mia held out her left hand, showing everyone her simple diamond solitaire.

"Very nice," Katie said, leaning in for a glance.

"Married," Grandma Tessa said with obvious delight. "To that nice boy, David? He's not Italian, but he's very handsome. Is the family Catholic?"

"Mama Tessa, you worry too much," Mom said as she kissed her daughter's forehead and brushed her streaked hair off her face. "My baby is going to be married. I'm so happy."

Katie watched the show and fought tears of happiness. "Way to go, Sis," she called when Mia looked at her. "Make the weekend all about yourself."

Mia grinned. "I'm really excited, Katie."

"That's all that matters."

Francesca pushed off the counter she'd been leaning against and joined the affection competition. "Congratulations, Mia."

"Don't be sad," Mia implored, grabbing her hands and squeezing them. "Please, Francesca."

"I'm not sad," her sister protested. "I'm thrilled for you."

Katie knew Francesca was telling the truth, even if the Grands wouldn't believe it. Eight years ago, right on schedule, she and Brenna, her fraternal twin, had been married in a lovely double ceremony. While Brenna was still happily married to Jeff, Francesca had become a widow at the tender age of twenty-one. Busy with getting an education, Francesca preferred staying single and independent. A philosophy that violated everything the sisters had ever been taught.

Grammy M clapped her hands for silence. "When is the wedding to be?"

A hush fell over the kitchen. Francesca and Katie glanced at each other. Katie remembered the fund-raiser she'd just agreed to organize and tried not to panic. Not soon, she thought silently. The fund raiser was going to take all the free time she had.

Mia reached for a cherry tomato and popped it into her mouth. "We're not sure," she said after she'd finished chewing. "This summer. Probably sometime in July."

Katie did the math. The fund-raiser was at the end of May, which meant if the wedding was in mid-July, there would be only six weeks left. Which meant she wouldn't be sleeping much between now and then.

Grammy M nodded. "We'll have to get started right away."

Grandma Tessa sighed. "July is so pretty with the vines and the leaves. You'll be a beautiful bride, little one."

Katie's mother grabbed a pad of paper from the stack under the wall phone. "We need to start a list. How many people? What kind of food? Mia, have you thought about invitations yet? I suppose we need an actual date for that."

"In case anyone is interested, David and his father are coming over for dinner tonight," Mia said.

That set off another flurry of activity. The two grandmothers returned their attention to the cooking. Katie's mom shrieked something about the dining room table not being set right and rushed out of the kitchen. Francesca excused herself, leaving only Katie and Mia with nothing to do.

Mia sidled up to her. "So what do you think? I mean, really."

"I remember the day you were born," Katie said softly. "Mom and Dad were desperate for a son, but I wanted you to be a little girl. They even let me name you. And now you're all grown up. I can't believe my little sister is getting married."

Mia's dark eyes widened. "So you're happy for me?"

Katie thought about how Mia had always known what she wanted from a very young age. Not only was she intelligent enough to be considered gifted, she had the uncanny ability to choose exactly the right path for herself.

Mia had found her handsome prince. Did it get any better than that?

"I'm thrilled for you," Katie promised. "I want you to have the most beautiful wedding ever, and I want you to be delirious with joy for the rest of your life."

"I will be. David is so great."

"How old is he?"

"Eighteen, like me. We met during orientation." She wrinkled her nose. "He's a freshman, which is kinda weird, but okay, too."

Katie swallowed. Eighteen? Somehow she'd assumed that her sister's fiancé was older—maybe a grad student. Mia had started college at sixteen, which meant she and David weren't in the same class. "But you're a junior. What happens when you graduate? Don't you still want to go to Georgetown for your master's?"

"Sure."

"What about David? He won't be finished with his undergraduate degree. Won't that be a problem?"

Mia dismissed her concern with a flick of fingers tipped in bright purple. "We'll work it out." Her expression turned pleading. "Be happy for me, Katie. I really need that."

Katie gave in with a smile. She'd never been able to deny Mia anything. If her sister wanted to get married, then Katie would make sure that happened.

"You got it, kid," she said.

"And you'll help plan the wedding? And help me when Grammy M wants to put me in too many ruffles and a thirty-foot train that went out of style like twenty years ago?"

Katie made an X above her left breast. "I swear. I'll defend you against ugly wedding gowns. We'll pick out something really special and all of us will make it for you. This will be the best wedding ever."

"Thanks." Mia hugged her. "There's just one more thing."

Katie laughed. "Why am I not surprised?"

"Because you and I have a special bond and there always is." Mia glanced around to make sure they were still alone, then leaned close. "Can you take care of David's dad tonight? I've met him and he's really great, but he's, you know, a dad."

"And?"

Mia sighed. "Katie, come on. This is us. The Marcellis. We're not exactly average. The Grands are going to fuss, and Mom and Dad will probably want to check his teeth or something. I don't want to think about what Grandpa Lorenzo will say about me getting started on having babies right away. You're so normal. Just be nice to him. You know, be charming."

Katie remembered that David's father was single. "Great. So you're using me as bait."

"A distraction. Remember, you're the one who's so good with people. So keep him busy enough that the rest of the family doesn't freak him out." She arched her eyebrows. "He's not that old and he's really cute. Well, in a Dad sort of way. You might really like him."

"I might."

Of course, there was the problem of having just convinced the female members of her family that she'd already met the perfect man in the form of Zack Stryker. Still, she wasn't opposed to helping out her sister.

"I'll see what I can do," she said.

"Great. You're the best." Mia twirled in place. "Tonight is going to be so amazing."

Zack Stryker consciously relaxed his hands on the steering wheel. As he and his son drove steadily north, he struggled to find the right words and the right to say them.

"What the hell do you think you're doing?" came to mind, along with, "Could you be *more* successful at screwing up your life?"

He reminded himself that anger and sarcasm would only make David dig in his heels. His son had inherited many good qualities from his father, but he'd also inherited a large dose of Stryker stubbornness. In the eyes of the law Mia and David were both adults. There was nothing to prevent them from running off and eloping. Zach was determined to keep that from happening. Which meant playing along with the engagement . . . for now.

"Have you met Mia's family before?" he asked.

"Sure."

"Do her parents know about the engagement?"

Some of David's teenage confidence slipped. "I, ah, don't know. Mia said she was gonna tell everyone today. You know, before we got there." He shifted uncomfortably in his seat.

Some of Zach's tension eased. If Mia's parents didn't know about this idiotic engagement, then there was a chance they would object. What normal parents would want their eighteen-year-old daughter marrying a kid with no life experience and no job? Mia was David's first girlfriend, for God's sake. He knew as much about being a husband as he did about solving the issue of global warming.

"We'll just have to see how it goes," Zach said, striving for noncommittal. "So tell me about the family."

David shoved his too-long blond hair off his forehead and slumped down in the seat. "Mia's the youngest of four sisters. Katie's the oldest. Brenna and Francesca are a year younger. They're twins, but they don't look alike."

"Any of them married?"

"Brenna. Her husband's a doctor. I don't know much about Francesca except she's like really hot. Mia said she could have gone into modeling, but she's not that shallow."

David continued to talk about parents and grandparents, but Zach wasn't listening. None of this information was new to him. When David had first admitted he was serious about someone, Zach hadn't been concerned—not until his eighteen-year-old son had asked for money from his trust fund so that he could buy the girl in question an engagement ring.

At that point Zach had been tempted to lock David in his room for the next five years or until he came to his senses. Whichever happened first. Reality had prevailed. Instead of searching out a secure location, he'd learned as much as he could about Mia's family and had come up with several plans to keep the happy couple from tying the knot. One of those plans had already been put into action.

Katie Marcelli had *not* been hired by accident. She was going to owe him big time for her new contract, and she intended to use that to his advantage.

Zach was determined to keep David from screwing up his life. If the kid wanted to get married in a few years . . . like ten or twelve . . . when his career was established and he knew what he wanted, that was great. But not now. Not like this.

"That's the exit," David said, pointing to the sign above the highway. He fished a sheet of paper out of the front pocket of his khakis and read off the directions.

Zach drove along two-lane roads. It was already dark, and the small country signs were difficult to read. A rock clunked against the side of his car, and he winced at the thought of a chip in his paint job. He didn't have many personal pleasures in his life, but his one-year-old dark blue BMW 540i was one of them.

They made a left after the railroad tracks, then drove for three more miles. Finally David pointed at a well-lit wrought-iron arch and a small street sign reading PLEAS-URE ROAD.

"There it is."

Zach slowed. The high beams from his car illuminated cultivated grape vines for as far as the eye could see. He recalled the multiple offerings from the Marcelli Winery in his local wine emporium. Even the low-end stuff sold for over ten bucks. None of the research he'd done on the family and the winery had indicated there was any financial trouble. Between the Marcelli legacy and David's trust fund, it was going to be a hell of a prenuptial agreement.

Five minutes later he parked his car next to several others. The side door of the house burst open and Mia Marcelli raced into the night.

"You're here! I told everyone about the engagement and they're so excited. Hey, Mr. Stryker."

That was as much as Zach heard. David had already sprinted from the car toward his intended. The teenage lovebirds embraced, then kissed. Zach's stomach tightened in a combination of anger and frustration.

He slowly stepped out into the cool February night. Light spilled from the house. He saw several people standing by the open door, no doubt trying to get a look at the man who'd raised such a crazy kid. He wanted to defend his son, and himself, but that wouldn't accomplish anything useful. Instead he was going to make nice, act friendly, and size up the opposition. Once he figured out who was on his side, he would suggest they get together to come up with a plan to break off the engagement.

Katie heard Mia run outside. The rest of the family gathered around the back door while she started opening the bottles of wine that had been chosen to accompany dinner.

"That should send David and his father screaming into

the night," Francesca said as she leaned against the counter. "Families like ours should only be allowed to greet people in groups of two."

Katie grinned. "Mia's already sweating that. She asked me to be nice to David's father. Actually, I think I'm a sacrificial distraction so the Grands don't scare the life out of him."

Francesca raised her eyebrows. "Won't that be difficult with your attention so firmly riveted on your new job and the hunk-in-a-suit you'll be working with?"

Katie knew Francesca was only teasing, but she still felt embarrassed. "I know. I shouldn't have lied, but they make me crazy. If I'd told them I wasn't seeing anyone, they would have tortured me endlessly. Besides, the guy who hired me *is* all the things I claimed, and more."

"Like what?"

"Like a first-class player. He dates starlets and models and society types. From what I've read, no relationship lasts longer than thirty-five seconds."

"Hardly the kind of material to get your romantic heart to thumping."

Katie wished that were true. "The bad news is, he's really sexy. I can't explain my hormonal reaction to him, but it's amazingly powerful. How can I lust after someone I don't even like?"

"Do you know him enough to make that kind of judgment?"

Katie shrugged. "I'm reasonably confident I won't like him no matter how much we know each other."

"As long as you're not prejudging the situation."

Katie laughed. "Good point. I'll try to keep an open mind, while resisting the need to rip off my clothes in his presence."

Outside car doors slammed. "Here they come," Francesca said, then pushed off the counter. "I'll leave you to comfort David's father. I have to go make a quick call to my adviser."

"Chicken."

Francesca glanced over her shoulder. "Not even close. I just have really good timing."

"You're the one who likes to rescue people," Katie called after her. "So rescue me."

"This is definitely a save-yourself-first moment. I'm outta here."

"Come in, come in," Grandpa Lorenzo called from his place in the doorway.

Katie stayed in the kitchen, where she continued opening bottles of wine for their dinner. The Marcelli kitchen was generally a happy place, but tonight there was a festive air. As if the wine with dinner wasn't enough, their father had already set several bottles of their best champagne to chill in the small wine refrigerator tucked under the counter by the alcove.

She glanced up and saw her parents surrounding Mia and David as the young couple entered the house. David's father had yet to make an appearance.

Katie looked at David's blond hair and pale skin and tried to picture the man. Maybe an older version of his son, she thought. If Mia was worried about him, he was probably shy and quiet. She frowned as she realized she didn't know what he did for a living. A professor, maybe? She would like that. They could talk about books and—

A man walked into the kitchen and seemed to look straight at her. Instantly her stomach dived for her toes.

She'd read the expression in books and had never believed it, but at that moment all her internal organs zipped down her legs and splatted onto her feet.

She couldn't breathe. She couldn't think, which was probably a good thing. Panic flooded her. While she was willing to accept being punished for lying, she resented the punishment not fitting the crime. This *so* wasn't fair.

Zach Stryker, smooth sophisticate, powerful lawyer, and her newest client, stood in the center of the Marcelli kitchen.

Horror joined panic as she remembered all the things she'd told her mother and grandmother about him. She wanted to scream. She wanted to run. She wanted to disappear into a puff of black smoke.

Instead she was forced to just stand there, immobilized by frozen muscles, while Zach raised one eyebrow in obvious surprise.

"Katie?"

Her mother looked at her. "You two know each other?"

Before Katie could come up with some swell lie to cover the other lie she'd already told, Zach spoke.

"My law firm recently hired Katie to plan a big charity party for us."

Katie braced herself, but it didn't help. Not when Grandma Tessa scurried close and clutched Zach's arm. "Ooh, so *you're* the handsome man she was telling us about."

Zach's other eyebrow joined the first. Katie moaned softly as heat raced up her cheeks to her hairline. Oh, God. Now what?

Well, this being her life, it got worse.

Grammy M took Zach's other arm. "Our Katie says you're a very special man."

"I—" She swallowed and tried again. "Not really."

The corner of Zach's mouth quirked. "You don't think I'm special?"

"No. I mean—"

"Katie." Grammy M's gaze turned reproachful. "Don't be insultin' our guest."

She wanted to die.

To complete the thrill of the moment, both Grands chose to release Zach and leave her alone with him. She clutched the last bottle of Cabernet to her chest and wondered what would happen if she hit herself in the head with it.

Zach shoved his hands into his slacks pockets. "Small world," he said easily.

Of course, it was easy for him, she thought bitterly. He'd been invited to a free, live show.

"Just my luck," she muttered, then sighed. The best course of action was to pretend none of this had actually happened. "So you're David's father?"

"Guilty."

"But you're so . . ." She hesitated, not sure how to phrase the obvious.

"I was seventeen when David was born," he told her, answering her question without her having to ask it.

He leaned toward her. "You told your family you thought I was hot, huh?"

She winced as the heat on her face returned. "Those exact words never crossed my lips."

"But something close."

Obviously the man didn't have an ego problem. Unfortunately she was hardly in a position to put him in his place.

For a second she thought about explaining why she'd

said what she had, but he was unlikely to believe her. Women threw themselves at Zach. Why would he think she was any different?

"I'll recover," she said, striving for a light, cheerful tone. "Don't sweat it."

"Maybe I want to."

His low words rubbed against her skin like velvet. Man oh man, he might be not her type, but did he know how to use what he had to the greatest advantage.

"We have a working relationship," she told him. "I intend to respect that."

"All work and no play . . ."

"I'll risk being dull."

"Want to bet I can change your mind?"

Yes! Her hormones had already taken a vote and offered their opinion. Part of her couldn't believe he was coming on to her. And while sex without emotional commitment had never tempted her, she was suddenly all aquiver to find out if it had any redeeming qualities at all.

She was saved from answering when her father came up and claimed Zach.

"Let's leave the cooking to the women," he said.

Grandpa Lorenzo joined his son, slapped Zach on the back, and led him to the study.

Katie set down the bottle of wine and breathed a sigh of relief. She'd just survived the most humiliating experience of her life and deserved some kind of tasteful award.

Instead, Grammy M winked at her. "David's father seems very nice. A strong man."

Grandma Tessa picked up the refrain. "Smart, too. A lawyer. I can see why you liked him."

Katie wanted to protest that "like" didn't begin to describe what she felt, but she couldn't at this late date.

Okay—if God was trying to show her why it was stupid to lie, she'd learned her lesson.

Her mother leaned against the opposite side of the island. "Mia says David told her that Zach never remarried after his wife left. Could be he had a broken heart."

"Time heals," Grammy M said.

"A man who loved once is more likely to love again," Grandma Tessa pronounced.

"One marriage leads to another." Her mother beamed at her.

Katie leaned her elbows on the counter and covered her face with her hands. "Stop, I beg you."

Grammy M patted her arm. "I'll sit him across from you at dinner. He'll spend the entire meal gazing into your pretty eyes, and by dessert he'll be yours."

Not knowing if she should laugh or cry, Katie contented herself with a strangled moan. "There are no words to describe my joy," she whispered.

Her grandmother kissed her cheek. "I know, child."

3

"The cannolis can't wait forever," Grandma Tessa complained, checking the casserole dish in the top oven. "Where *is* that girl?"

Katie was about to explain about Brenna taking her husband to the airport when the back door opened and Brenna breezed inside.

"Sorry I'm late," she said. "Traffic getting out of the city was awful. It's the whole Friday thing."

Brenna kissed her two grandmothers and mother, then hugged Katie.

"I saw a Beamer parked outside. Who's the company?"

Katie laughed as the older women rushed to the window and peered out into the darkness.

"I can't see it," Grammy M complained. She straightened and looked at Brenna. "Was it nice?"

"Very."

The two grandmothers exchanged a look of satisfaction, then turned their attention to Katie. "Good-looking *and* well off," Grandma Tessa said with a wink. "Good for you, Katie."

Brenna looked confused.

Katie pulled her toward the dining room. "Remember

Mia's boyfriend? You met him around Christmas. Tall, blond hair, blue eyes, a little skinny?"

"Sure."

"They're engaged. He and his father have joined us for dinner, and we're doing the celebration thing."

"Wow! That's great. So why is that good for you?"

They stepped into the dining room. A table that seated twenty filled the center of the room. Two hutches lined one adobe wall, while a long buffet sat against another. Two wrought-iron chandeliers illuminated the sparkling crystal and elegant china. Katie sat on an extra chair pushed under the high window.

"God is punishing me," she said, and told Brenna about her attempt not to be bugged about her current boyfriend-free status.

Brenna covered her mouth to hold back hysterical laughter.

"It's not funny," Katie told her.

"Sorry, but it is. Something like that would only happen to you. So how bad was it? Did the Grands completely humiliate you when he walked in?"

"Absolutely."

Brenna sank down next to her. "Oh, Katie. I'm sorry."

Katie glared at her sister. "Yeah. Sorry you missed the show."

"Well, that, too." Brenna touched her arm. "Is there anything I can do to help?"

"Shoot me now."

Francesca came into the dining room. "So you two are hiding out here? What did I miss?"

Brenna rose and hugged her twin. "Katie was telling me about her recent humiliation. I think it's pretty funny."

"Ha ha," Katie said glumly.

Francesca shrugged. "So he knows you think he's hot. What's the big deal?"

Katie couldn't believe she was even asking. "I have to work with the man."

"He'll pay more attention to your legs than what you say. What's your point?"

"That he isn't the least bit interested in my legs. Which makes all this not just humiliating, but also pathetic."

"Oh, I'm willing to bet he was interested." Brenna sat back down and took Katie's hand in hers. "I think you should sleep with him."

Katie stared at her. "What?"

"Sleep? Have sex? Get laid? It can't have been so long that you've forgotten the word."

"I know what you meant, I just can't believe you're saying it. Zach is not a nice man. He's shallow and superficial."

"Technically, those two characteristics are the same," Francesca said helpfully. "And perfect qualities for a one-night stand. Besides, you don't know him well enough to be sure."

Katie glared at her, then returned her attention to Brenna. "Why would you suggest that?"

"Because you obviously want to. Katie, you've been a good girl all your life. We all have. Maybe it's time to be bad."

Katie pulled her hand free. "I don't think so. If my punishment for one little lie was that swift and severe, I'd hate to think what would happen if I actually did something wrong."

"If Zach is everything you say, maybe it would be worth it."

"You've lost your mind," Katie told Brenna. "Your brain fell out of your head while you were sleeping."

Francesca stretched. "Don't dismiss Brenna's suggestion. Zach may not give you the happily-ever-after romance you're looking for, but he'd be good for some hot, quickie sex. Brenna's married and I don't date, so it's up to you to provide us all with the vicarious thrill."

"That is not possible. For one thing, he's a new client. The job is huge and could easily take my company to the next level. I'm not going to mess with that. For another—in case you've forgotten—his son is marrying our sister. That makes him an in-law. I can hardly spend the next forty years sitting across from him at Christmas and Thanksgiving, knowing we've seen each other naked."

"But—"

Francesca started to protest, but Katie cut her off with a flick of her wrist.

"It's like a double yellow line," Katie said.

Brenna and Francesca looked first at each other, then at her. "Want to explain that?" Brenna asked.

"Sure. You can cross one yellow line, no problem. But if you cross two, things get ugly."

Francesca grinned. "Katie, honey, we're talking about sex, not a moving violation."

Katie wanted to pound their heads together. Fortunately she was saved from coming up with a response by Brenna's groan. "Geez, Francesca, do you have to be so damn skinny? You've lost more weight, haven't you? Let me guess. You've been so busy, you've forgotten to eat."

"It happens," Francesca said, sounding only a little defensive.

"Not to me." Brenna poked at her own thigh. "I can honestly say that I've never missed a meal by being too busy. There's always time for pasta. It's these Italian genes. Every mouthful heads directly south of my waist. Why couldn't I take after Grammy M like you?"

Katie studied her sisters. Francesca was taller, slimmer than her twin, with small bones and lighter eyes. Brenna took after Grandma Tessa and Grandpa Lorenzo. Large bones filled out her five-foot, seven-inch frame. She had thick dark hair, brown eyes, and olive skin. Despite her Irish name, she appeared to be all Italian.

"Stop whining," Katie said. "You're both pretty."

"Yeah, and I outweigh my taller twin by nearly thirty-five pounds," Brenna said. "You're tiny, too. I hate you both."

The sound of footsteps in the hallway broke up the conversation. Their father and Grandpa Lorenzo entered with Zach, Mia, and David. Katie introduced Brenna and Francesca, then wished she could excuse herself to the other side of the planet. But no. Seconds later Grammy M was urging everyone to their seats. And just as she'd promised, she put Katie directly across from Zach so her oldest granddaughter could spend the entire meal reliving the humiliation.

Dinner with the Marcelli family was like a scene out of a Merchant Ivory film, Zach thought nearly an hour later. A beautiful setting filled with charming, interesting, slightly odd characters in nice clothes, all accompanied by classical opera in the background. He had a sudden yearning to go find a Starbucks and take a call on his cell phone.

They were a party of eleven at a table built for a much larger group, so there was plenty of space between each place setting. Dozens of dishes lined the center of the table—each filled with something more delicious than the next. He hadn't known there were that many ways to serve pasta. And even better than the food was the wine.

He took another drink, appreciating the fullness of the Cabernet, the rich middle and mellow finish. The family served their own private blend. The handwritten label contained notes about year of harvest, location in the vineyard, the type of barrel, and how long it had been aged.

Lorenzo Marcelli noticed Zach's interest.

"We make a few cases the old-fashioned way," the patriarch of the family explained, raising his voice to be heard from his seat at the head of the table. "They're pressed separately from the main harvest and then aged. This is for family."

Mia, sitting next to Zach, giggled. "Grandpa means that someone stomped the grapes with his feet."

Brenna smiled at her sister. "Mia's not into the process— only the product. Crushing the grapes by hand . . . or by foot, as it were . . . is a more delicate way to achieve the end result. Less juice is extracted from the grapes. Most harvests are pressed by massive machines that can crush a grape to sawdust. We don't go to that level, but for our commercial wines the old ways are too expensive and slow."

Lorenzo turned to Brenna. "You remember."

She sighed. "I still love the grapes, Grandpa."

"Then why aren't you here? Working with me? Of all your sisters you're the only one with the passion for what we do."

"I have to be in L.A. You know that. Jeff's medical training was there and now his practice is. I'm married. My place is with my husband. Haven't you always taught us that?"

Lorenzo snorted, obviously unconvinced. Lorenzo's wife, sitting at the opposite end of the table, flapped her napkin at her husband and her granddaughter. "Zach does *not* want a lesson in wine making. You can be boring another time. Tonight we celebrate the young lovers."

Her beatific smile made Zach uncomfortable. His half hour or so alone with Mia's father and grandfather hadn't given him the opportunity to casually discern opinions on the potential union. Instead Lorenzo had talked about the land, showing Zach a map of the winery grounds.

Since sitting down to dinner, however, the family had offered multiple toasts to David and Mia's happiness. Didn't anybody else think the marriage was a damn stupid idea?

He studied the various family members. Mia's parents seemed engrossed in each other, as were Mia and David. Not wanting to observe young love in full bloom gave him plenty of time to check out the rest of the family.

He glanced at the Marcelli daughters. Francesca had the face and the body of a cover model. She reminded him of Ainsley, his ex-wife, and he instantly dismissed her as high maintenance. Brenna, the only married sister, seemed torn between her devotion to her husband and the pull of the family business. Which left Katie.

Katie, who sat across from him but refused to look at him. Katie, who had apparently told her family all about their meeting in such terms that her grandmothers had practically picked out china patterns. Katie, who had great legs and the kind of mouth that made a man fantasize about being taken advantage of.

Kathleen Elizabeth Marcelli—age twenty-eight, never married. She had a bachelor's degree in business from UCLA, and had started working for a party planner/organizer type during college. Five years ago Katie bought out the client list and opened Organization Central. She had three full-time employees, seven working part-time.

No illegal vices—from what he could find out, no vices at all. She was smart, organized, reasonably successful, and while she visited her family regularly, she didn't make them her life.

He'd hired her to get her in his corner. Based on the chemistry clicking between them, all was going according to plan.

At least the wedding wasn't for a few months. That would give Zach time to stop things. His son was too important for him to lose this battle. He was the best at what he did for a reason.

"So, Zach," Lorenzo said, motioning with his wineglass. "We have the big wedding this summer, then next year, the bambinos, eh?"

Babies? Zach nearly spit. Mia and David were still babies themselves. Damn. The last thing he needed was Mia getting pregnant.

Mia rolled her eyes. "Grandpa, I have school. I'm not getting pregnant until I have my degree."

Tessa frowned. "But being a mother is more important than a few classes at a university. You're a woman, Mia, not a computer. You don't need to fill yourself with more learning. You're a smart girl. Wouldn't you like to have some babies?"

"There's plenty of time for that," Zach said hastily, earning a grateful smile from Mia.

"I disagree." Colleen Marcelli, the girls' mother, spoke up. "I had Katie when I was nineteen and the twins the following year. But Mia didn't come along until ten years later. I have to say, that pregnancy was a lot more difficult. A woman's body is built to have children early."

Even petite, grandmotherly Mary-Margaret had an opinion. "I suppose if you're waitin' until summer to get married, there's no hope of an unexpected bundle of joy?"

Zach nearly choked.

"We need a son," Lorenzo said, pounding his fist on the table.

Zach glanced from the old man to his equally aging wife. Even with all the advances in fertility research, there was no way that was going to happen.

"Brenna." Lorenzo turned his attention to his grand-daughter. "You're married nine years and no babies."

"Grandpa, we've had this discussion before. Jeff had to get through all his medical training first."

"*Bambinos* come first," Lorenzo insisted. "Besides, he's a doctor now. Why are you still so skinny?"

"If only," Brenna muttered.

"My granddaughters—you all let me down. Katie—my beautiful Katie. Why haven't you found a nice boy?"

"Lorenzo," his wife warned. "Leave the girls alone."

He ignored her. "Francesca—you have a face like an angel. For many years you mourned the loss of your husband, but it is time to move on." He motioned to the table. "Only little Mia goes out of her way not to break her old grandfather's heart."

"Pop, back off," Marco told his father. "If the girls are happy, we're all happy."

Lorenzo didn't look convinced.

Zach glanced at the sisters. Their expressions were identical masks of long-suffering. Apparently this wasn't an unusual outburst. Still, he felt a strong need to grab David and make a break for the car.

Their mother straightened in her chair. "We're nearly

finished with the new labels. They're very impressive," she said, and suddenly everyone was talking about wine.

Mia leaned toward him. "Welcome to the family. It's not always like this. Just when someone mentions something about a wedding."

Great. So in addition to worrying about David screwing up his life, Zach also had some concerns about mental stability in the older generation.

When the meal ended, the sisters quickly cleared the table. Brandy was brought out, along with trays of cookies.

"Bring in some paper," Colleen called. "I don't know when we're going to all be together again. Let's work out some of the details of the wedding while we have the chance."

Zach swore silently. "Isn't there plenty of time for that? Maybe we should enjoy the engagement for a while."

Colleen looked at him as if he'd lost his frontal lobe. "Zach, I'm sure you're a whiz in the courtroom, but like the average male, you don't know anything about planning a wedding. Think of it as invading a small country. We need to plan, organize—"

"Shop," Katie offered helpfully as she stepped back into the dining room. She carried several pads of paper and a handful of pens. Instead of circling to her seat, she paused by his chair, and for the first time since dinner had started, actually looked at him. "You might want to take notes, just so that later, when you're finally home, you don't try to convince yourself that this was all just a bad dream."

A smile teased at the corner of her full mouth, making him want to smile in return. When he'd met her in his office, he'd thought she was attractive and sexy as hell. Now he was impressed by her ability to recover. Most women he knew couldn't get over a broken fingernail in less than twenty-four hours. Katie had survived what even he had to admit had to have been a pretty humiliating experience, and she'd done so with grace and style.

She was tough. He liked that. He took the pad of paper she offered, along with a pen. As she turned away, he admired the curve of her hip and the length of bare leg exposed by her dress. Tough, together, and more than a pretty face. Exactly the sort of ally he needed to keep his son safe.

The rest of the sisters returned to the dining room. All the women grabbed pads from Katie.

Mia knelt on her chair. "We've talked about July," she said, drawing a big heart in the center of her paper. "Maybe the nineteenth."

Six pens dutifully scratched out the date. Zach's good humor faded. Ally or not, how the hell was he going to stop this damn wedding?

"You'll have the ceremony here," Marco, Mia's father said. "The vineyards will be beautiful then, and all the flowers will be in bloom."

"An arch by the east garden," Colleen said.

"Exactly."

Husband and wife smiled at each other. Zach's stomach knotted. Until then, Marco hadn't said much, and Zach had been holding out hope that at least one person in the Marcelli family had a brain. Unfortunately Marco seemed just as enthused by the idea of the wedding as everyone else.

He glanced at David. "This is moving pretty fast. You okay with this?"

His son beamed. "It's great, Dad. Didn't I tell you this was the best family?"

Oh, yeah. Just peachy, Zach thought grimly.

"We were thinking of afternoon for the ceremony," Mia continued, after kissing David's cheek.

"Late afternoon," Tessa said from her end of the table. "You'll want a nice dinner. We could have it outside. Lorenzo, do we have enough champagne?"

He dismissed the question with a wave. "What kind of man would I be to not have enough champagne for my youngest granddaughter's wedding?"

In a surprisingly short period of time, the family had worked through a number of points. At this rate the wedding would be planned by ten that night. If they were going to work fast, he would have to work faster.

Mia drew more hearts on her paper. "I haven't had time to start looking for dress ideas yet, Grammy M. Maybe we can go out next week."

Mia's petite Irish grandmother shook her head. "My hands aren't steady enough anymore," she said quietly. "It's time for someone else to be in charge." She turned to the granddaughter sitting next to her and clasped Katie's hands. "Katie will make your dress."

Make? Zach blinked stupidly. Couldn't they just buy it . . . and return it when the wedding was canceled?

There was a second of silence, followed by an explosion of conversation. Mia raced around David to hug and kiss her sister. Colleen wiped away a tear. Katie simply looked stunned.

Apparently not, he thought grimly.

"Are you sure, Grammy?" Katie asked.

"Yes. You were always the most patient and the best seamstress. You'll make your sister a beautiful dress."

Mia pulled Katie from her chair and hugged her again. "We can go shopping together and find the absolutely best pattern and then come home and make it. I'm so happy!"

Chairs were pushed back as the family collected for a

group hug. Once again all Zach wanted to do was grab his kid and bolt for freedom. Instead a surprisingly wiry Grandma Tessa pulled him to his feet, where he was ushered into the crowd.

David owed him for this, he told himself as Lorenzo grabbed him by both arms and kissed his cheeks. David owed him big time.

4

Zach and David didn't escape until well after midnight, although Zach doubted his son viewed their leaving as an escape. David had seemed genuinely sad to go.

Zach congratulated himself on having the foresight to have his assistant, Dora, make reservations at a nearby hotel. After the post-dinner brandies, not to mention an impromptu sing-along with a *Barber of Seville* CD, he was in no shape to face the long drive back to Los Angeles.

Instead he and David bedded down in adjoining rooms in a small beach-front hotel that had probably been fashionable back in the nineteen-forties.

He'd barely turned out the lights and shifted on a mattress that had seen better days when he heard footsteps rustling on the carpet. He clicked the light back on.

David stood in the doorway between their rooms. Sometimes his son seemed so grown-up. He was capable and competent. But tonight, wearing the hotel's too-big bathrobe, with his hair mussed and a thousand questions in his eyes, he looked like a little boy. Zach shoved several pillows behind his back so he could sit up, then motioned to the room's only chair.

"Let's talk about it," he said.

David shifted his weight from foot to foot, then slowly headed for the dark blue armchair. He sat down, legs parted, hands hanging between his knees.

"So what'd you think?" he asked, not quite looking at his father.

Zach considered the question. There was no way he was going to tell his son what he *really* thought about anything. "They're nice people."

"Yeah?" David glanced up, his expression hopeful. "I really like them all," he admitted. "I mean Mia's great and I love her a lot, so the family's just a bonus, you know?"

"Sure. Kind of like finding a plastic race car in the cereal box."

David grinned. "Exactly. I like spending time there."

He hesitated. Zach waited patiently, knowing that his son would get to whatever he had to say eventually.

"I don't remember my grandmother very well," David admitted softly, speaking of Zach's mother.

"You were what, six, when she died?"

David nodded. "And I never met your dad, or my mom's parents."

Zach figured the day had been crappy enough without him having to think about Ainsley, or his ex-in-laws.

"I really like the idea of a big family, Dad," David continued. "It took me three visits to figure out Mia's grandparents. Grandpa Lorenzo is always talking about vines and grapes. I don't get the whole wine thing, but it's fun to listen. He tells great stories about going back to Europe during the Second World War and smuggling out cuttings from French and Italian vineyards. Mia's grandparents found these really old architecture plans based on some house for a Spanish nobleman and used them to design the house."

Zach listened without saying anything. He was just a single father—a lawyer who worked in an office. No way he could compete with Spanish noblemen and war stories.

He wanted to slam his fist against a wall and demand a fair trial. He'd done the best he could. Ainsley had been the least maternal woman known to the human race, and when she'd bailed, he'd been left alone with a child. He and his son had grown up together. Sometimes Zach even allowed himself to think he'd done a damn fine job.

"I was an only child as well," he said casually. "I know what it's like to want a big family. But we've done okay together."

David swallowed uncomfortably. "I'm not complaining, Dad."

"I know you're not. You're saying that your attraction to Mia isn't just because she's a pretty girl who makes your heart beat faster."

David nodded.

Zach didn't want to hear that. It meant breaking them up was going to be more difficult than he'd first thought.

"You were really great tonight," his son said. "I could tell you were sort of, you know, uncomfortable, but you did good."

Zach didn't know if he should be pleased or insulted by the compliment. "Gee, thanks."

"No, I mean it. You're trying to keep an open mind about everything."

Warning bells went off in Zach's head. "What do you mean?"

David crossed and uncrossed his legs. "Just that you're not a huge fan of the whole wedding thing. At least not for me." He grinned. "Dad, you haven't said anything. But I'm your kid. I know you. I'd have to be a complete moron not to guess that you're a little nervous about the idea of me getting married. You probably want to ship me off to an island somewhere on the other side of the planet. I appreciate that you're really listening to me, to what I want."

He rose and headed for the open door between their rooms. "Some parents would lay down the law, but you're willing to let me go my own way. I know you think I'm making a mistake, but you're wrong. Mia is absolutely the one for me. So thanks for being supportive." He gave a small wave. "Night."

"Good night."

Zach could barely speak, what with the way his throat was closing. When David climbed into his bed and turned out the light, Zach clicked off his as well. But he didn't slide back down in bed. Instead he stared into the darkness and mentally ran through every swear word he'd ever heard.

He hadn't fooled David for a minute. He supposed it was a testament to his child's intelligence . . . or maybe it was just that he hadn't done a good job of concealing his feelings. Either way, he was going to have to be more careful than ever. If David was alerted, he would be on guard. Zach was still determined to stop the wedding at any cost. The trick would be getting David to think it was his own idea.

"My client had an excellent grade-point average while she was in college," Zach said.

Wayne Johnson, the attorney for the opposition, sighed in mock disgust. "She was studying sculpture. Are you trying to tell us that she plans to get a master's in sculpturing? I wasn't aware there were that many openings for professional sculptors. Or is it sculptress?"

Zach ignored the question. He knew Wayne. They'd been on opposite sides of the negotiating table many times. The thing Zach liked most about Wayne was that the man didn't learn. He had yet to figure out that Zach always won.

Zach glanced at his client, a small, quiet woman in her forties. Her husband, a successful accountant with a practice specializing in movie stars and doctors, had left her for a much younger woman. He wanted to dump the old and used, and marry the trophy wife. Obviously it didn't bother him that the future Mrs. Allen Franklin was two years older than his oldest child.

Zach turned away from Wayne and spoke to the judge overseeing their mediation session.

"Mrs. Franklin was a promising young artist when she met Mr. Franklin. She'd just received her B.A. and was expecting to start on her master's in the fall. She'd had two showings, had sold several pieces, and had been given a grant. When Mr. Franklin proposed, he requested that they start a family right away and asked my client to give up her art."

"She could have said no," Wayne pointed out.

"She could have. Or Mr. Franklin could have respected her talent. Your honor, my client's request that her husband support her while she returns to college to get an advanced degree isn't unreasonable. She plans to get a master's in elementary education, thereby allowing herself to find a job and be a contributing member of society."

Zach knew that the request was a little unusual, but it was what his client wanted.

Wayne slapped several folders onto the conference table. "Your Honor, Mr. Stryker and his client have passed from reasonable to greedy. It's one thing to talk about helping Mrs. Franklin get back on her feet, but between the request for alimony and the ridiculous property split, Mr. Franklin is the one who is going to need assistance."

The judge looked at Zach.

Zach shrugged. "I'm sorry Mr. Franklin feels he doesn't have the resources necessary to aid his wife."

"He does not."

Zach shifted a file from the bottom of the stack in front of him to the top. "Perhaps if Mr. Franklin were to liquidate some of the assets he purchased for his new lifestyle, he wouldn't feel the financial pinch quite so much." Zach casually pushed the folder toward the judge. "Assets he purchased with community property, Your Honor. Actually, under California law, they're technically half Mrs. Franklin's."

Zach gave Wayne a slight smile. Both the lawyer and his client paled suddenly. Mr. Franklin had a heated conversation with his attorney that wasn't as quiet as it should have been. Zach caught a couple of choice phrases along the lines of "You told me no one would find out about the beach house" and "You mean I have to pay her for half the jewelry I bought Sara?"

"Mr. Franklin was not as forthcoming as he could have been on his financial statements," Zach said unnecessarily.

The judge was not amused.

An hour later they reached a settlement that would ensure that Mrs. Franklin would have ample funds to support her while she studied for her advanced degree. If she didn't spend her days on Rodeo Drive, she wouldn't need to work again at all.

After Wayne and a very angry Mr. Franklin stormed past them, Zach turned to his client.

She shook her head. "I didn't think you could get it all."

"You gave me your wish list. I did my best to achie
Your husband was stupid. Hiding money in a commu
property state is guaranteed to make the courts angry.
Once I found out what he'd done, I knew we'd win."

"Thanks to you."

"Do me a favor," he said.

She smiled. "Let me guess. Pay your bill on time?"

"I'll be going after your ex-husband for that. Don't forget the judge slapped him with the fees. Actually, the favor is—before you get married again, give me a call. I'll write up a prenup that will protect you so you don't have to fight so hard next time."

"I'm not getting married again."

"Right. Just give me a call."

They shook hands, then parted. Zach headed for the elevators that would take him to the underground car park. He would bet money that they were both remarried within two years and divorced the following year. He'd seen it happen a thousand times. On one hand, it kept him in business . . . on the other hand, it was a hell of a way to run the world.

Katie walked into the waiting area three minutes before her appointment with Zach. She'd crammed her briefcase as full as possible, but all her notes weren't going to ease the fluttering panic in her stomach.

There weren't enough words in the universe to describe how much she didn't want to be here. Not after what had happened nearly a week ago at the hacienda. She still cringed whenever she thought of it, which was about forty-seven times a day.

The thing was, she couldn't tell Zach the truth. If she

explained why she'd mentioned him to her family, he would think she was lying, trying to downplay her attraction to him. Saying she wasn't attracted to him *would* mean lying, and she wasn't about to risk more cosmic interference. Saying she was attracted, but not sure she liked him, was just plain tacky.

"Deep, cleansing breaths," she murmured to herself. "I am confident, professional, and more than ready to take on this challenge."

After squaring her shoulders, she reminded herself of her greater purpose. This fund-raiser would put her company onto the A-list of party planners. Once there she would be able to expand, pick and choose her jobs, and start saving to buy a house. All that was more than worth a few awkward moments with a client. Besides, rather than focusing on what she'd done, she should think about what she had to do. Putting together a charity event of this magnitude in an impossibly short period of time would tax her and her staff to the point of insanity. If she wanted to sweat something, worrying about the party was a whole lot more productive.

Feeling completely calm and centered, not to mention attractive yet professional in a forest green suit and another pair of killer heels, Katie crossed to the receptionist and gave her name. The young woman there told her to go right back. Mr. Stryker was expecting her.

Zach's assistant sat outside his office. She stood up as Katie approached and eyed her bulging suitcase.

"I can't believe he volunteered to be in charge of the annual fund-raiser," Dora Preston said cheerfully. "If he starts to glaze over when you talk about the details, slam something hard against the coffee table. Loud noises help keep him awake."

"Thanks. I'll keep that in mind."

Katie really appreciated the other woman's friendly nature, but didn't think she would be using the advice. If Zach fell asleep during her presentation, she would take it as a sign that she was supposed to run for the hills and never be heard from again.

"Go right in," Dora said.

Katie nodded once, took a deep breath, sucked in her stomach, and opened the door to Zach's office.

He sat behind his desk, engrossed in paperwork.

"Knock, knock," she said as she entered.

He glanced up, then rose. He was even better looking than she remembered. When he smiled, she nearly stumbled, what with all her blood rushing around her body like so many lost bumper cars.

Just perfect, she thought, more annoyed than embarrassed. Couldn't the horror of their previous encounter have chased away her visceral and inappropriate hormonal response to him? Was this fair?

"Katie." He sounded delighted to see her.

"Hi."

"Thanks for coming by." He walked around the desk and moved close to her.

"Ah, no problem."

She was about to point out that the meeting had been her idea when he put his hand on her upper arm and guided her toward the leather sofas in the corner.

"Coffee, tea, soda?" he asked as she settled onto the slick seat.

"I'm fine," she said as she set her briefcase next to her.

"Let me know if you change your mind."

Zach sank onto the sofa next to hers. As they were both sitting on the side closest to the corner table, they were actually fairly near each other. Knees had the potential for bumping. Which, of course, she noticed.

For about three or four seconds she thought about pretending the other night had never happened. But there wasn't just the party to consider. After David and Mia were married, Zach would be her brother-in-law's father. She didn't need to deal with undercurrents for the next fifty years.

"I have to explain something," she said.

He leaned toward her, his forearms resting on his thighs. His expression was attentive, his dark blue eyes fixed on her face. "Yes?"

Her throat went dry. "I, um. I need to apologize for what happened. You know. At my folks' house."

One corner of his mouth twitched. Then the other. Then his whole mouth curved in a smile. A lock of dark hair fell across his forehead in a sexy, mussed look that tempted her to push it back into place.

"You mean when you told your entire family you were hot for me?"

She winced. "That wasn't exactly what I said, but yes. It was completely unprofessional of me."

"I thought it was charming."

"Really? I would have thought a man like you would get tired of women saying things like that. They practically line up to be taken advantage of. Doesn't it get old?"

As soon as the words were out, she wanted to call them back. She slapped a hand over her mouth, but it wasn't enough. Oh, God, she hadn't really said that, had she?

Horror and humiliation blended into what was becoming a familiar feeling. Zach leaned back in the sofa and shook his head.

"I see you've been doing your research," he said evenly.

She couldn't tell if he was just annoyed or completely furious. "Sort of. A little. I do like to know about the people I'll be working with, and you have something of a reputation." She shook her head. "But I don't mean that in a bad way. I'm sorry. I can't seem to engage my brain and mouth together."

He looked at her. "Is it circumstances or me?"

"I don't know. Maybe both."

Humor brightened his eyes. "Want to start over? Clean slate on both sides."

In this case she wanted more than a fresh start; she wanted to travel back in time and do the whole thing over. But as that wasn't available, she would accept what he offered.

"Absolutely."

He held out his hand. "Then we'll ignore the fact that you think I'm irresistibly sexy, and I'll do my best not to come on to you. Deal?"

She'd been about to put her hand in his when his words sank in. Come on to her? As in he thought she was . . . well, attractive?

It wasn't that she had a low opinion of herself. Men found her appealing. She had dates, boyfriends. But Zach wasn't just any guy. He was a world-class player. His women were starlets and models. In the smorgasbord of women available to him, she was little more than an appetizer.

"Deal," she said and slid her hand against his.

The heat that flared, along with the sparks arcing up her arm, nearly made her laugh. Okay, one problem solved, but the issue of the wayward hormones needed more work.

She pulled her hand free and reached for her briefcase. "Ready to talk about the party?"

"Sure. It'll distract me from the hell of my day."

"Stressful case?"

"Mediation." He dropped his hands to his lap. "The couple had been married for over twenty years. The wife stayed home to take care of the kids. He hit his forties and decided he wanted a new-and-improved spouse. Fairly typical."

Katie wasn't sure what to do with the information. "Who were you representing?"

"Her. She got a decent settlement. I guess the real question is why she married the guy in the first place."

"Probably because she loved him."

Zach looked at her. His dark blue eyes seemed to flash with anger, and there was a cynical twist to his mouth. "I don't see a whole lot of that in my line of work. In my world, relationships don't work, and the kids nearly always pay the price for that."

He shook his head. "Sorry. I'll step off my soapbox for now."

"No, it's okay. You're obviously concerned about the people you deal with. I think that's good."

He smiled. "Katie, I'm a mean, hard-assed, son-of-a-bitch lawyer. I don't do 'concerned.' "

He was right—she'd heard he was a tough opponent. Word had it he was smart, ruthless, and never gave away any advantage. Between that and his reputation with the ladies, she'd assumed he was self-absorbed and someone she really wouldn't like. But he'd surprised her twice in less than five minutes. First with his gracious offer to forget what had happened at the hacienda, and just now with his comments about kids getting caught in their parents' problems.

Maybe she'd judged him too quickly. Maybe there was a real person under the sharkskin. Maybe she liked him.

"Okay. Enough about the law. I have a very large charity event to plan." She pulled several folders from her briefcase. "I looked over the notes you gave me and went to see the hotel that had been reserved. Apparently no one had arranged for a contract, so nothing was firm."

A tickle of nerves swept across her chest, but she ignored it. She was the professional here. Zach had hired her to make the fund-raiser a success. That's what she intended to do.

"I want to change venues," she told him. "The original hotel is older, and while the architecture is lovely, the ballroom isn't very big. With a crowd of over two thousand people to consider, space is important. We need spillover rooms. Also, I thought it would be fun to make the locale more of an integral part of the party, rather than just the background."

She glanced at Zach to check for some kind of a reaction, but his expression was unreadable. Assuming silence meant agreement, she passed him a brochure.

"The West Side Royale Hotel?" he asked. "It's new, right?"

"Refurbished. What I like best about it are the gardens. They start by the ballroom and flow throughout the property. The man in charge is a botanist. He's done amazing work. A cancellation cleared the weekend we're interested in. They've got a big hole in their schedule, and they're willing to deal to get it filled. They're offering a great price to give us the rooms we need."

Zach flipped through the brochure. The hotel had been done Art Deco style.

"What do you mean rooms?" he asked. "Isn't there one ballroom?"

Okay, now came the selling part. This is where she proved she was worth what he was paying her. "There can be. That's more traditional. I've pulled articles on different fundraisers held in Los Angeles. They've ranged from funky with organic food and barefoot guests to elegant black-tie. I wanted something different, something special. Something successful. To that end, I'm thinking of a two-tiered system."

Zach raised his eyebrows. "Excuse me?"

"The cost of a ticket is a thousand dollars per couple, right?"

"Yes. The partners set the price."

"So that can stay the same. The cost of the party is about two hundred dollars a person, leaving a good chunk of money for the charity. But out of the two thousand to twenty five hundred people who will attend, at least three hundred and as many as five hundred are serious players in the charity game. They give away millions of dollars every year. Why not to your charity?"

"We're not going to invite them to the party and then go begging for additional donations."

"Agreed. But you could charge them more up front."

"What?"

She held up a hand. "I'm suggesting that a few hundred special guests receive an invitation to attend the fundraiser, but that they are invited to a more exclusive party held at the same time. They'll have the same dinner and the same entertainment, but there will be separate activities both before and after the meal."

"Such as?"

Katie opened a pale blue folder and unfolded a map of the hotel grounds. She pointed to the main ballroom, and the gardens beyond, then showed a small ballroom flanking the main one.

"I was thinking of games of chance," she said, "but not gambling. That's so overdone. More like carnival games, but instead of winning a goldfish at the ring toss, you could win a diamond bracelet worth, say, five grand. We could do ski vacations in Gstaad and balloon trips in France. If we keep the prizes around five to ten thousand a piece and charge the couples twenty-five thousand to participate, we're still coming out ahead of the thousand-dollars-a-plate donation."

She couldn't read his face. He was listening and he hadn't started screaming. She figured that was all good news.

"Go on," he said evenly.

"Okay. Well, I thought we'd go with a whole dipping-for-charity theme. The menu would be dipping foods and finger foods. A lot of kabobs, which would mean small grills set up all over. We can do all kinds of exotic meats and fun vegetarian kabobs for those who don't do the animal-product thing. We can grill bread and have make-your-own appetizers, then do chocolates from around the world in fondue pots for dessert. We'd have entertainment in the ballroom, and then put tents in the gardens. Each tent would be a different food station."

She stopped talking and surreptitiously crossed her fingers. Yes, it wasn't the usual kind of party, but Katie figured her best chance of success was to make the event her own rather than trying to do what every other party planner in the city had already done and done well.

Zach tapped the brochure for the West Side Royale Hotel. "We've never had a party like that before."

"I know. Different can be good."

"I'd have to run it by the partners."

"Of course."

He smiled—a slow smile that made the corners of his eyes crinkle and her heartbeat zip into an aerobic state.

"I like it," he said.

She nodded briskly, determined not to show her intense relief. "I'm glad. I think it could be fun. At least the larger venue will keep the party from feeling crowded. That seems to be a big problem with mega events."

He tossed the brochure onto the table and settled back into the sofa. With one ankle resting on the opposite knee, he looked dangerous and masculine . . . or maybe one went with the other. Could a man look masculine without appearing dangerous?

She found it impossible to stop staring at him, especially when he began loosening his tie. It was only an insignificant length of silk, yet the way his fingers worked the knot, then tugged it free made her thighs go up in flames.

"I'll present the idea to them in the next day or so and get back to you."

"Good. The hotel will hold the facilities until the end of the week. As long as I hear by Friday, we'll have our space."

"Fair enough."

She collected her various folders, but left him with the brochure. Their work now concluded, Katie felt she should make her escape as quickly as possible, before she put her foot in it again. Still, one thing continued to bother her.

"I'm more than a little surprised by the coincidence of all this," she said. "You hiring me to plan this party. Your son getting engaged to my sister. What are the odds of that?"

His relaxed posture didn't change, but she would have sworn something inside of him shifted. He shrugged.

"Things like that happen."

Until that moment she'd never thought anything else, but suddenly she wondered if there had been some kind of manipulation behind the scenes.

Don't be crazy, she told herself. That wasn't possible . . . was it?

"So you didn't hire me on purpose?" she asked, speaking slowly. "You didn't hire me *because* Mia is marrying David?"

"Why would I do that?"

"I have no idea," she said honestly.

"Unless I wanted something from you."

She stiffened. Every nerve ending went on alert and not in a good way. "What do you mean?"

"My son is my world, Katie. He's a good kid. But there's no way in hell he's ready to get married."

She blinked several times. "What? Why are you telling me this?"

He pointed toward her stack of folders. "This job represents a lot of money to your company. It would change your life. What would happen if word got out that you weren't up to the task?"

Her chest tightened. Half-formed sentences flashed through her brain. Nothing made sense. "Are you threatening me?"

"Do I have to?"

Confusion turned to anger. "Let me get this straight. You deliberately hired me because I'm Mia's sister. Now you're telling me if I don't get Mia to somehow back off from marrying your son, you'll destroy my company?"

"That sounds melodramatic."

Not to her. "Do I have it wrong?"

"I'm helping you achieve your goal. I expect you to help me achieve mine."

Outrage joined fury. "Mia loves David. You want me to sacrifice my sister's happiness because you don't approve?"

He leaned forward and pinned her with a gaze that could have cut metal. "It's not about approving. It's about my son's future. Do you know the odds of a marriage surviving past five years? Any marriage? They're less than ten percent of that when the couple is under twenty. If you're so damn worried about your sister's happiness, think about how well she'll survive a divorce."

"Zach, I—"

"No. This isn't personal, Katie. I think Mia's great. But David's too young to marry anyone."

"He's eighteen. Isn't that his decision to make?"

"Legally, which is why I haven't delivered an ultimatum."

Of course. Because being upfront wasn't his style. Katie gritted her teeth. To think she'd actually felt badly about judging him. She'd bought into his nice-guy act, but he was just as much of a slimy player as she'd first thought. *And* he was trying to ruin her baby sister's life. The bastard.

She shoved the folders into her briefcase and snapped it shut. "I appreciate that you're worried about David. You care about him, just like I care about Mia. But here's the thing. I won't go behind my sister's back. She loves your son and she wants to marry him. That's good enough for me."

She rose and glared at him. "If you thought you could force me to do what you want for the price of this job, you were wrong. And if that means you're going to try ruining me, then have at it. Anyone who would be swayed by your opinion doesn't matter a damn to me."

She started for the door. Her high heels and the thick, plush carpet slowed her down, so it wasn't a surprise when

Zach caught up with her. He grabbed her arm, holding her until she stopped and faced him.

"What?" she demanded.

His mouth twisted. "You're saying you can't be bought."

"Amazing, isn't it?"

He stunned her by grinning. "You're tougher than you look."

"Gee, that's nearly as nice as saying I'm smarter than I look."

"That, too."

"You're a bastard, Zach."

"Not technically, but maybe in spirit." He released her and shoved his hands into his slacks pockets. "I had to try, Katie. He's my son. I love him."

Two seconds ago she would have sworn there was nothing he could say that would have made her want to do anything but hit him upside the head with a two-by-four. But with six simple words, he knocked the mad right out of her.

"Then tell him you're worried. Won't he listen?"

"No. He already knows what I think." Zach shook his head. "I tried to keep it from him, but I didn't do much of a job. He's determined to marry your sister, and I know it's going to be a disaster."

"What if you're wrong?"

"I'm never wrong."

The mad returned. "I'm guessing no one has ever accused you of being humble."

"Not really."

"Color me surprised." She shifted her briefcase to her other hand. "I won't get between them. David and Mia want to get married, and I think it's a great idea."

"Are you open to persuasion?"

She hated that her first thought was sexual. This man was slime and she still found him attractive and intriguing. There was definitely something wrong with her.

"I'll listen," she said, "but only if you'll give equal time to the opposition."

"Fair enough."

As he made his living arguing his side, it didn't sound fair to her at all.

"You still doing the party?" he asked.

She narrowed her gaze. "Are you going to threaten me again?"

The smile returned. "I was bluffing. I wanted to see how far I could push you."

That had been a bluff? What would he do if he was serious? "Don't do it again."

"Agreed." He looked at her. "Friends?"

She reached for the door. "Uneasy business associates."

"I was hoping for more."

"Hope away," she said as she stepped into the hallway and walked toward the elevator.

5

Mia stepped out of the bridal shop dressing room and headed for the platform in front of the three-way mirror. The stiff satin gown flowed out around her as she walked.

"Shoes will help," Katie said, grabbing a pair with three-inch heels from a row of bridal pumps in front of the mirror.

Mia held up her skirt, then slid into the shoes. They were too big. Like a little girl playing dress up, she shuffled the last couple of feet to the platform and stepped up. Katie moved around her, adjusting the dress.

"How are you two doing?" the salesperson asked as she breezed in front of the mirror. She tilted her head as she studied Mia. "She's just lovely. What a beautiful dress."

Katie agreed with her on both counts. The strapless satin gown hugged Mia's full breasts, rib cage, and waist before flaring out to the floor. The heavy fabric flowed into a train. The dress was a little big on Mia, so Katie reached for a box of pins tucked on a shelf by the side mirror.

"We'd like to see what it would look like if it was fitted," she said to the saleswoman. "Is that all right?"

"Of course."

The woman watched for a couple of seconds, then smiled. "You seem to know exactly what you're doing. I'll leave you two to discuss possibilities."

Katie circled Mia, taking in a bit of fabric around the waist, then fluffing out the skirt. "What do you think?"

Mia looked at her reflection. "I like the style, but there's something wrong."

Katie nodded. Mia looked like a princess, despite her streaked hair and big eyes. The white satin set off her skin. Yet it didn't look . . . perfect.

"What do you like about it?" she asked.

Mia shrugged. "That it's strapless. I like the lace." She brushed her hand against the lace sewn across the waist and rising toward her breasts. More lace decorated the hem and the train.

Katie squinted, trying to imagine her sister walking down the aisle of a church. The way she would move and the dress would move with her. The flow of the fabric. The—

"The satin's too heavy," she announced. "It's not going to look right on you. We should have seen it before. You're only five foot three and despite having the biggest boobs in the family, you're really small. Don't move."

She hurried back to the dressing room, where they had already tried on and discarded five other wedding gowns. She returned with one covered in tulle and lace.

It was an off-the-shoulder style that had made Mia's neck look as wide as a fullback's. But the fabric was perfect. Lace decorated the bodice of the dress, becoming more scattered closer to the bottom. A lace trim finished the hem.

"Imagine the dress you're wearing," she continued, "but with this material. It's soft, it flows better, and it won't overwhelm you. I would do a band of satin at the top, to give the bodice structure, but the rest of the gown could be in this lacy tulle. What do you think?"

Mia kicked off her shoes and spun around on the platform. "Yes. That's exactly right. It will be perfect for summer, too. I love all the lace." She beamed at her sister. "You're the best."

"Yeah, yeah, I know." Katie couldn't help smiling. "Okay. If you're sure, then go get changed and we'll grab some lunch. After that, I want to have you pick out the lace."

Forty-five minutes later they sat across from each other at a Beverly Hills bistro. While Katie didn't normally shop in this part of town, she'd wanted Mia to see as many lovely gowns as possible before making her choice.

"Are you sure about the dress?" Katie asked after they'd given their order. "We can keep looking."

Her youngest sister tucked her shoulder-length hair behind her ears. "I swear, I love your idea. I'll have to start working on my arms, though, so they're buff."

"They're pretty buff now."

"Thank you." Mia picked up her soda and took a drink. "I can't wait to see the look on David's face when he sees me walking down the aisle. He's gonna die."

"Let's hope not."

Mia grinned. "You know what I mean." Her smile faded a little. "Katie, are you okay? You've been kind of distracted today."

"I'm fine."

"Really?"

Katie nodded because there was no way she was telling the truth. What Zach had done yesterday still made her furious every time she thought about it, which was far too often. Okay, he loved his son and was worried about him, but that didn't excuse threatening her or wanting her to betray her family.

Whatever his plan had been, he'd blown it, because she was more determined than ever to see Mia and David happily married.

"Are we counting calories?" she asked to distract her sister. Mia shook her head. "Not even close."

"Good."

Katie flipped back the white napkin covering the bread basket between them and groaned when the smell of freshly baked rolls drifted to her. She offered the basket to her sister, then took one for herself.

The flaky crust scattered crumbs everywhere when she tore it in half. Katie braced herself for a religious experience. A dab of sweet butter completed the moment. She took a bite.

Heaven. Pure heaven. Who needed men when there was perfect French bread in the world?

And speaking of men . . .

Zach flashed back into her brain. Go *away*, she told the image. She refused to find him attractive after what he'd done. He was not good-looking, not sexy, and certainly not her type.

One out of three, she thought wryly. Not bad odds. He'd been a jerk, and she would be wise to forget about him. There was only one problem—a couple of things he'd said had made sense.

Oh, she didn't want that to be true, but there it was. Young marriages didn't often make it.

"Do you ever think it's strange that our parents have always pushed us to get married so young?" she asked her sister.

Mia shrugged. "I never thought about it. It's not really our folks, it's much more Grandma Tessa and Grandpa Lorenzo. It's an Italian thing."

"That and they want a male heir for the winery."

Mia laughed. "Granny M shares that. I couldn't believe she sounded disappointed when I said I *wasn't* pregnant. Most grandparents would be relieved."

"Not ours."

Katie thought about all the subtle and not-so-subtle hints she'd received over the years. About how she would be so much happier if she was married and had children of her own. Preferably *male* children.

Mia leaned toward her. "Why can't they leave the winery to Brenna? She cares about wine making and stuff."

"Brenna lives in L.A. That makes it hard to run things on a day-to-day basis. I have my own business, Francesca is studying psychology and sociology, and—"

"And I plan to take over the world," Mia said lightly. "Brenna is the right one, if you ask me. Now that Jeff is out of medical school, he could start a practice up close to the hacienda. Plus, then we'd get to see them more."

"Good point. I wonder if they've discussed it. Or if Jeff would be interested."

"I don't know." Mia planted her elbows on the table. "That's one thing I really like about David. He sees me as an equal. He knows I'm smart and capable and that I have goals. And he's okay with that."

Zach's words drifted through Katie's brain. She could hear him saying that Mia and David were too young to make it.

"You're making a pretty big decision," she said, even as she hated herself for bringing it up in the first place. "Marriage is forever. I envy you knowing it's right."

Mia's smile faded as she reached for Katie's hand. "Is all this wedding talk making you think about Greg?"

Oops. Not the direction she'd wanted the conversation to go. Ex-fiancés should best be forgotten. She squeezed her sister's fingers. "I'm fine with Greg. To be honest, I'm not sorry we didn't get married. I don't think it would have worked. I guess my concern is that you have so much of your life in front of you. I want to make sure you're marrying David because it's what you want and not because of family pressure or feeling that it's time." She grinned. "After all, it would be much easier to rule the world if you were single."

"I think I can handle a marriage *and* world domination. I'm a great multitasker." Mia studied her. "Katie, I love him. He's everything I've ever wanted. As for being pressured by the family, that's impossible to escape. *You* know. You get hassled every time you walk in the door."

"Tell me about it. I swear I've dated every single guy over the age of twenty in a fifty-mile radius. Well, except for the ordained priests."

"If Grandma Tessa didn't think it was a sin, she'd dragging them home for you, as well."

"One of these day's I'll find the right man."

Mia smiled. "Your own handsome prince?"

"Sure."

"I hope so. I found mine."

Katie looked at her sister's pretty face. Contentment radiated from her expression and happiness brightened her eyes.

"Of course you'll be happy with David," she said, wondering why she'd ever thought differently. Zach might have his reasons for worrying—in his line of work, who could blame him? But statistics were about other people. Marcelli marriages were forever.

• • •

Mia collected the mail, including a copy of *Cosmo* in French, and ran up the stairs to her apartment. She'd already seen David's truck parked on the street, so she knew he was waiting for her. She burst into the front door.

"We picked out a dress," she announced, tossing her mail and backpack on the floor and slamming the door shut behind her.

David lay stretched out on the sofa. He grinned at her and motioned for her to come closer. "Hello to you, too."

"Hello."

She kicked off her Nikes and straddled him, bending low to kiss him. His arms came around her.

She loved looking into his face. His eyes were a deep, true blue and made her melt a little inside when she gazed at them. In his arms she felt sure and safe. While everyone in the world thought she was so smart and together, what they didn't see was she was always afraid of being just the baby. She'd been the baby her whole life, and getting out on her own and growing up hadn't been easy. With David around, she didn't have to try so hard.

"Tell me about your day," she said, brushing his mouth again and feeling heat fill her body.

He nipped her lower lip. "Tell me about the dress."

"I can't. You know that. It's a surprise. But it's beautiful and we picked out the fabric and the lace. Katie's going to make the pattern from a couple of different ones. In the meantime, we all start the beading."

"What beading?"

"All the lace gets beaded by hand. The flower petals are outlined in seed pearls and filled in with little beads. It's what we do. You know—a tradition."

"Cool." He kissed her jaw. "So who is Robert Anderson?"

She raised her head. "Who?"

"I asked first. He called while you were out. There's a message. Something about him coming out to L.A. in a couple of weeks and wanting to know if you'd like to have dinner."

Mia bounced off the sofa to her feet and raced for the machine. Sure enough, the red light blinked steadily.

"He called!" she crowed. "He called, he called, he called."

David sat up slowly. "Mia, who's the guy?"

She spun around and grinned at him. "Oh, don't give me that look. This isn't *personal*. It's about my career. Robert Anderson is that guy I met last summer at the Arabic language course I took. Remember? He went to Georgetown, too. We've been e-mailing and he said if he got out here, we could hang out. He's willing to write me a letter of recommendation to both Georgetown and the State Department."

"Yeah, right." David looked anything but convinced.

"David, don't act like that. The man is in his forties. He has a daughter close to my age. Plus he's married and I met his wife and they're a totally cool couple. They took me to dinner a couple of times."

David didn't look convinced.

She hurried back to the sofa and squeezed onto his lap. "You're the one I love."

"I don't like the idea of you having dinner with other guys."

Mia really, really wanted to roll her eyes, but that never led to meaningful conversation with the opposite sex. She also wanted to smack David upside the head. Another bad idea. Instead, she kissed his face, all the while murmuring phrases like "lovey dovey" and "kissy wissy." It usually worked. Just not today.

He moved her off his lap and set her on the sofa next to him. David might be tall and skinny, but he could sure push her around without breaking a sweat, which was one of the things she really hated about being short.

"Mia, I'm serious," he said.

She sighed. "I'm serious, too, David. Robert Anderson is someone who can help me. I'm in my junior year, which means I'll be applying to grad schools over the summer. Getting into Georgetown isn't a sure thing. Robert can help. If you're so concerned that it's more than just that, then come with us to dinner. I don't care."

Instantly his face brightened. "You wouldn't mind me being there?"

"As they say in the Valley, well, duh. Of course you're welcome. It's going to be boring, but if you want to be there, then be there."

"Okay. Great."

He reached for her, but instead of falling into his embrace, she rose and crossed to the window. Once there, she stared out at her view of the side street and the apartment building across the way.

"I don't know why you don't trust me," she said softly, folding her arms over her chest. "You're going to have to get over that, David, or we're going to be in trouble."

"I do trust you."

Mia didn't say anything. Although she and David were the same age, sometimes she felt years older. Maybe all that crap about girls maturing more quickly wasn't exactly the crap she thought it was.

"I know things are different for you," she said, not wanting to fight. "You're in your first year of college. You haven't even picked a major yet."

"A lot of people haven't."

"I know." She turned to face him. "I'm not being critical. I mean, most kids don't know what they want when they enter college. I happen to be one of the ones who did."

"You also started college when you were sixteen. What was that all about?"

He grinned as he spoke, reminding her that this was a familiar point of discussion. He accused her of being too smart for her own good while she called him a lazy bum who couldn't pick a direction of study.

But what if they weren't really kidding?

Mia didn't know where the thought came from. She also didn't like it.

"I love you," she said intently.

David rose and crossed the floor. When he reached her, he pulled her close. "I love you, too. I want to be with you for the rest of my life."

She leaned into him, parting her lips for his kiss. When he picked her up to carry her into the bedroom, she found she sometimes quite liked that he was big enough to push her around.

6

The delivery guy from the Thai place arrived thirty seconds before Katie did. Zach paid the bill and added a generous tip for speedy service, then waited by the open front door while Katie parked her convertible in front of his house.

She turned off the engine, then collected her ever bulging briefcase and stepped out onto the street.

It was nearly seven, and long since dark. The night was cool and damp. Winter, such as it was, had returned to Southern California, keeping daytime temperatures in the fifties. In deference to the change in season, Katie wore a lightweight coat over slacks. As she approached, streetlights illuminated the red in her hair.

"I wasn't sure you'd show up," he called.

She stepped onto the walkway. "This is business. Besides, I don't scare off that easily." She glanced at the large bag he held. "Am I too early? I thought you said seven."

"I did." He held up the bag. Already the smell of Thai food made his mouth water. "It's a peace offering."

She sniffed once, then smiled. "I could be persuaded."

He was hoping she would say that.

Zach ushered her into his tall, narrow house. The split level entry led down to the main living area and up toward the bedrooms.

"How long have you lived here?" she asked, glancing around. "It's a fabulous location."

"Two blocks from the beach with a perfect view," he said. "David and I moved in two years ago. We'd been living on the west side for a few years and wanted a change."

They walked into the kitchen and Katie set her briefcase on the granite counter. Bleached birch cabinets lined two walls. Aside from the Sub-Zero freezer and six-burner stove, the previous occupants had left behind a built-in under-the-counter wine cellar and Jenn-Air cooktop in the center island.

Katie did a slow turn. "I'm not a huge cook, but even I could envy this setup." She glanced at him. "Let me guess. You only order take-out."

"Something like that." He set the food on the counter. "Let me take your coat."

He moved behind her as she slipped out of her jacket. Beneath, she wore tailored black slacks and a soft-looking sweater in emerald green. She'd piled her long hair on her head, leaving her neck bare.

Zach draped the coat over his arm, ignoring the scent of Katie's body and the warmth lingering in her coat. He hung the garment in the hallway closet and returned to the kitchen. He had to keep his mind on business. At least for now.

But when he found her leaning against the counter, looking at several pictures of David on the refrigerator, he found thoughts of business fading. Instead he focused on the curve of her hip as she rested her weight on one foot, and the way her fingers gracefully skimmed the collection of photos.

He could imagine those fingers touching other things—namely him. He would do some touching in return. Naked, he thought. He wanted her naked.

He mentally cuffed himself. Time for a distraction.

"So you didn't call me up and tell me to go to hell," he said.

She glanced at him. "Was I supposed to?"

"You could have. You were mad."

"I've always been more of a 'living well is the best revenge' kind of person. I'm going to throw you a party so incredible, you'll have to eat your words."

He appreciated that she'd twisted the situation to her own advantage and that she wanted to win.

"Until then, let's eat Thai," he said, grabbing the bag of food and moving toward the table in the corner. "You willing to put business on hold until after dinner?"

"Sure."

He plied her with noodles and Thai chicken, all the while asking questions about what it was like to grow up at the winery.

"Four girls," he said. "Any complaints about not having a brother?"

"It's a bit of a sore spot," she admitted as she scooped up more noodles. "My grandparents are old-fashioned and want a male heir. That's why there's some pressure to marry and have grandkids. Jeff, Brenna's husband, is a sweetie and we all adore him, but he wasn't interested in wine. Instead he wanted to be a doctor, if you can believe it."

"You never married."

Her brown eyes widened slightly. "Was that a question or a statement?"

"Which isn't going to get me in trouble?"

She smiled. "I think it's too late for that. As for me being married, I was engaged when I was eighteen, but things didn't work out."

"What happened?"

She took a bite of food, then chewed. After she swallowed, she said, "He joined the service three days before the wedding. I always thought it was pretty tacky of Greg to prefer the possibility of going to war over marrying me."

"He dumped you?"

She raised her eyebrows. "Thank you for putting it so delicately, but yes."

"Are you okay with that?"

"It's been about ten years. I've managed to get on with my life."

"Without getting married."

She put down her fork. "Marriage is one of those topics we should probably avoid."

She held her own with him—he liked that. "So let's talk about me."

"Your favorite subject?"

"Absolutely. Ask me anything."

"Who do you prefer to represent in your work?" she asked, leaning back in her chair. "The husband or the wife?"

"I take on whoever asks me first."

"So you don't care about being on the side of right?"

"We're talking about divorce. There's almost never a 'right' side. I've yet to see a marriage fall apart all because one person is inherently evil. Usually both parties have some claim to the blame. In the case of drugs or alcohol, the nonabusing spouse doesn't usually deal with his or her problems because the substance issue is bigger than both of them, but that doesn't mean it's not there."

"I never thought about it," Katie admitted. "There hasn't been any divorce in our family. I guess we're just lucky."

"Luck helps. In my line of work I don't see very much of it."

"Why a divorce lawyer? There are a lot of ways for a lawyer to make a living in this town. Why'd you pick that specialty?"

"Let's move to the living room first," he said easily, rising, then pulling out her chair for her. "It will be more comfortable."

She reached for the empty plates on the table, but he brushed her hands away. "I'll get that later." At her look of surprise, he shrugged. "I can be domestic when the situation calls for it."

He put his hand on the small of her back. She didn't move away. Score one for his side, he thought, pleased that she liked being close to him. He didn't find her nearness a hardship, either, which meant being charming to get his way had plenty of perks. Pleasant working conditions always improved his attitude.

The sunken living room had west-facing, floor-to-ceiling windows. Katie walked toward them.

"You must see amazing sunsets," she said, staring into the darkness.

"If I'm home in time."

"If I lived here, I'd make sure I was home."

"The hacienda overlooks the Pacific. You see the sunsets from there."

"That's where I grew up, so it's different."

She started toward the sectional sofa. As she passed a

hip-high table, she paused. He saw that her gaze had settled on several framed photographs. Zach shoved his hands into his pockets and waited for the questions. So far everything was going according to plan.

A beautiful blonde smiled out from one picture. The same woman laughed in two other pictures. She and a much younger Zach were together in a fourth.

"She's stunning," Katie said, a question in her voice.

"David's mother."

"Oh. She's really lovely."

"On the outside. On the inside—" He shrugged. "She walked away from David when he was four, and I don't think she's seen him more than twice since."

Katie's gold-flecked brown eyes widened. "I don't understand. How could she not want to be with her child?"

"She never wanted children."

He hesitated, more to figure out how much to tell than because he was reluctant to share his past. He didn't usually spill his guts to people he just met, but extraordinary circumstances called for extraordinary measures. He needed Katie as an ally, but he had to be careful.

He motioned to the sectional sofa. Katie sank down onto the cushions. Zach settled across from her. He schooled his features into his "I'm concerned but I'm okay" look.

"I met Ainsley in high school. She was the head cheerleader, prom queen. You know the type."

"I've met one or two," Katie said with a slight smile.

Zach nodded. "I thought Ainsley was a princess. So I wooed and won her. Boy meets girl, boy falls for girl, boy gets girl pregnant."

Katie winced. "How old were you?"

"Just seventeen. We got married. David came along nine months later. It wasn't how I planned to spend the summer after graduating from high school. But we learned how to be parents. It wasn't easy."

He didn't go into details. There was no point in discussing the fights, the anger that had flared between them as they struggled to take care of their son. They'd both felt trapped. Whatever infatuation they'd once shared had quickly burned away.

"I had some money from a trust fund," he continued. "That paid for our living expenses, although there wasn't much left over for more than basics. Ainsley's parents paid for her college. I had a scholarship. Both our moms helped out with daycare. It was still tough."

Tough didn't begin to describe what it had been. Ainsley had made his life a living hell. She'd resented David and being married. She had been young and beautiful, and she wanted to be out in the world.

"The day I graduated from college, Ainsley had me served with divorce papers," he said flatly. "She'd hired one of the best lawyers in the city. *My* lawyer had been recommended by a friend. He wasn't in the same league. Ainsley got everything. I fought for custody of David, which turned out not to be a problem. Not only did she not want to see her son, she wanted compensation for the pain and suffering of having to have a child in the first place. She claimed she'd wanted to have an abortion and that I'd talked her out of it. She even had notes from a clinic visit she'd made while she'd been pregnant."

Katie frowned. "I don't understand. Had she wanted an abortion?"

"I don't know. She never said anything to me. In the same breath she told me she was pregnant, she announced we were getting married. I'd been raised to believe a man took his responsibilities seriously, so I never thought otherwise."

He rested his elbows on his knees. "Let's just say Ainsley got her pound of flesh and then some. I was to come into the lump sum of my trust fund when I turned twenty-five. She got all of that *and* didn't have to pay child support. When it was over her lawyer took me aside. He slapped me on the back and told me next time I needed to get a better lawyer. At that moment I vowed to *be* a better lawyer."

Katie looked stunned. Zach knew it wasn't a pretty story, but every word of it was true.

"So Ainsley simply disappeared from your life?"

"She showed up to collect her checks, but once she had all the money she was due, she disappeared. I heard she moved back East. I don't care where she is."

"Why do you keep her pictures out?"

"They matter to David. I packed them away once, but he asked me to let them stay. He has trouble remembering her and the photos help."

Katie had never had a child, so she was unable to comprehend the depth of Zach's feeling for David. Still, there wasn't a doubt in her mind that this man loved his son with every fiber of his being. His intensity, his steadfastness, not only made her quiver on the inside, they confirmed her belief that Mia had made a good choice. David Stryker had an amazing role model guiding him through life.

Now that she'd heard Zach's history, she understood his concerns for the engagement. She approved of his concern, even if she didn't appreciate his tactics.

"Did you tell me this to explain your position or to win me to your side?" she asked.

"Both."

"Because threatening me didn't work? Now you're going for the heart?"

"Am I getting close?"

"No, but I have extreme respect for your skill level in court. Can you see the other attorneys trembling or do they hide it?"

He grinned. "They try to act cool."

Katie leaned back in the sofa. "So if you're so smart, why did you tip your hand with me?"

"I told you, I wanted to see if you would call my bluff."

"If I'd caved in, you would have accepted the victory."

"Of course. And solved the wedding problem."

Katie didn't appreciate her sister's engagement being referred to as "the wedding problem," but she knew what Zach meant.

"Have you considered that I could rally the entire family to my side?" she asked.

"It crossed my mind, but I'm not worried."

"Why?"

He smiled slyly. "You can't risk your grandmothers and mother resenting me. What if the wedding goes through? I'll be a part of the family. You wouldn't want to be responsible for screwing up that relationship."

Her mouth dropped open. She closed it with a conscious thought, but that didn't stop her from being stunned. "How did you figure that out?"

"Men get over things. Women remember forever."

He was right, she thought, still amazed. About all of it. Her first instinct had been to call home and let everyone know what he was planning. But she'd reconsidered when she'd realized her mother and grandmothers would hate Zach from that moment on.

He was good. Maybe too good. She was out of her league with him in more ways than one. He was also annoying, what with always being one step ahead of her.

Zach stood up suddenly and held out his hand. "Come on. I'll buy you a drink and we'll talk about your plans for the party."

It took her a second to decide if she wanted to switch gears. But what was the point in arguing? "Actually you're supposed to tell me that everyone loved my ideas, that they think I'm so incredibly brilliant that they might have to pay me more, and they're waiting breathlessly for the event to occur."

"How'd you guess?"

After telling herself not to do anything stupid, Katie placed her hand in his.

Despite having braced herself for the impact, she still felt it all the way down to her toes. Her heart rate quadrupled, her skin flushed, and rational thought fled. She might not trust him, but that didn't mean there wasn't chemistry between them.

Zach led her back into the kitchen. He released her hand, which allowed her to catch her breath and try to remember what it felt like to be an adult. While he cleared the table, she pulled the paperwork out of her briefcase.

The good news was that alternating between being annoyed by Zach and being turned on by him kept her from being nervous about planning the party.

"What will you have?" he asked, opening a cupboard and revealing several bottles of liquor.

"I'm driving, so I'll pass, but please have something yourself. If you pour me ice water in a pretty glass, we can pretend I'm drinking hard stuff."

"You got it."

They sat down at the table. Katie spread out her various folders, then turned her attention to Zach. They were close enough that she could see the tiny lines by the out-side corners of his eyes and the various shades that made up his deep blue irises. He was handsome, and he smelled good. A potent combination.

"So talk," she told him. "Tell me the truth—I can han-dle it."

He took a sip of the single malt scotch he'd poured for himself. "They love your ideas. John's pregnant wife thinks everything is, and I quote, 'Too precious for words.' That's a good thing," he added. "She also wants you to call her. She has the names of a couple of jewelry designers who would be happy to come up with some original designs for various prizes."

"Great. I hadn't been worried exactly, but I'll admit to being relieved now."

"I had every confidence."

She blinked at him. Was it her imagination, or had he just shifted closer to her?

"I'll, ah, call the hotel in the morning and finalize the contract. Menus will be next. Do we want to schedule a tasting for everyone?"

"No, thanks. I trust your judgment. And I don't want to have a heated conversation about flowers, napkin colors, or table placement." He leaned toward her. "You're the expert. Dazzle me."

"You got it," she said. "I'll line things up, make some selections, and then run everything by you. While I'll agree to skip the massive tasting, there are some things I'm going to want you to try."

"I'm open to that."

His low and seductive voice made her think of tan-gled sheets, champagne, and chocolate. Was there a more enticing combination? Throw in a good-looking man . . . preferably dressed in nothing, with an eager-to-please attitude, and an evening couldn't get much more perfect.

Just not *her* evening.

"So if threats and heartfelt stories aren't going to work, you'll try seduction?" she asked.

He looked amused rather than embarrassed. "Will it work?"

"Not on me."

"Too bad."

A lesser man would have been rattled by being shot out of the water, she thought. But not Zach. Figures.

"Okay, then." She began to pack up her briefcase. "That's all I need for now. I'll just get out of your hair so you can have the rest of your evening to do whatever it is you do."

She half expected him to invite her to stay, and when he didn't, she tried to be relieved rather than disappointed. She was about fifty percent successful.

Zach collected her coat, then held it out for her. As she slipped into it, she said, "I know you're worried about Mia and David, but I wish you'd relax. I thought a lot about what you said, about young marriages failing and I know it happens, but not to everyone. I come from a long line of people who get it right."

"I'm a worried father," he said, staring deeply into her eyes and making her want to throw herself at him. "I can't help it."

"You're a good father, too," she said instead. "Trust that and trust your son. If that doesn't work, remind yourself that Marcelli marriages never fall apart. I promise."

"And if you're wrong?"

"I won't be. You can—"

He cut her off with a kiss. Katie supposed she should have seen it coming, but she hadn't. One second they'd been talking, and the next she was in his arms, and his mouth had claimed hers.

The brush of his firm lips sent her senses into a tailspin. Heat surrounded her, as did need and passion. He didn't deepen the kiss, which only made her want more, and when he stepped away, she found it impossible to speak.

He picked up her briefcase and put his arm around her, then led the way to the front door. By the time they reached it, she'd regained the power of speech.

"Why did you do that?" she asked.

"I wanted to. Should I apologize?"

"Would you mean it?"

"No."

She tried to work up some righteous indignation, but she tingled too much. "Zach, we have a business relationship."

"You're irresistible."

"You're lying."

"Am I?"

Pathetically, she wanted him to be telling the truth. Right. Because she was exactly Zach's type. Not.

"You can't use sex to get what you want from me," she told him.

"What can I use it for?"

She ignored him, grabbed her suitcase, and stalked out of the house.

"You didn't answer my question," he called after her.

"Go to hell."

He laughed. "I had a good time, too, Katie."

She fumed all the way to the car. When she was

inside, she put the key in the ignition. The man made her insane.

She couldn't wait to see him again.

Seed pearls multiplied in the night. At least that was Katie's conclusion Tuesday morning when she dumped out bags of them onto the dining room table at the hacienda. Along with the seed pearls were tiny beads and stacks of lace appliqués.

Four pairs of eyes turned accusingly from her to Mia. The eighteen-year-old shrugged.

"So the dress has a lot of lace. It's gonna be beautiful."

Grandma Tessa fingered the stack of lace, then glared at her granddaughter. "We'll be beading for months. My fingers will fall off."

Mia remained uncowed. "I'm your favorite. You love me. You want my dress to be beautiful."

Grandma Tessa smiled. "You girls are all my favorite, but yes, I do want you to have the most beautiful dress ever. Who needs fingers, right?"

Mia laughed and hugged her. "I knew you'd understand."

Francesca wasn't so easily swayed. "How will we get the blood out?"

Katie grinned. Francesca had many wonderful qualities, but she couldn't sew for spit, and whenever she sewed there were always drops of red scattered on the delicate fabric. It was amazing that she hadn't bled to death when she'd taken a quilting class a couple of years ago. But then Francesca was a hobby junky. If there was a craft/cooking/decorating class within a fifty-mile radius, she had taken it.

"I can get it out. Don't worry about it."

Katie glanced at her watch and frowned. Brenna was late. Maybe traffic had been bad up from the city.

"Let's get started," Katie said. "I'll show Brenna the design when she gets here."

She opened the sketch pad, exposing the drawing she'd done of Mia's dress.

"It's beautiful," Grammy M said. "So delicate. Just perfect for you, Mia."

"That's what I thought."

Their mother fingered the stack of lace flowers. "I love how you've scattered the lace over the dress."

Even Francesca had to admit that the gown was lovely, before grumbling about the amount of work they were all going to have to do.

Mia, knowing her family, ignored the teasing and discussed hairstyles and shoes instead.

Katie reached for the first lace appliqué. "It's pretty simple," she said. "Outline the flower in seed pearls. Fill in the petals with beads. I did one over the weekend. It took me about four hours."

Four hours she'd spent *not* thinking about how complicated Zach was and how much she hated that she'd enjoyed their kiss.

Silence descended. Francesca blinked first. "For one flower? How many are there?"

"About sixty or seventy for the skirt, a hundred and fifty for the hem, twenty-five or so for the bodice."

"Then we'd better get started," Colleen said, reaching for several lengths of seed pearls and bags of beads.

Just then Brenna burst into the room. Katie turned to chastise her for being late, but the stark expression on her sister's face stopped her before she could start.

Their mother moved toward her. "Brenna, honey, what's wrong?"

Tears pooled in Brenna's dark eyes, then trickled down her cheeks. "Jeff l-left me," she managed as a sob caught at her throat. "This morning. H-he says he wants a d-divorce."

7

By the time everyone stopped talking and Grammy M had prepared tea, Brenna's sobs had settled into hiccups. The seven women huddled together in the living room, with Brenna sitting in the center of the green sofa by the window, flanked by her mother and Grandma Tessa. Katie sat on the coffee table in front of the sofa, Francesca next to her. They each held one of their sister's hands. Mia and Grammy M hovered.

Katie felt sick to her stomach. How could this have happened? Brenna and Jeff were always so happy.

"Tell us what's going on," their mother said firmly. "Start at the beginning."

"I don't know when it started," Brenna said, then pulled her hands free and clutched at the crumpled tissues on her lap. "I thought everything was great. I didn't know—"

She squeezed her eyes shut, but that didn't stop a tear from trickling out of each corner. She brushed them away impatiently.

She swallowed. "Jeff's been working long hours, but he always does. His practice is new and he has to make rounds at the hospital. I never suspected . . ."

Katie gasped. No! She refused to believe it. Bad enough for Jeff to want a divorce.

"Another woman?" she asked in disbelief.

Brenna nodded and dropped her chin to her chest. "He says he's loved her for a l-long time."

Katie turned toward Francesca, who looked as heartsick as she felt. Tears filled Francesca's eyes.

"This can't be happening," Francesca whispered.

"It is," Brenna said with a sob. "It hurts too much not to be real."

Katie pressed a hand to her stomach. "Who is she?"

Brenna glanced at her, then shrugged. "I don't know exactly. He didn't say much, except . . ." Her voice thickened. "She's a lot younger. Like twenty."

Brenna sprang to her feet and slipped out from between the sofa and coffee table. She paced the length of the room, still twisting the tissues in her hands.

"I can't believe it. I just can't. I gave up everything for him. I loved the winery. I'm the only one of the four of us who gave a damn about it, and I walked away because of him. I worked hard, I supported him and cared about him, and he *left* me."

Grandma Tessa half rose to her feet, but for once she didn't chastise her granddaughter for her language. "Brenna, it wasn't like that. You were getting married. Jeff was going into medical school. Supporting your husband the way you did is a sign of a loving wife."

Brenna brushed away more tears and shook her head. "It's the sign of a fool. I can't believe I was such an idiot. I sacrificed my whole life for him and he walked out on me for a younger woman. I'm a twenty-seven-year-old cliché."

She crumbled into a wing chair. The Grands and Mom headed to her side. Katie shared a glance with Francesca.

Neither of them knew what to say. Katie had friends who had divorced, but that was different. Friends weren't family. Friends' husbands weren't Jeff.

Francesca sucked in a breath. "We loved him like a brother," she murmured. "We joked with him and confided in him. He betrayed us all."

Katie nodded, but couldn't speak. She felt as if she were going to throw up.

Grandma Tessa stroked Brenna's hair. "I know it sounds like the end of the world, but it isn't," she murmured. "Married couples sometimes say horrible things to each other. Or do horrible things. Occasionally men stray. Time heals—we forgive."

Brenna made a sound that was either a strangled sob or a very scary laugh. "Don't get your hopes up, Grandma Tessa. There's no way I'm ever forgiving Jeff."

Their grandmother clucked her tongue, then pulled her ever-present rosary from her pocket and kissed the cross. "Don't say such things. You weren't raised to be so cruel. Your husband will come around. I think you two need to talk about having babies. That will makes things right between you."

Katie felt her grandmother's advice was poorly timed, at best. Not to mention overly optimistic. Her mother didn't take it so well.

"Mama Tessa," Colleen said, glaring at her mother-in-law. "For once leave babies out of this."

"But *bambinos*—"

Grammy M pulled her granddaughter close. "Ah, my poor darlin'. The pains of the world seem bigger than usual today, don't they?"

Brenna clung to her. "You don't understand," she said harshly. "There aren't going to be any babies. There isn't going to be any marriage. Jeff told me he already filed for divorce, and when it's final, he's getting married. To the bimbo."

A fresh storm of sobs overtook her. Katie rubbed her temples, fighting a sudden headache. Even Mia was subdued for once. This couldn't be happening. Not to Brenna. Not to the family. Francesca was right. Jeff had betrayed them all. She wanted to kill him.

Brenna raised her head and looked right at Katie. Anger glittered in her eyes. "I want you to call Zach."

Katie stiffened. "What?"

"I need a lawyer and I want a good one. You said he's a shark. That's what I want. I want Jeff to suffer."

Grandma Tessa winced. "Brenna, please. Do you have to be so hasty?"

Brenna ignored her grandmother. "I mean it, Katie. Will you help me?"

Katie's first thought was to protest. Zach was ruthless. He was a take-no-prisoners man who would stop at nothing to win. Not to mention she wasn't ready to face him after that kiss. Then she thought about her sister and her pain. Ruthless sounded about right.

"I'll call him right now."

"Good. Tell him I need to see him as soon as possible."

Manna from heaven, Zach thought when he hung up the phone. So much for Katie's promise that Marcelli marriages never fell apart.

He buzzed Dora, his assistant, and had her clear his calendar for the afternoon. Right after his eleven o'clock partners meeting, he would head north.

It was nearly one when he finally drove onto the freeway

and close to three when he exited. Tidy rows of grapevines stretched for as far as the eye could see in every direction. A fancy sign at a T-intersection directed tourists to the public buildings of the winery and indicated that the facility was open for tasting seven days a week, even in winter.

Zach turned the opposite direction and soon found himself driving under the massive arch over the road that led to the main house.

The three-story, pale yellow hacienda stood on the crest of a small hill. His first visit had been at night, when he'd been unable to appreciate the vivid colors of the main structure and the surrounding buildings. Flower boxes hung from several windows. The red and orange blossoms matched the tile roof. Wrought iron provided counterpoint, the gleaming black metal scrolled and swirled in intricate patterns forming balcony railings and lampposts on the driveway.

He pulled up to the side of the house and parked. Katie must have been watching for him because she was on the front porch even before he'd closed his car door. Her expression was both sad and wary. No doubt she thought he was going to say "I told you so."

Zach didn't believe in wasting breath on the obvious.

"Thanks so much for coming," she said by way of greeting. She hurried down the front steps and crossed to stand in front of him.

"I won't say it's my pleasure to be here," he told her, taking in the troubled expression darkening her eyes and the way she bit on her lower lip. Her lashes were damp and spiked. She'd been crying.

"It all really sucks," she admitted. "Everybody liked Jeff. I know Brenna's the one he's divorcing, but we all feel kicked in the gut."

"I'm sorry," he said, and realized he meant it. "This is never easy on anyone."

"You would know."

He put his arm around her. "I know it's a cliché, but time heals. It's going to get worse before it gets better, but it *will* get better."

She glanced at him. "Promise?"

He thought of her promise that Marcelli marriages lasted forever, but didn't mention it. "Absolutely."

She looked like a grown-up version of Alice, after her journey to Wonderland. A headband held her long, wavy hair away from her face. She wore a simple cotton dress, matching cardigan, and sandals.

"Staying calm is important," he said. "Brenna needs that. She's in shock and it's going to be a few days until she fully comprehends what's happening."

Katie shook her head. "Brenna's not the only one in shock." She glanced up at the house. "We should probably go in."

She led the way into the house. All the Marcelli women huddled together in the living room, not saying much as they sewed. Only Brenna stood separate from the group, her back to the room as she gazed out the window.

Zach watched the flash of needles through lace. Nearly invisible thread hooked beads, securing them in place. Light caught the iridescent pearls, glinting off them like sunlight off dew on a spiderweb. He stiffened slightly, seeing these women as spiders, weaving a trap to snare his son.

Mia glanced up and saw him. "Zach! You're here."

She rose and hurried toward him. The grandmothers rose as well, but stayed in place, as did Francesca. Colleen moved across the room.

"Zach, thank you for coming." She touched his arm. "We appreciate you driving all this way to help."

Zach wasn't sure that representing Brenna as she divorced her husband technically qualified as help, but he didn't dispute Colleen's description. He was here because he wanted the family to owe him. He planned to build up a damn big credit. When the time came, he would cash it in, take David, and escape.

Brenna was the last one to turn toward him. He recognized the stunned disbelief in her eyes. She was a woman who felt as if she'd just walked through a war zone. It was his job to tell her all she'd survived was the opening salvo of the very first battle. The war was far from over.

"You hungry?" Grandma Tessa asked. "There's pasta."

He had a feeling there was always pasta in her house. "I'm fine."

"Some tea?" Grammy M asked. "Fixin' it is no trouble a'tall."

Brenna walked toward him. "Let's not drown Zach in food or drink," she said. As she got closer, he could see that her eyes were red, and her mouth trembled when she spoke.

"I appreciate the hospitality, but it's not necessary."

Brenna swallowed. "You got here pretty fast. After Katie called, I realized I probably shouldn't have asked you to come all this way."

"In my business, house calls aren't all that uncommon." Actually they were for him, but she didn't have to know that. He might be taking advantage of a miserable situation to find a way to keep his son from screwing up his life, but that didn't mean he wasn't going to give Brenna his best.

"There's something wrong when divorce lawyers make

house calls but doctors don't," Brenna said. "Let's get this over with."

"Sure."

She glanced around at her family, then pointed down the hall. "There's a library just over there. Second door on the left. I think that would be the best place."

Colleen moved to intercept her. "Do you want one of us with you? Me or Francesca or Katie?"

"No. It's going to be ugly enough without witnesses." She gave her mother a very shaky smile. "I'm fine."

Grandma Tessa pulled out a string of rosary beads and began speaking softly under her breath. Colleen hugged her daughter. "Call if you need anything."

"I will."

Brenna led the way down the hall. She and Zach entered a good-size room with bookshelves lining three walls. A large desk sat near the bay window, and two leather sofas faced a stone fireplace.

"We might as well make this official," Brenna said, motioning to the desk. "Why don't you have a seat?"

Zach set his briefcase on the surface, but instead of settling in a chair, he leaned against a corner of the desk. Brenna paced to the window, then back to the door she'd closed when they entered the room. Her body screamed tension. She hunched her shoulders, as if against a blow, and looked a lot like the other wives he'd met over the years. Wives who had been left; wives who weren't sure if they wanted revenge or a second chance.

"Why don't I go first," he said easily, as if they were about to discuss the weather. "I'll tell you how I like to handle things, and you can let me know if that agrees with you."

She nodded without speaking. Nor did she stop pacing.

"You don't have to get a divorce," he began.

The words were familiar—he'd given the speech countless times. It served two purposes. First, having him start things usually put his clients at ease. Second, he was blunt about the divorce process, which often shocked the ambivalent back into their marriages for a year or two. Divorce was ugly, destructive, and expensive. Those who weren't sure shouldn't get involved.

"If you decide you want a divorce, you don't have to do anything about it today."

Brenna reached the window and turned to look at him. "If this is your standard line, how on earth do you stay in business?"

"That's not a problem."

She sighed. "Let me guess. Because the world is filled with foolish women who marry bastards?"

"Something like that." He waited, and when she didn't speak again, he continued. "Whatever you tell me is private. Attorney-client privilege means I won't be discussing your personal business with anyone." He allowed himself a slight smile. "Not even your family."

"They have their ways of making people talk."

"I'm pretty tough."

"Katie says you're the best."

"I'm not afraid to go for the gut. But know this. Divorce is going to change your life in ways you can't begin to imagine. I'll start the process if and when you say you want to. However, if you change your mind, I have no problem stopping."

She paused in mid-pace and stared at him. "You're a divorce lawyer. Why aren't you pushing me to do this?"

"Because if we go through with the divorce, I'll need your cooperation. That doesn't happen if you're ambivalent."

He continued with his standard speech, going over everything from the length of time to the dissolution of marriage to the potential hazards of a court-mandated property settlement. Brenna listened intently and didn't wince when he named his hourly fee.

When he was finished, he moved behind the desk and sat down. "Now you talk," he said. "You can tell me you need more time, tell me to go to hell, or just cry."

One corner of her mouth twitched slightly, as if she had almost smiled. "You must be pretty used to female tears."

"I've had plenty of male clients lose it."

She walked to one of the chairs across the desk from his and collapsed onto the soft leather. He guessed she was a year or two younger than Katie, but right now she looked old and very tired.

"There's no question about the divorce," she said flatly. "Jeff cheated on me."

"That doesn't have to be a hanging offense."

"It is to me." She looked at him. "He's not remorseful and he's not coming back. He told me he's already filed for divorce."

Zach pulled out a pad of paper. "That means you'll be served in the next day or so. Brace yourself for that."

"Great. So the hits keep on coming?"

"I can help you hit back. If that's what you want."

"Revenge sounds really good right about now. I guess one bright spot in all this is I don't have to change my name back. I never took his. A voice inside told me not to. I guess there was a bigger message I should have listened to."

Zach leaned forward. "I need to ask you a lot of questions about your marriage, what property the two of you own, that sort of thing. Do you want to deal with that now?"

She nodded.

He pulled out a form and handed it to her. "I'll need this information as soon as you can get it."

She read the paper. "Bank account numbers and balances, credit card accounts, car license information." She glanced up at him. "I guess you're going to want to know a lot of personal details."

"So will the court if we don't come to a settlement privately. California's a community property state. Everything gets split fifty-fifty."

"Works for me."

"Good. Now tell me about the relationship."

Brenna wanted to curl up in a ball and have the entire world go away. Some kind of oblivion didn't sound so bad, right about now. One minute her heart raced so fast she thought it was going to jump out of her throat, the next she couldn't even find a pulse. She felt both hot and cold. Her body ached.

Less than twenty-four hours ago she'd been blissfully happy. Stupid, but happy. Twenty-four hours ago she'd been working at the job that she hated to pay off medical school for a husband who had been busy screwing someone else.

Anger filled her. Anger and rage and frustration and shame. She felt humiliated. She felt old and used.

None of which was going to help Zach Stryker with her divorce. So she did as he requested and gave him a thumbnail sketch of her marriage to her soon-to-be ex-husband.

"You've been sharing a residence," he said.

"Right up until I walked out this morning."

"And a bed?"

She glanced at him, but he wasn't looking at her. Instead he scribbled notes on his pad. Heat flared on her cheeks. At that moment she wanted to get on her knees and thank God for her Italian genes. They might have given her chubby thighs, but at least her olive coloring prevented her blush from showing too much.

"If you're asking if we're sleeping together, then yes. Every night." She frowned. "Except when he's gone for his conferences." Which there had been a lot of lately, she remembered. Tears burned in her eyes. "If you're asking about sex. Not very often."

Not even once in the past four months, she reminded herself. Jeff had had so many really good excuses. Her hands clenched into fists. To think he'd wasted his time coming up with reasons to avoid making love. All he'd had to do was tell her the truth. If she'd known about the other woman, she wouldn't have bothered asking.

Humiliation clawed at Brenna's throat. That's what really got her. That she'd asked. She'd known there was something wrong, and like a fool she'd assumed it was the pressure of finally finishing up his residency or the stress of interviewing with different doctors about joining their practices.

"You and Jeff don't have any children together, right?"

"Right."

"Are you pregnant?"

The question raced through her like electricity. Her skin seemed to shrink a size and it was hard to breathe.

"Why do you want to know?"

"Because a child means a whole new set of legal complications. Are you pregnant?"

"No."

She pressed her lips together to maintain control, but it was useless. Tears spilled from her eyes.

She jumped to her feet and circled around the desk. A

box of tissue sat in a bottom drawer. She pulled out the box and returned to her seat.

"Sorry," she said, her voice throaty.

"No problem. I take it this is a sore subject."

"Yeah." She sniffed and wiped away her tears. "I wanted kids, Jeff kept saying we had to wait. Wait until he was done with medical school, then wait until he finished his internship. Then wait until he had his own practice. I was working eighty hours a week, so it's not like I had time to brood or anything, but God." She leaned back in the chair and closed her eyes. "I wanted kids."

She still did. The difference was now she didn't have a husband. No husband, no babies. Her heart twisted.

"Any prenuptial agreement?"

She straightened and stared at him. "No. We never discussed it."

"Did either of you bring any money into the relationship?"

She laughed humorously. "No. Jeff brought plenty of debt, though. Student loans from college. Those just got bigger as time wore on."

"So basically you supported him through his medical training and paid for debt he'd incurred before the marriage."

"You got it."

"Did he work also? Part-time or summer jobs?"

"No. He studied. We agreed that was his job." Because she'd been so damn stupid, she thought grimly. Being the perfect, supportive, loving wife had been all she'd aspired to. If that meant two jobs and no free time, hey, she was married. She'd walked away from her family, from the vineyards, and for what?

She balled up the tissue she held. "He didn't do anything. I worked, I cooked, I cleaned, I picked up his dry cleaning." Just talking about it made her furious. She rose to her feet and crossed to the window. "I can't believe it. All these years of my life given over to him, and I have nothing to show for it. I certainly didn't go to college. I have no education, nothing. I have no life, except for being his wife." She spun to face Zach. "I gave him my entire being and this is my reward."

"You loved him."

"I was a fool." She rubbed her temples. "I can't believe I put my husband through medical school and now he's left me for a younger woman. That wasn't supposed to happen for at least another ten years."

Zach didn't respond. Brenna knew there wasn't anything he could say. Instead he asked, "What do you want from Jeff?"

"Blood," she said flatly. "I want him to pay. He used me and he cast me aside." Worse, he'd hurt her, but she wasn't about to say that. The irony of the situation didn't escape her. Jeff was a cardiologist—he'd known exactly how to break her heart.

"Are you sure there's no chance of a reconciliation?"

She tried to laugh. "He's not interested. He's already moved on. I'm not interested, either. He screwed some bimbo—probably in *my* bed. Let her have him."

"He could change his mind."

"I don't think so. I think the chances of him leaving his bimbo for an old, used wife are pretty remote."

"What about you? What if he came to his senses and realized he was an idiot. What if he begged you to let him come back? Would you let him?"

Brenna considered the question. This morning when Jeff had casually announced that their marriage was over, that he had filed for divorce, and oh, by the way, would she please leave the dry-cleaning ticket on the table when she left, she had felt as if a meteor had destroyed her world. She'd been crushed—broken into a million pieces with no hopes of ever being whole again. In that moment she would have done anything to have her life restored.

Since then she'd been on a roller coaster of emotion, up and down, turning at breakneck speed until she didn't know what she wanted or where she was going to end up. But she did know one thing with complete certainty.

"I don't want him back," she said with a conviction that came from the very depths of her being. "It's not only the infidelity that I can't forgive. It's that he wasn't even willing to try. I didn't get a vote or a hearing. He decided it was over, so he filed for divorce. I would never trust him again. What's been broken can't be fixed." She leveled her gaze and stared at Zach. "I want him punished."

Zach nodded. "I can do that. It's something I do very well."

8

~

The printer spit out page after page. Mia glanced at David, who looked just as lost as she felt. The perfectly dressed woman in the bridal registry department smiled as she tore off what looked like an endless list.

"Now, these are just some ideas. Obviously you don't need to register for *everything* on the list."

Mia took the offered papers. "Okay. Great. We'll, um, just look around?"

"Exactly. Write down your choices as you make them. I'll be right here if you have any questions." She smiled again, her perfectly made-up features barely moving. "Do you need a pencil?"

Mia patted the small purse she'd slung over her shoulder. "Got one, thanks." Then she grabbed David by the arm and hurried away.

"She's scary," Mia muttered when they were out of earshot. "Aren't people's faces supposed to move when they talk?"

But David wasn't paying attention. Instead he stared at a large display of china with all the enthusiasm of a vegetarian facing a steak dinner.

"So we have to pick one?" he asked, desperation tinting his words.

"That's the basic idea." She scanned the list. "My God. Just the dish section—which they call china—is broken down into sections. Plates, bowls, side plates, dessert plates, fruit nappies."

David stared at her. "What the hell is a fruit nappy?"

Mia giggled. "Don't the British refer to diapers as nappies? Maybe it's some weird kind of fruit diaper."

David rolled his eyes. "Yeah, right."

She continued to scan the list. "Serving pieces. Then we move into flatware. I think that's like knives and forks. Oh, and there's everyday china or stoneware, which I guess means we're supposed to have two sets." She thought about her postage-stamp-size kitchen. "I don't think we're going to have room for all this."

David grabbed the list. "Water glasses, wineglasses, highball glasses, tumblers. What's a highball?"

"A type of cocktail." She drew in a deep breath. Somehow she had thought that shopping for future presents would be more fun. "Okay, let's just start with the china. We don't have room for one full set, let alone two, so we can find a pattern we like and use it all the time. Later, when we have a house or something, we'll deal with two sets. How's that?"

"Great." He eyed the wall displaying over a hundred different patterns. "What do you like?"

Twenty minutes later Mia was ready to choke the life out of her intended. She liked flowers, he didn't. She wanted color, he thought beige was enough color for anyone. Then he'd picked a pattern with three dimensional fruit that made her want to gag. They'd discovered that fruit nappies were basically cereal-size bowls, and that they both hated anything with a gold rim, but otherwise, they couldn't come close to an agreement.

Rather than shed blood right there in the middle of fine china, Mia suggested a compromise.

"Let's start with something different," she said, refolding the list to the section entitled: "Stocking your kitchen." "What about small appliances?"

"Sounds good."

They headed for that department, passing flatware on the way. If they couldn't pick out china, Mia figured they'd better avoid any department with sharp knives.

However, kitchenware had knives. It also had dozens of appliances she'd never seen before. Nor did she have any idea as to their purpose or usefulness. She stood in front of a multitiered device that was supposed to dry fruit.

"Who eats dried fruit?" David asked.

"I do." Mia studied the machine. "Wouldn't it just be easier to buy it?"

"Or eat chips." David poked at a massive box containing a pasta maker. "Dad never cooked much. I sure didn't learn anything from him."

"Don't look at me. The Grands have always done the cooking at our house."

He looped an arm around her and grinned. "You're gonna be the wife, Mia. I guess you'll have to learn."

She shrugged free of his embrace. "That is *so* not going to happen. Just because I'm the female here, don't assume I'm going to be taking care of you. As far as I'm concerned, household chores will be split fifty-fifty, and that includes cooking."

Suddenly David wasn't smiling. "I'm not going to learn to cook."

"Why not?"

"I'll be busy with school."

"And I won't? While you're still trying to figure out your major, I'll be applying to grad school, taking my regular classes, and working part-time at one of the consulates, assuming I get into that internship program."

"Mia, I'm a guy."

She eyed the selection of knives on a nearby wall. But as her father liked to say, violence was the refuge of the incompetent.

"I guess if you don't cook and I don't cook, we'll be buying a lot of take-out," she said lightly.

"Works for me."

"The good news is there are a ton of great places by campus. And when we're in D.C., there will be all-new places to try." She saw a display of coffeemakers. "Hey, I could use a new one of these. What do you think?"

But David didn't follow her to the display. Instead he stood in the center of the aisle, feet braced, hands in his pockets, an unruly lock of hair falling across his forehead.

She turned to him. "What?"

"You're talking about Georgetown."

"Of course. I know I have to apply to other grad schools, but that's the one I really want." She frowned at his stern expression. "David, it's not like this is news."

"Are you applying to UCLA?"

She felt the ground turn into quicksand. Actually, she was not. Although she was enjoying her undergrad experience there, she wanted to attend a different school to continue her studies. Preferably somewhere on the East Coast.

"I haven't decided," she hedged.

"When you graduate, I'll still have two years left there."

She shifted her weight from foot to foot, hating that she felt almost . . . guilty. "I know." She had known. She just didn't like to think about it.

Then she reminded herself she had nothing to feel guilty about. This was her life, her dream, her career. She'd wanted to go into the State Department since she'd first learned what it was nearly six years ago. She'd already compromised. Wasn't it his turn?

"Look," she said. "I wanted to take that Japanese language class in Japan, and you agreed it would be fun. We talked about it being our honeymoon. Then you changed your mind and didn't want to go. So we switched to D.C. Now I'm taking the language class and you're just going to hang out for six weeks. I'm okay with that. Why can't you be okay with me *not* getting my master's at UCLA?"

"Because it means I have to change schools."

"Which you already said was fine with you." She tried not to scream. "Is this *all* about you? *You* need a wife who can cook, and *you* need a wife who won't study a foreign language in a foreign country, and you need a wife who has no dreams of her own, except you don't have any dreams or plans, either. You don't even have a fucking major."

They glared at each other. Mia refused to be the one who blinked first.

David sighed, then shrugged. "I don't know what I need, Mia. You're the one with all the answers. Maybe you should tell me."

Suddenly picking out items for their gift registry didn't seem like such a good idea. She carefully folded the sheets of paper in half.

"Look. I have a report I have to work on. You want to do this another time?"

David shrugged. "Sure."

They headed for the escalator. Mia had the weirdest feeling that she couldn't catch her breath. It wasn't supposed to be like this, she thought frantically. Was it? She and David were engaged. Shouldn't they be happy?

The first time Katie had walked into Zach's office, she'd been excited about the job offer of a lifetime. The second time she'd been dealing with post-humiliation repercussions. Now she had to wrestle with the fact that he was not only her client and a future in-law, but a man who had rocked her world with a simple kiss (annoying but true). He was also her sister's divorce lawyer. If they got any more involved, they would become symbiotic beings.

She was determined to make sure that didn't happen. She would be wary, on guard, and *completely* professional. No visceral reactions allowed.

Dora Preston sat outside of Zach's office. She smiled when she saw Katie. "He's waiting for you," Dora said. "Go right in."

"Thanks."

Katie straightened her spine, tried her "You're the best" mantra for good measure, and stepped into the shark's lair.

Zach rose when he saw her. And smiled. As she had yet to receive her Zach-smile vaccine, she found herself instantly melting.

Stop! No melting, she told herself. No being excited to see him. *Nada!*

"Katie, what a pleasure."

He walked around his desk and approached her.

Instead of shaking her hand, he squeezed her upper arm and sounded genuinely pleased to see her. Uh-huh. Sure. Cool, she told herself. She was ice.

"I come bearing paperwork," she said calmly, holding up her stuffed briefcase. In her other hand she held a portable file box.

Zach led her to the desk, then offered coffee, which she accepted. While he walked over to a small tea tray by his credenza and poured her a cup, she unloaded her briefcase and started on the file folder.

"Cream? Sugar?"

"Just black," she said.

By the time he returned to sit next to her, she had spread out several sample invitations.

"We need to get the order into the printer," she said. "I like this one." She pointed to a thick paper invitation edged in black and gold.

Zach laughed. "The last invitations I picked out had toy soldiers on them. I think it was for David's eleventh birthday party. You go with what you like."

"I'm happy to pick, but do you want to run the selections by your partners?"

"Not even on a bet."

She forgot herself for a second and smiled. "Okay. So you're not party planners."

She pulled out her master list and noted the invitation number. "Now, before I can do anything, I will need one thing from you. And that's budget approval."

The five-page document listed every possible expense, although some items, such as liquor, had to be estimated. Zach took the document and scanned it.

"You're very thorough," he said after a minute.

"I try to be. As I noted at the bottom, should there be an

unexpected expense of more than three hundred dollars, I'll send out written notice immediately."

"Fair enough." He read a little more. "Goody bags for adults. Isn't that a kid thing?"

"Not at all. I'll do a smaller, less expensive bag for the regular guests and a dynamite one for our high rollers." She shrugged. "I can't explain it, but there is a serious thrill in getting something for free. I practically shimmy in delight when my favorite makeup lady offers me a sample, even if it's something I'll never use. I thought a goody bag would be a fun way to leave our guests with warm fuzzies about the party."

He continued to study the budget. As he read, she watched him. There was something so sexy about his eyes, she thought. And of course, his smile. She also liked the way he seemed comfortable in his own skin all the time.

She groaned silently. Damn. What happened to being ice? Ignore him. Which was easier said than done, considering how the man turned her on. Her resolve seemed to have all the tensile strength of potato chips.

He tossed the budget down on the desk. "I'll take it to my partners right away. When do you need to hear back?"

"Within a week. The invitations need to be engraved. Some of the food has to be ordered well in advance, and I won't even go into the trauma of picking out flowers."

"Please don't." He leaned back in his chair. "I guess this means I need to get my tux into the dry cleaner."

"Don't complain to me about that," she told him. "You know exactly what you're going to wear, while I have the challenge of finding the perfect dress. I need to fit in, and yet not look like a guest."

He raised his dark eyebrows. "What about your date?"

She hardly needed the pressure. "It's a working night for me."

"No Mr. Right?"

She couldn't tell if he was making idle chitchat or trying to figure out if she was seeing someone. The possibility of the latter made her thighs tingle.

"Not even a Mr. Adequate. And you? Who will you bring?"

"I haven't decided. How's Brenna doing?" he asked.

"She's hanging in there. Her mood seems to swing between a strong desire to get revenge and feelings of devastation."

"The loss of a marriage is like a death. It takes time to move through the grieving process."

His insight surprised her until she reminded herself that this was what the man did for a living. Of course he would be familiar with the process.

"Brenna said you won't be meeting with her for a few weeks."

He nodded. "We'll speak regularly, but there's no need for a face-to-face. I've filed all the papers. We're going to have to deal with the settlement, and that's what's going to take the planning."

"Do you know Jeff's lawyer?"

Zach smiled again, but it wasn't the least bit friendly. "I've dealt with him before. Not to worry. I'm a whole lot better."

"Will you think I'm a complete bitch if I say 'good'?"

"No. She's your sister. She's in pain and you want blood for that." He studied her. "You can't have it both ways, Katie. You can't complain about my tactics, then use them for your own self-interest."

"Actually, I can, but it's tacky." She shuffled through the papers she'd brought, pulling out three more sets of the budget. "So you don't have to make copies."

"Very thoughtful."

She returned to the issue of her sister's divorce. "While there might have been a snag in the 'all Marcellis stay married forever' theory, I'm still not on your side about breaking off Mia and David's engagement."

"I'm okay with that. However, I reserve the right to use any means at my disposal to change your mind."

Hardly news, she thought wryly. "Why me?"

He leaned back in his chair and considered the question. "Two reasons. No, three. First, I have the most access to you. That means plenty of time to work my charm."

She widened her eyes in surprise. "Is this charm? I hadn't noticed."

He grinned. "Second, your family listens to you. If I convince you, you'll convince them, or at least Mia, and she's the one who matters."

"Never going to happen."

"I'm taking bets."

"Sure you are. What's number three?"

He turned his gaze fully on her. Dark blue eyes narrowed slightly, and his expression turned predatory. "You're the Marcelli who interests me the most."

Two parts intrigued and one part terrified, she did her best to act unconcerned. "You're saying spending this much time with Grandpa Lorenzo wouldn't blow your skirt up?"

"I don't wear a skirt, but if I did, no."

"Those are really fabulous reasons. Thanks for sharing." She began to pack up her briefcase.

"Leaving so soon?"

"I have another meeting."

"What if I wanted to take a few minutes to work on convincing you?"

"No, thanks."

He chuckled. "You haven't heard what I had in mind."

Oh, but she could imagine. "I don't need to know."

"You're tempted."

"Not even close."

She had a feeling they both knew she was lying. She finished with her briefcase and went to work on the file box. When she was done, she turned back to him.

"Thanks for taking the time to see me today, Zach."

He leaned forward and rested his hand on hers. "I'm always happy to see you, Katie. You know that."

Was it her or had it just gotten really hot in here?

"How nice," she said primly and stood. She'd wondered if he would kiss her again. Now that he hadn't, she told herself she was happy. Really.

He stood. "You're not easy."

"That's not much of a compliment, but thank you anyway."

He grinned. "I'm not easy, either. If we manage to get through the next couple of months without killing each other, I'd like you to be my date for the fund-raiser."

The phrase about being knocked over by a feather had never been more appropriate. A date? With Zach? Only a fool would say yes.

"I'll be working," she said instead.

"That's okay with me." He winked. "I like to watch."

Zach never left work early and he almost never took Pacific Coast Highway home. But at three o'clock that afternoon, he did both. He drove west to Lincoln and turned south. The congested street met up with PCH in Marina Del Rey. It was a warm, sunny afternoon, with a hint of salt in the air. He opened his car's sunroof, as well as the windows, inhaling deeply.

Despite his busy schedule, he felt restless. As he headed toward the airport, he saw jets taking off toward the ocean, heading west. Where were they going? Who was on board and what would they do when they arrived? He didn't want to be going with them, but he did want something . . . A woman?

He had an answer to the question before he even asked it. Yes. A woman. And not just in bed, although he wouldn't mind an hour or two of pleasure in a pair of willing arms. No, what he wanted was more than sex. He wanted to talk to someone long enough to grow comfortable. He wanted rhythms and patterns and familiarity.

How long had it been since he'd had a relationship that lasted more than two dates? A year? Longer, he thought. Although he'd never been interested in getting married again—Ainsley and his belief that long-term relationships didn't work had cured him of that particular desire—he'd always enjoyed the company of women. Generally one at a time, and often for as long as a few months, then he walked away. He might not do marriage, but he was deeply committed to serial monogamy.

It had been a long time since anyone had tempted him for more than a night or two. He couldn't remember the last woman who had surprised and challenged him. Some of it was his own fault. His position in a prominent law firm and his growing bank balance brought out a certain kind of woman. Those who were more interested in what he had than who he was. He'd gone out with enough of them to earn a reputation. Once he'd dated the shallow, those with substance didn't think he was worth the effort. Which meant *he* had to go find *them*.

Or wait on fate.

Is that what had happened with Katie Marcelli? Had fate dropped her into his lap? Maybe. Maybe not. Either way, he intended to take advantage of the situation, because that was what he did. Fate might have brought her to him, but he would be the one getting her into his bed.

9

⌒

"*Maybe we could* figure out a way you could just borrow my hips and thighs," Brenna said as she shifted to get more comfortable on her sister's lumpy double bed. Not only was the mattress more like a rocky path than a place for restful sleep, the only light in the room was diffused by heavy lampshades, making it difficult for Brenna to bead as neatly as she would like. She had no doubt that if she did a less than perfect job, Katie would reject the lace appliqué out of hand.

Francesca smiled in response to Brenna's comment, but didn't speak as she continued to work on her face. Not her makeup . . . her *face*. While the light in the bedroom might be dim enough to qualify for a mood-lit nightclub, that in the bathroom rivaled the intensity of an operating room. Several bulbs illuminated the bathroom mirror from nearly every angle possible. Francesca had placed an eighteen-inch-wide board over her pedestal sink to give herself a work area for her array of cosmetics.

While Brenna found the various pots, jars, and pencils interesting, what really captured her attention was the fat suit hanging in the open doorway. The foam . . . what, she thought—Garment? Creation? *Outfit*—consisted of padded shoulders, full breasts, a bulging tummy and thick thighs. Actually it was everything Brenna hated about her own body. If only she could unzip the extra fifteen or twenty pounds she carried around.

Talk about a miracle, she thought glumly.

She reached for another bead from the small bag and sewed it into place. So far she'd completed fifteen lace flowers. She hadn't been back to L.A. since Jeff had announced he wanted a divorce. She'd called in her resignation to the job she'd always hated and had only taken because the pay was decent. She clenched her teeth. Just thinking about all she'd gone through with Jeff made her furious. She wanted to scream. She wanted to throw something. She wanted to stab an ice pick through his two-timing heart.

Instead she beaded lace. And fumed. Because if she allowed her anger to fade, she found herself feeling lost and alone, not to mention slightly panicked about the future.

She glanced around Francesca's tiny bedroom. "I can't stay here forever," she said more to herself than to her sister.

"Sure you can." Francesca applied a grayish-taupe shadow under her eyes. She instantly looked tired and drawn. "I like having you around."

Brenna smiled. "That's because you like rescuing people. But if I spend many more nights on your sofa, I'm going to be in physical therapy for the rest of my life. It's not exactly comfortable."

"Are you thinking of going back to L.A.?"

"For what? I don't have any real ties there. I quit my

job. I guess I need to get my stuff out of the apartment, but other than that . . ." Her voice trailed off. She'd been too busy working and taking care of her husband to make friends. God, her life was damn empty. Why had she allowed that to happen?

"We should have him killed," Francesca said, sounding calm enough to be scary.

While Brenna appreciated the support, she wasn't sure Jeff's death would make up for much. It would be too easy. In a perfect world, he would have to suffer.

"Are you sure he's worth prison time?" she asked.

"Good point." Francesca turned and shrugged. "It's just he's such a bastard. I know your pain is the worst and I want to make it better, but on a personal level, and for the family, I want revenge."

"We could brainstorm a plan."

"Works for me."

"I'll come up with some ideas while I bead." Brenna returned her attention to the lace in her hands. "In the meantime, I need a place to live."

"You could move home."

"Yeah. Maybe."

Moving back to the hacienda wouldn't be her first choice, but at this point what options did she have? There wasn't any money. She had worked her ass off to cover the monthly bills and keep up with Jeff's student loans. Savings had been a luxury they couldn't afford.

"You know Mom and Dad would be thrilled to have you back. The Grands would treat you like a princess."

"I could use a little pampering," Brenna admitted. "Although I'd have to redecorate our old room. It looks exactly the same as when we moved out. My tastes have changed in the past few years."

"Mine, too."

"You were smart to stay single after Todd died," Brenna told her. "You learned your lesson early."

Francesca shrugged. "My marriage wasn't all good times and laughter. I'm much happier on my own. Now you get to make that choice if you want to."

"It's already made." Fall for another guy who would only use her to get what *he* wanted? No, thanks.

"So we'll be unmarried into our dotage," Brenna said. "People will think we're lesbians."

Francesca smiled, but didn't look up from the mirror. "Can you imagine how many rosaries would be said by the Grands if they suspected that? They'd need a hotline to heaven."

As Brenna watched, Francesca used a sharp eyebrow pencil to draw in tiny lines which thickened her eyebrows. She'd already applied fake skin along her jaw line, to round out the shape.

"Are you going for the ugly look on purpose?"

Francesca glanced at her over her shoulder. "I don't want to be recognized."

"No chance of that." Brenna eyed the fat suit. "Doesn't it freak you out to gain weight instantly?"

"Not really. I know it comes right off."

Which was true, but made Brenna feel cranky. "I know this is all part of your studies, but I have to tell you that wearing a fat suit is a weird way to get a doctorate."

Francesca shrugged and returned her attention to the mirror. She shaded more of her face. "Actually today I'm going out in a wheelchair. I'll use the padded suit later. As for my doctorate, my purpose is to document how people react to me, based on different physical appearances."

"Oh, I get the theory," Brenna told her. "I just think it's strange."

Francesca reached for a lip pencil that matched the color of her skin. She carefully outlined her mouth, making the curves appear smaller. A tiny dot of a line at each corner drew the shape of her mouth downward, giving her a pinched appearance.

She applied a flesh-colored lipstick which made her mouth practically invisible. Then she reached for her hairbrush.

Several strong strokes tamed her thick, dark hair. She pulled it into a severe bun, after which she sprinkled baby powder on her hands and smoothed it over her sleek hair. Dark brown faded to muddy gray. Heavily rimmed glasses and a shapeless dress completed her transformation. She turned to face her sister.

"What do you think?"

Brenna wrinkled her nose in distaste. "You're my sister and I really love you, but I have to tell you, sometimes you scare me."

Several tables clustered together on one side of the vast hotel ballroom. Try as he might, Zach couldn't imagine the space filled with two thousand guests, nor did he have any interest in the china chosen for the event. But when Katie had asked him to drop by the hotel to make the final seating choice, he'd found himself agreeing. Maybe it was because hotels were filled with beds and he was determined to get her into one.

"There are different philosophies," she was saying. "Tables of eight are more intimate. People can actually talk around the table. It's also easier for couples to buy a table when there are only eight seats to fill. Tables for twelve can make for an easier seating plan in a room this size. They're more efficient for the serving staff, but they make it virtually impossible to speak with anyone but immediate neighbors."

Katie indicated a large round table set with everything from water glasses to salt shakers.

"With our 'cook your own dinner' menu, we have to consider allowing people to move in and out of the area. A table for ten falls somewhere in the middle of the two. Obviously." She shot him a quick smile. "As an aside, tables for eight mean more linen rentals and centerpieces. I could work out the cost differences if you would like."

Zach already felt his eyes glazing over just hearing her talk about it. A spreadsheet on the subject was about as appealing as a root canal.

"You're the expert, Katie," he said. "It's your call."

She grinned. "I had a feeling you'd say that. Somehow I suspect this isn't all that interesting to you."

"You think?"

Her grin turned into a chuckle. He leaned a little closer to better hear the soft sound. In the process he caught a whiff of feminine fragrance . . . something sweet and just a little sultry. Tempting—much like Katie herself.

As usual she dressed for success—slacks and a cropped jacket in black, with a red silk blouse. Her hair had been piled on top of her head in a style that was probably supposed to be professional. But it was late afternoon and too many tendrils had escaped for the look to be anything but sexy.

She was doing the "I'm a businesswoman" dance, and all it did was make him want to see her naked. If she knew, she would smack the crap out of him.

"Okay, so you have no vote on the table size," she said, making a note on her ever-present pad of paper. "Do you want to express an opinion on the color and style of linens?"

"Do you want to have a detailed conversation about torte law?"

She glanced at him out of the corner of her eye. "Gee, Zach, if I'd known you were going to be so difficult, I wouldn't have asked for your opinion on anything."

"Sure you would. You like hanging out with me."

She raised her eyebrows. "No wonder you drive such a big car. You need room for your ego. What do you do when you fly? Will it fit in the overhead compartment or do you have to check it into baggage?"

"You know what they say. Big ego, big . . ."

"Idiot?" she offered with a smile and walked toward her briefcase, which rested on a chair. After opening the bag, she pulled out a thick folder.

"Back to the subject at hand," she said. "I have a list of the prizes for our high-end donors. I've spoken with the jewelry designers Sara recommended. They're—"

"Who?" he interrupted.

"Sara." Her eyes twinkled with humor. "Probably better known to you as 'John's wife.' "

"Okay. The pregnant one."

"Right. She recommended a few jewelry designers. They all agreed to sell us unique pieces at cost. Of course their names will be prominently displayed in the program, and I'm sure we'll start a fashion trend or two that night." She looked up from the paper. "I don't suppose you want to look at the design sketches."

"Not really."

"Then how about a list of the various prize packages? I've worked up a ski vacation in Europe, golfing in Scotland and Pebble Beach, and a lovely weekend in Napa, complete with a private dinner with the three top wine makers there." She closed the folder. "I used family connections on that last one."

"I'm impressed."

"It's all a matter of knowing who to call. Now, about the centerpieces."

Zach held up his hands in front of him and took a step back. "Absolutely no flower decisions," he said. "Order whatever you like in any color or style. I'm sure they'll be wonderful."

Katie slid a little closer. "Is the big, bad lawyer frightened of a few orchids?"

He was saved from replying by the arrival of a tall, painfully thin man in a white coat. The dark-haired stranger crossed to Katie, spoke her name in a tone of delight, and kissed the backs of both her hands.

She disentangled herself with grace and a small laugh. "Jerome, you spent way too much time in France. Stop acting so Continental, or I'll tell my client that you're actually from Nebraska."

The tall man winced. "Katie, don't even joke about that." He turned to Zach and held out a hand. "I'm Jerome. I'm the head chef here at the hotel, and I'll be in charge of the food for the charity event."

"Nice to meet you." Zach shook hands with the man, then glanced from one to the other. "You two have worked together before?"

"Several times," Katie said easily. "Jerome is a perfectionist. Fresh produce is practically a religion with him, and his food is the better for it. He's creative, yet willing to work within the confines of my ideas and, just as important, my budget. That's unheard of at his level."

"You flatter me," Jerome said with obvious false modesty. "I'm simply gifted."

"I know. And *brilliant* and all those other lovely adjectives you adore so much. Did you bring the menus?"

Jerome held out several sheets of papers. Katie moved next to Zach so that he could read them as well. They were detailed food selections for the charity dinner. Handwritten notes filled the space by the typed items, detailing everything from possible condiments, to notations on availability and cost per serving.

"You'll have to pick the chocolates quickly," Jerome said as Katie flipped a page. "Some are easy enough to get, but if you're serious about chocolate from around the world, some of my suppliers require a month's notice."

"No problem."

When he started talking about the availability of produce, Zach excused himself and stepped into the hallway to call his office. Dora assured him there were no emergencies. He slipped the phone back into his jacket pocket and watched Katie work.

His mind returned to all the possibilities available in the large hotel. A small room with a smaller bed? A luxurious suite with a Jacuzzi tub? The sauna?

He found he really liked the idea of both of them slick with sweat, sliding against each other, burning from the inside out. He imagined himself pumping into her, then quickly shifted the fantasy so she was on top, riding him, her breasts—

He swallowed a sudden laugh. What the hell. His vivid images had produced a predictable and physical response. He was hard, horny, and couldn't remember the last time he'd gotten an erection during business hours. Work generally consumed him. Just not lately.

Katie made notes as Jerome talked, narrowing down the list of possible choices to something manageable. She would get all the information onto spreadsheets that evening. It would seem less unwieldy that way.

"What about a tasting dinner?" she asked. "When do you want to do that?"

He pulled a Palm Pilot from his jacket pocket and pushed a couple of buttons. "You want it here, or you want to take it with you?"

"Either works for me." She looked around and saw Zach in the hallway. "You're not escaping that easily," she called to him. "Come on. I won't make you decide on the items for the tasting dinner, but you did promise to help me with the actual eating."

Zach returned to the ballroom. He moved with an easy masculine grace that left her mouth dry.

He annoyed her, impressed her, charmed her, and surprised her. And *she* was supposed to be the people person.

"We have two important issues regarding the tasting dinner," she said, determined not to let him know how much he affected her. "Do you want to eat it here or get it to go, and when do you want to have it?"

"Let's get it to go," he said. "Then we won't be rushed."

"Sounds great." Maybe they could make it a very long evening. One that ended with . . .

She mentally slapped herself into paying attention to the moment at hand. Rather than deal with Zach, she focused on Jerome. At least he was completely safe. "What dates are good for you?"

He named off several.

Zach pulled out his own Palm Pilot and pushed buttons. "I'm pretty open. What about you, Katie?"

She ignored the suggestive tone of his voice. "Same here."

Jerome pushed more keys. "The fifth?"

"Works for me," Zach said.

She nodded in agreement, noted the date, and volunteered to pick up the food. They would deal with the "where" they would be eating another time.

Jerome excused himself and returned to the kitchen. Katie pulled seating charts out from her briefcase and held them up to Zach. He shook his head.

"Not in this lifetime."

"You have no opinion? Isn't there someone you're dying to sit next to? A rich divorcee? A female rock star? The latest Hollywood 'It' girl?"

"I prefer women to girls," he said. "And despite the rumors, I'm more into substance than style."

She laughed. "Just once I would like to meet a man willing to admit he likes his relationships simple and his women easy."

His gaze narrowed. "You don't believe me?"

"Not for a nanosecond. Come on, Zach. You're successful, good-looking, and rich. I've seen the photos in the press. Tabloid text may not always be accurate, but you know what they say about pictures speaking a thousand words. Are you trying to tell me you haven't dated all those women?"

"No. I'm saying there's a reason I walked away from all of them."

It was a semi-decent comeback. "So you've been converted? Now intelligent, articulate conversation is the way to your heart? Big breasts and long legs no longer work? Imagine my surprise."

He shook his head. "I'm not going to win this conversation, so let's change the subject. Why don't you show me these fabulous gardens I've been hearing about?"

She couldn't believe it. "You're conceding defeat?"

"I'm making a strategic retreat."

"Wow. I *must* remember to put a star by this day on the calendar when I get home."

He grunted in response. Katie was still delighted with her victory as they stepped outside into the landscaped gardens of the hotel.

It was late afternoon on the sort of day that made postcard photographers drool. The sky was the color blue only ever seen on the California coast. A warmish breeze chased away any clouds that might want to linger. Dappled sunlight illuminated the perfectly green grass, while elegant trees provided patches of shade. A few colorful leaves decorated the stone path, and birds offered commentary on the events. All the moment needed was an orchestra playing something dreamy and a quick, magical clothing transformation during which she would shed her sensible business attire for something diaphanous.

But that wasn't likely to happen. Rather than push her luck when she'd already scored for her side, she went for a safe topic.

"How's David doing in school?" she asked.

"He's starting to panic. It's nearly time for finals again. The quarter system is proving to be a challenge for him. He's used to being the smartest kid in his class and not having to work very hard, but suddenly everyone around him was the smartest in each of their high school classes. But he's doing okay. I think by the third quarter, he'll be more relaxed."

There was pride in Zach's voice. And love. He might

have a million faults, but his relationship with David made up for a lot.

"I'm surprised you didn't have more children," she said idly.

Zach paused, giving her a startled glance. "I never thought about it," he said slowly. "I like kids. But I was so busy being a single parent, I never considered having more."

"You didn't have to stay single."

"Another marriage wasn't in the cards for me," he said easily, his blue eyes staring directly into hers. "What about you? Why aren't there a dozen or so Marcelli grandchildren running around? It's not as if your parents wouldn't have approved."

She sighed. "They would love it. As you've already experienced, the pressure to marry and have children is pretty relentless in our family."

"Yet you resisted."

"Probably because a dozen kids seems like a few too many."

He smiled. "Okay. How about four? It's a nice round number."

"I'll agree." She'd always wanted children and four sounded perfect. "However, in my world, children require me to be married, and as I've yet to find the right guy . . ."

"You're kidding?" he asked.

"What? That I think there's a 'right one'? "

"Yes. That's a myth of popular culture."

She laughed. "So speaks the man who has never risked marriage after one youthful mistake. I don't think that makes you an expert."

"My career does."

"No. Your career makes you an expert on why marriages fail, not why they succeed. You know everything a couple shouldn't do, but very little about what they *should* do. In my family, marriages have always been forever." She glanced at him. "Brenna's recent troubles to the contrary."

His gaze narrowed. "You argue a lot."

"Actually I don't. I'm a very pleasant person."

"You argue a lot with me."

She nodded. "You're right. Ask yourself why."

"I already know why. You're fighting the chemistry between us."

As he spoke, he moved close. Very close. Close enough that it seemed unnecessary for her to keep breathing. There was also the matter of his arms going around her and drawing her next to him.

She knew what he was going to do, and she didn't even consider stopping him. Not when she'd secretly wanted another kiss ever since he'd ended the first one. Oh, she knew she should resist, but this was one of those times when being bad felt so good.

His lips moved against hers with the best combination of tension, pressure, and softness. Firm yet yielding, sweet yet masculine. She found herself melting into the sensation, savoring every exquisite millimeter of contact. She wanted to part her lips, to have him plunge inside of her, but she also wanted to continue the kiss, drawing out the moment, enjoying the need and hunger building inside of her.

He moved his mouth back and forth, gently discovering her. When he bit on the full center of her lower lip, she gasped in both shock and delight. A quick brush of his tongue on the sensual injury made her shiver in anticipation. She raised her hands to his shoulders, for balance as well as to hold him in place. Her fingers rubbed against the smooth fabric of his suit.

Slowly, as if to give her time to get used to the idea, he slipped his tongue inside. She waited for some voice to call out the need to be sensible, but there was only silent anticipation. Hadn't Brenna told her she needed to be more bad? Kissing Zach sure had to qualify.

She surrendered to the wanting and parted her lips fully to admit him.

The arms around her tightened. He held her close enough that his heat warmed her, yet she didn't feel trapped. They moved together, as if they had performed this particular dance a thousand times before. There was no awkwardness, no bumping of noses and knees. Just mind-crushing desire. It swept through her like a tornado, sucking the air from her lungs and making her want to beg him to let her surrender.

Her skin felt too hot and too tight. Every erogenous zone she knew about and some she had yet to discover sent up warning signals that if they were not touched and soon, she would have to die right then. The taste of him, the pressure, the sweet sensations were all more than she had expected.

All her fantasies about Zach, both funny and serious, hadn't prepared her for the reality. His hands moved up and down her back, making her want to purr. When he slipped lower, cupping her rear, she instinctively arched against him, wanting to feel all of him. The hard proof of his arousal nearly made her scream in delight.

The rational part of her brain, which should have been telling her this was a big mistake, began to gauge the distance to the front desk of the hotel and calculate the embarrassment factor of checking in for a couple of hours of hot monkey sex. The alternative was doing it right here in the garden, but she'd never been one for public displays of affection.

Before she could decide if she could overcome her inhibitions, Zach drew back just enough to break the kiss. He rested his forehead on hers. She had a feeling he'd come to his senses, which really pissed her off. At least he was breathing just as hard as she was. She would hate to be the only one in the throes of uncontrolled passion.

He rubbed his thumb across her swollen lips. "You're full of surprises."

She tried to smile, but had a feeling it came out a little shaky at the corners. "The same could be said about you."

"No way." He cupped her face and kissed her again. "I've been kissing on and off for the past twenty years and I know I haven't felt anything like that before. So it must be you."

Even as she told herself his smooth line didn't mean anything, she found herself desperately wanting to believe it. Okay, Zach had promised to do whatever he could to change her mind about Mia and David, but she didn't want to believe he would go so far as to seduce her to his side. Except she had a feeling he just might.

The fact that she didn't know should have sent her running for the hills, or at least her car. Instead she felt only regret that they hadn't hooked up under slightly less charged circumstances.

"This is going to be complicated," he said.

"Not for me."

He grinned. "You're tough, Katie. I like that. I like it a lot."

His words made her shiver, which only proved she was a fool.

She stepped back and straightened her jacket. "This was great and all, but I really have to run."

"You could come back to my place."

The invitation, delivered in a sensually husky voice, made her knees melt. She had to consciously force her muscles to tighten so she wouldn't collapse in a heap.

"I could, but I won't. Thanks for asking, though."

"Want a rain check?"

She risked glancing at him. His dark blue eyes were bright with passion, his lips were still swollen. He looked impossibly sexy and irresistible. Giving in made perfect sense. No one would blame her.

"This is L.A.," she said. "We don't actually get rain."

"You're afraid."

"I'm smart."

"And scared."

As they both knew that was the truth; she didn't see any point in admitting it. "Let's just say I don't trust you."

She picked up her briefcase and made a timely retreat. Because ten more seconds in his company would put her on the verge of giving in, and she couldn't risk that.

Mia stood up from her place at the kitchen table and stretched to relieve the muscles in her back. Too many hours spent hunched over a book, she thought. She crossed to the calendar posted on the refrigerator door, where she checked off another two-hour block of study. She only had a week until finals. As usual, she'd prepared a schedule dividing up her non-classroom time into review sessions. Also, as usual, she was right on schedule.

Thanks to Katie, she thought, her gaze straying to a picture of all four Marcelli girls standing together in the middle of a vineyard. Her sister had always been the most organized student, and she'd passed all her tricks along to Mia.

A knock on the door made her turn. She knew instantly who stood in the hallway of her apartment building. She wrestled with two parts anticipation and one part apprehension.

She crossed to the door and opened it.

"Before you say anything," David told her as he entered, "I'm only staying thirty minutes. We need to stay focused on finals. But I've missed you."

"I've missed you, too."

She studied his familiar face, the blue eyes that she'd noticed right off, and the way his blond hair always fell across his forehead.

He held up a white bag. "I got your favorites," he said. "Just yesterday I was reading that sugar helps with mental acuity."

She glanced from the bag containing Baskin-Robbins ice cream to David. Apprehension faded as love swelled to take its place.

For the past few weeks, ever since they'd tried to shop for the gift registry, things had been kind of twisted between them. Not wrong, exactly, but not right, either. The fight had changed things. They'd been seeing each other, but the seeing had been strained.

Suddenly everything felt right again. She wrapped her arms around him and held him close. He dropped the ice-cream bag and pulled her hard against him.

"I'm sorry," she whispered, suddenly fighting tears.

"Me, too." He kissed her. "I love you, Mia."

"I love you more."

He smiled at the familiar joke. She continued to cling to him, needing to crawl inside and be a part of him. Whatever else went wrong in her life, being with David was always right.

10

Zach arrived at the Marcelli hacienda shortly before five. The house calls were killing his billable hours, but he willingly accepted that. After all, there was a greater good to consider. Besides, he could feel time ticking away. It had been six weeks since David and Mia had announced their engagement. Six weeks during which he'd made little progress toward breaking up the happy couple.

A recent spat between them had given him hope, but David had called to tell him they'd made up. Katie had yet to see the light, and he found himself spending as much time thinking about getting her into bed as getting her on his side.

Brenna was a potential ally, but she was too caught up in her own personal grief to be of much help. So despite a plan to find a fellow dissenter in the enemy camp, he was still on his own.

He parked and collected his paperwork, then walked to the front door of the hacienda. Brenna met him there, looking dark-eyed and tragic. Despite her olive complexion, she appeared pale. Shadows stained the skin under her eyes, and there were new lines by the corners of her mouth. Divorce did not agree with her.

"Thanks for coming," she said as she stepped back to invite him into the house. "I know I really need to start driving down to L.A., but right now that seems like an impossible task."

"You haven't been back to the apartment to collect your belongings?"

She gave a strangled laugh. "What is there to collect? Some old clothes and costume jewelry?"

"Stereo, television, a clock radio, whatever was yours to begin with."

She frowned slightly. "I hadn't thought of it that way, but you have a point. I guess I should force myself to check out the place. I can't imagine Jeff would do anything to my things, but then I never thought he'd want a divorce, either."

He'd heard of a whole lot worse. "If you find anything missing, I'll need a complete inventory of what's not there. Wanting to end the marriage doesn't give him the right to destroy your personal property."

She nodded listlessly, as if the entire process would take more energy than she had, then pointed to the living room.

"Do you want to work in there?"

"Somewhere with a table would be better."

He had plenty of papers for her to review and some news that wasn't going to brighten her day. It would piss off the family, as well.

Brenna led the way into the kitchen. Zach was surprised to find it bustling with activity. The taller of the two grandmothers—Tessa, he thought—stirred something at the stove, while Mary-Margaret O'Shea kneaded bread dough. Neither woman noticed them.

Grammy M, as Katie called her, used her forearm to brush back a loose curl. "I'll be needin' the oven, Tessa. When I've finished with the bread, the sweet rolls will be wantin' to bake."

Grandma Tessa peered at the temperature setting. "It's ready now." She started to say something else, but spotted him and Brenna instead. "Zach, how good to see you."

She abandoned her efforts at the stove and hurried toward him. Between his briefcase and the stack of files he carried, he didn't have a free hand. Not that he would be able to ward off her enthusiastic greeting. He was summarily hugged, patted, and cheek-pinched. Grammy M— so tiny she barely came up to his chest—followed, although she only squeezed his arm instead of his cheek. They both spoke at once, one offering tea, the other Italian cookies, or maybe a nice dish of pasta. The combination of warm Italian staccato and lilting Irish brogue should have jarred his ears, but he'd grown used to the odd melody.

"Nothing for me, thanks. I'm fine," he said, depositing his briefcase in a chair and his files on the table.

They both ignored his statement. Within a minute a steaming cup of tea had been set at the head of the table and right next to it was a plate piled high with cookies. A mug of tea was pressed into Brenna's hands. She cradled it as she took a seat next to his. Zach settled into the chair obviously assigned to him and reached for his paperwork.

Grandma Tessa and Grammy M hovered by the table. He glanced at the bread dough now resting in a covered bowl, then at the stove. Nothing else appeared to be cooking. And whatever Grammy M had put in the oven was there to stay for a while. He hesitated, not used to conducting business with an audience, but Brenna didn't seem to notice. Finally he glanced at his client.

"Will we be in the way here? Should we move to another room?"

Brenna roused herself enough to shake her head. "I like the emotional hand-holding. Besides, they're going to find out everything anyway," she said quietly. "Having the Grands here will mean two less tellings of the story. You're lucky the whole family isn't attending." She glanced at her watch. "Katie's not coming because she's busy with work, but Francesca should be here any minute. Not that we have to wait for her. I didn't tell Mia because she's busy with finals this week and I didn't want to upset her."

He had a couple of socialite clients who brought their rat dogs to meetings, and a famous actor who traveled everywhere with a publicist, business manager, and assistant, but very few people had a familial entourage. Somehow he thought the Grands were going to be a whole lot more helpful to Brenna than a pet or a personal assistant.

Zach was about to begin when Colleen Marcelli walked into the kitchen.

"Have I missed anything?" she asked, moving first to her daughter, where she bent low and kissed her cheek, then to Zach. She lightly touched his shoulder and gave him a warm smile before taking the seat across from Brenna and settling in to listen.

"We're just starting," Brenna said.

Colleen nodded. She was a well-dressed woman in her mid-forties, although she looked much younger. She'd inherited her mother's blue eyes, along with Grammy M's delicate build.

"I thought it best not to include your father," she said, nodding when Grammy M offered tea. "You know how much he can yell. Marco and your grandfather are already talking about altering Jeff's manhood—such as it is." She sighed. "I didn't think any of us needed to hear the details again."

"I'd rather not," Brenna said ruefully. "Everyone welcomed him into the family when I married him, but now all I hear is how you all had your suspicions."

Colleen nodded sympathetically. She stretched her hand across the table to squeeze her daughter's arm. Zach waited it all out. He was used to emotional clients—sobbing, even fits of rage weren't uncommon in his line of work. Compared with that, a quiet, rational family looking on was no big deal.

He cleared his throat, but before he could speak, Grammy M put a cup of tea in front of her daughter, then took a seat at the table. Grandma Tessa did the same, but instead of liquid refreshment, she brought a basket with her. He eyed the container, wondering what on earth they could be planning—and then he knew.

Sure enough, lace flowers were passed around. Bowls of beads and seed pearls were set in the center of the table, and all the women, even Brenna, started sewing.

Light caught the tiny beads. Female fingers worked with a sure swiftness that came from hours of practice. Zach didn't want to think about what the lace was for, so he returned his attention to the business at hand—namely Brenna's divorce—and sorted through the files he'd brought.

He glanced at her. "Take a deep breath and relax," he said gently. "Most of what we have to discuss is fairly standard. The only unusual issue to turn up so far is that Jeff is claiming half of your share of the winery."

He braced himself as he spoke, knowing he'd just dropped a bomb on the entire family. As expected, conversation exploded around him. He didn't bother to compete, instead letting them express their outrage. Grandma Tessa sprang to her feet and announced that her late father-in-law (God rest his soul) had started the winery, breaking the ground with his own bare hands, and no lying, cheating— She began muttering in Italian. Grammy M's eyes narrowed in an expression of fury that made Zach want to inch away. Colleen looked just as ready to skin Brenna's soon-to-be ex-husband, while Brenna simply appeared stunned.

When the talk died down, he turned his attention to his client. "This is a ploy. Jeff and his lawyer want to distract us from the real issue—namely how long you supported Jeff through his medical training. Any inheritance you received wouldn't be considered community property unless it was commingled in some kind of joint account, with joint funds."

"That bastard," Brenna snapped. "He never cared about the winery. *I'm* the one who has always loved it. *I* gave it up for him and *this* is my reward?"

"This is a divorce," Zach told her. "Fair or right doesn't enter into it. This is all about money. Unfortunately, fighting his claim is going to chew up a lot. Was there an inheritance?"

"Not a penny," she said flatly. "Nothing has been turned over to me, and unless Grandpa Lorenzo has changed his will, nothing ever will be." Her mouth twisted. "He's giving up on a male grandson and holding out for a male great-grandson."

Grammy M leaned close. "Darlin' Brenna, don't you worry about this. The little ferret won't be gettin' so much as a single grape from this place."

Brenna nodded at her grandmother. "I know, but I can't believe he's doing this."

"As I said, Jeff wants to divert our attention from the real issue. I'm not going to let that happen. I'll let his attorney know there wasn't any kind of inheritance. He'll push back. Be prepared for that, but don't worry about it. I'll handle it. If that's the best they've got, we're in the clear."

He picked up a second folder. "*Our* attention will be focused on the fact that you supported your husband through medical school, his internship and residency, as well as paying off debt he accumulated before the marriage. The precedence for you to receive compensation is very strong. We have some tables that show—"

The back door opened. A blond-haired woman in jeans walked into the kitchen. She was tall and slender, but that wasn't what caught his attention. Instead it was the tattoos covering nearly every inch of exposed skin. There was even a small blue star by the corner of her right eye, just under the silver ring piercing her eyebrow.

The young woman laughed, then planted her hands on her hips. "Obviously it's working. Hello! It's me."

The grandmothers laughed, while Colleen rose to embrace the young woman. Brenna set down her sewing and studied the visitor.

"I thought the fat suit was next," she said.

"It was, but then I saw this guy with tattoos and it gave me an idea."

Grandma Tessa sighed heavily and dug in her pocket for her rosary. "For this God gave you the face of an angel? Did you color your hair? Francesca, it was so beautiful."

Zach blinked. Francesca? He tried to reconcile the tattooed woman in front of him with the sister he remembered. He supposed the shape of her face was familiar.

Brenna leaned toward him. "I know it's strange, but you'll get used to it. Francesca is studying social psychol-

ogy. Her doctorate explores how people react to appearance. She spends her day shocking people."

Zach shook his head. "She's good at it."

Francesca finished assuring both her grandmothers
that the blond hair was just a wig. She poured herself
some coffee from a pot on the counter, then sat next to her
mother and reached for a lace flower.

"So what's up?" she asked.

"Jeff wants a share of the winery," Brenna told her
sister.

Francesca's mouth dropped open. "That pissant, pin-
headed, sleazeball."

Grandma Tessa gave her granddaughter a warning
glance. "God listens to everything you say."

"Is he listening to Jeff's lies, too?" Francesca slapped her
hands against the table. "I can't believe this!"

"Me, either," Brenna said. "I shouldn't have said no
when you told me we should have him killed." She shook
her head at both her grandmothers. "Just kidding. Sort
of."

Zach waded into the fray. "Jeff is going to have to pay
up, ladies. Let's keep the big picture in mind. The best way
to get his attention is through his wallet."

He picked up the financial table he'd been holding and
turned it toward Brenna. "This gives you an idea of how
much of his income is up for grabs. You weren't married
long enough to cross the ten-year threshold. That's the
point at which you can petition for alimony for the rest of
your life."

"Not my style," Brenna told him. "I want him to suffer,
but I'm not going to sit on my butt."

"Good. The court will see it the same way. You're
young and capable. They'll expect you to want to make

something of your life. Marrying a jerk doesn't entitle you to a lifetime of support. However, the state believes that everything should be divided equally. And there is the matter of you supporting Jeff." He laid the financial paper aside. "It would help if you had some kind of plan, Brenna."

"Such as?"

"Goals for the future. A sense of what you want to do with your life. If you wanted to go to college or start a business, Jeff would most likely be required to ante up for some or all of that."

She nodded. "I'll come up with something."

"I think you should. In the meantime, you need to get back into the apartment and collect your things. Make a list of everything that's missing. Did you get the information on your checking account?"

"No."

Colleen looked up, but didn't say anything. Grammy M clucked sympathetically.

"Please check the current balance. Also, let me know what it was when you left. Oh, and would you get me a copy of your apartment lease?"

She nodded.

He handed her several papers he needed her to fill out.

"That's about it," he said. "Unless you have any questions?"

"Not really."

"Then I'll talk to you in a couple of days."

He started to put his folders back in order.

Grandma Tessa rose instantly. "Are you hungry? We'll be having dinner soon. You'll stay, yes?"

"I have to get back to Los Angeles," he said, a little surprised that he felt something close to regret. The idea of eating with the Marcellis, of spending the evening with them, wasn't unpleasant.

If not for David wanting to marry Mia, Zach would be pleased to hang out with the Marcelli clan.

"Then at least stay long enough to eat some of the cookies," Colleen said. "My mother will be crushed if you don't."

He nodded because it seemed easier to give in than fight. Grammy M rushed to get him more tea, while Francesca rose to check on the delicious-smelling baked goods in the oven.

Grandma Tessa continued her beadwork. "Katie called yesterday. She's working very hard on that fund-raiser for your law firm."

Zach shook his head. They were charming women, but not the least bit subtle. "She's a hard worker."

"Pretty, too," Grammy M offered from her place by the stove.

"Very pretty." Very sexy.

"Have you been seeing a lot of her?" Colleen asked.

He thought about the kiss in the garden. Not as *much* of her as he would like, but he wasn't going to complain to her mother. "We had a business meeting last week."

Colleen's mouth settled in a straight line. "Just a business meeting? Nothing more . . . personal?"

"No. Sorry."

He finished the cookie and rose to make his escape, before they started on a web for him. "Ladies, this has been terrific, but I have to head back to the city."

It took at least ten minutes to make his way out of the house. After he'd stowed his files and briefcase, he settled behind the wheel and started the engine.

They were good, honest people who didn't have a clue

about how financially vulnerable they were. To them, life was a sitcom. Easy problems wrapped up in twenty-two minutes. If Brenna hadn't inherited anything, then Jeff was out of luck. But what if she had? And what about the next Marcelli daughter who married? From where he was sitting he could see acres of vineyards stretching in every direction. Now the thick stalks were gray and wizened, but come spring . . .

He realized he didn't know what they would look like, come spring, but he could imagine. Each vine heavy with grapes. Grapes later transformed into wine. The Marcelli Winery was world famous. The family's wealth made David's trust fund seem insignificant.

They were all so gung ho on the wedding, but no one thought about what could happen after. There hadn't been a word of talk about a prenuptial agreement. They were too busy beading lace and spinning a web that could trap them all.

11

Katie juggled two "stay-hot" Styrofoam containers, along with her heavy briefcase, as she made her way up the stairs to Zach's front door. For the entire forty-two-minute trip from the hotel to his place, she'd lectured herself on the importance of staying cool, acting professional, and pretending that the passionate kiss in the hotel garden had never taken place. No matter what, she would *not* react to him again. Even if he opened the door naked.

Especially then.

In keeping with the "business only" attitude she'd decided was the most sensible—and safe—she'd dressed in a severe black pantsuit and a silk-blend turtleneck. Except for her face and hands, there wasn't an inch of exposed skin. She refused to give him any ideas.

Speaking of Zach, he must have been watching for her because he opened the door before she had a chance to knock. He grabbed both food containers and eyed her briefcase.

"Do you take that with you everywhere?"

"Just about," she admitted, unable to keep from smiling

at the sight of him. "I never know when I'm going to need to produce a chart or schedule."

He ushered her into the kitchen. He'd obviously arrived home some time ago. Not only was the table set, but he'd changed out of his suit into jeans and a long-sleeved shirt. Katie couldn't help noticing his butt as he turned to put the containers on the counter.

Most men had pretty decent butts, far better than most women's, and Zach's was definitely in the top ten percentile. Damn. Don't look, she told herself as she moved toward the containers of food. "Jerome prepared all the dishes we'd talked about tasting. Obviously they aren't as fresh as they will be at the party, so take that into account. Also, the presentation is somewhat lacking."

She started opening foil packages. Zach set Styrofoam containers on the table. Once the food was laid out, she pulled large, folded sheets of paper from her briefcase. She opened them to show mock-ups of the food displays. As Zach tasted, she explained what foods would be at which stations and how everything would be served.

"Some of the kabobs will be precooked," she told him, "but others will require guest preparation. Also, we're going to have a station of exotic meats, and vegetarian stations for those who prefer that sort of thing."

"Tofu on a stick?" he teased.

She laughed. "I hope it's more interesting than that, but yes."

She showed him computer-generated designs for the various carnival booths, then returned her papers to her briefcase and took some food for herself.

They discussed various ingredients, ranked their favorites, and narrowed the menu down to something close to its final form. Katie finished making notes while Zach prepared coffee.

"If only I could get you to care this much about the napkin selections," she joked as he collected two mugs from a cupboard.

"Never gonna happen."

"I suspected as much."

She pulled a flat plastic box from her briefcase. Before she could open it, Zach moved to the table and set her coffee in front of her. He then took the box and opened it.

In that second she realized she hadn't been thinking. Beading lace in the presence of the one person determined to stop the wedding was bound to get a reaction.

Zach lifted the half-beaded lace flower from its container and turned it over in his hands.

"You do beautiful work," he said, his voice not giving away his feelings. But then she already knew what was on his mind.

"I'm not doing a good job of convincing you to see my side of things," he told her.

"Not for lack of trying. You've threatened me, tried reason and seduction. What's next? Money?"

He set the lace back in the box. "Katie, it was one kiss. If I'd been trying to seduce you, things wouldn't have stopped there."

She snapped the case shut. Talk about arrogant. "You're assuming a lot."

His dark eyes locked on hers. "I know."

Heat boiled between them. Katie didn't want to be the one to blink first, but she could feel herself slipping under his spell. Better to retreat and live to fight another day than give in with a pitiful "Take me, I'm yours."

"So why can't you consider the possibility of being

wrong about David and Mia?" she asked in a feeble attempt to crank down the temperature in the room.

"Because I'm not. The only thing I feel more strongly about than keeping David from marrying Mia in July is keeping him from running off with her. He's stubborn enough to do it. I'm still building my case. When I have it together, I'll take it to him."

"I know you love your son. But Mia is so sure about David, and she rarely makes a bad decision. Can't you trust her?"

"No."

Not a surprise. Maybe a nice change of subject was due. "I spoke with my mom this morning. Everyone in the family is really impressed with how you're handling Brenna's divorce."

"Just doing my job," he said with a shrug.

"They're also furious with Jeff. I can't believe he had the balls to come after the winery. I'm half expecting Grandma Tessa to put some ancient Italian curse on him."

Zach chuckled. "Interesting plan. I prefer to take the legal approach, making him bleed every month as he writes Brenna a big, fat check."

"Is this where I hum the *Jaws* theme?"

"If it makes you happy."

She glanced at him. "So me thinking you're a shark doesn't bother you?"

"I am what I am. What I think isn't going to change your opinion."

"True, but my grandmothers adore you."

"They're fine women with excellent taste."

"What about the cheek pinching?"

He winced. "That's not my favorite trait."

"I'm used to the family, but I would guess you find us all

a little overwhelming." She put the lace flower back in the box. "The last dress I worked on was Brenna's. Well, Brenna's and Francesca's. They had a double wedding. Francesca's husband died a few years later, which left Brenna as the only married sister. Grandpa Lorenzo was constantly on her to have children. And now she's getting a divorce." She sipped her coffee.

"There are worse things," Zach pointed out.

"Not in our family. She's feeling a lot of guilt about all this."

"The divorce isn't her fault. Jeff is the one who left. From what I can tell, Brenna was willing to tough it out, even if things weren't perfect at home."

That surprised her. "She admitted there was a problem?"

"No, but she didn't have to. Happy marriages don't end in divorce."

"I suppose, but whatever the problem was, we never knew. Everyone liked Jeff, which made his leaving such a shock." She sighed. "Poor Brenna. She'd dealing with her own pain and knowing that this is the first Marcelli divorce ever."

"She'll recover."

"I guess people don't have a choice. It must be really hard on the kids. Didn't you mention that your parents were divorced? Or is that too personal to ask?"

Zach leaned back in his chair. "Katie, a few days ago I had my tongue in your mouth. It's not too personal."

She swallowed. She'd been doing so well, feeling normal around Zach, and with one sentence he'd made her *aware* of him again.

"My parents split up," he said. "Like most couples, they were in trouble years before that. I guess I was ten when I figured out something was wrong. I saw my dad kissing a woman who wasn't my mother. When I mentioned it to him, he said it was time I learned the facts of life and proceeded to tell me that every man who knew what was good for him kept a little something on the side."

Katie felt her mouth drop open. She closed it quickly, but knew she looked as surprised as she felt. "He said that?"

Zach nodded. "He thought he was hip. I told him he was a bastard. He only laughed. By the time I was twelve, he started introducing me to his flavor of the month. He never kept them around long, but there was always one waiting in the wings."

She shivered. "Did your mother know?"

"I never said anything. I was a kid and scared. She probably figured it out on her own." He hesitated. "Not that it mattered. My dad came from money and she didn't, so he had the power."

She heard the bitterness in his voice.

Zach picked up his coffee, but didn't drink. "He never worked a day in his life. Maybe that was the problem— too much time on his hands. I guess the cheating was the price my mother had to pay for the good life. But eventually the price got too high. They split when I was fourteen."

"Who did you live with?"

"My mother. After my father left, his money disappeared, too. She went to work, first one job, then two. She wouldn't touch the trust fund my father set up for me. She kept saying that was for my future. Ironically, despite his millions, my father never paid child support and my mother wouldn't take him to court to make him. So we went from rich to poor in short order."

"Why wouldn't she want him to pay child support? That was for you."

"I don't know. Pride? Shame? She was a hell of a woman—always there for me. Once I had David, she was a rock. She died my first year of law school." He paused, then glanced around the kitchen. "I wish she could have lived long enough to see all of this, and so I could have made her life easier."

"I'm sorry," Katie whispered, not sure what else to say. His childhood was light-years from her own. "Is your dad still alive?"

"No. He died a few years back. Turns out he left David a nice trust fund and the rest of the money to me." He laughed, but the sound had no humor. "Isn't that a bitch? Every stinking penny to me. But in the end I walked away from it. The old man put too many strings on his dollars, and I didn't need them that badly. So they went to some charity and I'm finally free of him."

Ever the man in charge, no hint of pain flickered in his eyes. She wondered if it was still there, or if he'd made peace with the past. Whatever doubts she may have had about Zach changing his mind about Mia and David getting married had just been squashed. No wonder he didn't think relationships worked.

He shrugged. "Okay, that's my sorry past. Let's talk about something cheerful. How about your dating history?"

She smiled. "Why is that a cheerful subject?"

"You being happily married would put a real crimp in my plans to seduce you."

Katie was glad she wasn't drinking. Had she been, she might have spit. "Okay, then. Thanks for making that clear."

"You're welcome. So tell me about all the Mr. Wrongs and how much more interesting I am than them."

"There's that ego again. I should have brought more food."

"You're stalling."

"I have nothing to say. My dating history is pretty much like everyone else's. I've dated men who are afraid of commitment, or men who want to commit for the wrong reason. Even some who should have *been* committed."

"That sounds interesting."

"Less so than you might think." She considered her dating past. "There were guys who could drive me crazy in three minutes and guys who just weren't as interested in me as I was in them." She leaned forward and rested her forearms on the table. "In all of that I never found the one who was . . ."

"Perfect?" he offered.

"I wasn't looking for perfect. Just a couple of bells."

He frowned. "What?"

"You know. Hearing bells or music or something. A cosmic sign that I'd found the right guy."

"You're way too romantic."

"I want what most women want."

"A free ride and a pool boy for sex?"

She shook her head. "That's cynical even for you."

"Okay. You're right. Not all women are on the take."

"On behalf of my gender, allow me to be flattered."

She rose and crossed to the sink, where she rinsed her mug. When she turned, Zach was standing right behind her. His dark gaze settled on her face.

"I never thought that about you," he told her. "I mean that, Katie. You're a class act."

"Thanks."

He was standing close. Too close.

He reached up and touched her cheek. Instantly heat spiraled through her, making it difficult to remember her plan not to react to him again. Somehow the importance of it all escaped her.

"What are you thinking?" he asked, his voice low and seductive.

"I, um, I'm not really thinking anything."

Which was true. She was using the moment to get lost in his blue eyes. They were the perfect color, she thought. She also liked the stubble darkening his jaw and the way he—

His mouth brushed against hers. All her senses went on instant alert. The sensible part of her knew this was a really big mistake. Kissing the last time could almost be considered an accident. But if they did it again, it might have significance . . . although she couldn't say exactly what that significance would be. And before she could figure it out, his tongue brushed against her bottom lip and she no longer cared.

He felt too good, she thought, surrendering to the moment. Her arms came up and rested on his shoulders as she took a step forward. Their bodies pressed together. He was hard to her soft—thick muscles and angles, unyielding where they touched. She liked that. She liked the scent of him, too. That heady masculine combination of skin and some unique elixir that was the essence of Zach himself.

He cupped her face, then slid his fingers into her hair. When he nipped her bottom lip, she gasped slightly, parting for him, wanting him to move inside of her. Her heartbeat quickened in anticipation. Heat flared between her thighs, and her breasts swelled. Every erogenous zone she owned prepared to party.

Their tongues touched in introduction, then circled each other. She dropped her hands to his back, where she could feel his muscles tensing. Was it suddenly hot in here, or was it her? She felt as if parts of her were on fire.

Zach must have read her mind because he tugged on the lapels of her suit jacket. She moved her arms to her side so he could push the garment over her shoulders. It slid soundlessly to the floor.

Her turtleneck suddenly seemed to be an unreasonable constriction. What had she been thinking? Wouldn't a silky camisole have been better? Something with thin fabric, lots of lace, and a style that exposed plenty of flesh. Or better yet a—

Her mind experienced thought gridlock when Zach put his hands on her waist and began moving them higher. As there weren't a lot of choices in the destination department, she had a good idea where he was headed. She also knew what was going to happen when he got there.

If his hot kissing was anything to go by, he would touch her with a combination of gentleness and experience that would rob her of several important abilities. So if she was going to stop things, this would be the moment. Right now. Right this second.

His fingers grazed the undersides of her breasts. Any master plan she'd had was lost, and she could do nothing but surrender to the sensation of his confident caress.

He cupped her curves, then brushed his thumbs against her already tight nipples. Even through the layers of clothing, she was exquisitely sensitive. Her breath caught and her pelvic muscles clenched.

As he gently squeezed her breasts, he drew back from her mouth. Before she could complain, he pressed his lips against her jaw, then moved lower to her neck. Soft, wet kisses made her arch her head back. He moved to the sensitive skin below her ears and gently sucked. She wanted him to keep going lower and lower, but her turtleneck was in the way.

She braced herself for the sensible fairy to burst into her brain and make her stop. She waited for Zach to come to *his* senses and stop making her whimper with the erotic pattern he traced over her breasts. Instead he dropped his hands to her waistband and started tugging on her shirt.

The first whisper of cool air should have made her reconsider. Under other circumstances—although she couldn't say what—it would have. Really. Instead she found herself helping him drag up her turtleneck. She slipped out of the arms, then tugged the tight neck over her head.

Even as she tossed it aside, his mouth reclaimed hers. She parted as he plunged inside her. Tongues circled, stroked, danced. He moved closer still so that their bodies pressed together, her bare midsection rubbing against the softness of his shirt. His hands brushed her bare back, then moved up to expertly unfasten her bra.

She felt the slack in the band, then the straps fell off her shoulders. He eased away just enough to slip one hand between them. That large, warm hand moved under her bra cup and engulfed her aching left breast.

Need flooded her. Need and wanting and passion that made her wet and ready in a heartbeat. Every part of her throbbed, but most especially the swelling dampness between her legs.

She quickly pulled off her bra and dropped it to the floor. Her hands moved restlessly, first to his shoulders, then to his back where powerful muscles bunched and released. When he bent down and drew her nipple into his mouth, she groaned. When his tongue flicked against the tight tip, she shook.

Her fingers went to work on his shirt, but his arms got in the way. She managed to pull a couple of buttons free, but that was all. He licked and sucked on her breasts until a steady pulsing beat began between her legs, and she knew that she was already heading for the edge of surrender.

He abandoned her long enough to pull off his shirt and step out of his shoes. She kicked off hers as well, but that was as far as she got before he reclaimed her with a deep, wet kiss that left her shaken down to her melting bones.

"I want you," he murmured against her mouth. "Katie, I want you. Now."

Simple words, but powerful. He drew her close and her breasts flattened against his bare chest. The hair there tickled erotically. He cupped her rear and squeezed. She tilted forward until her belly came in contact with his erection. They both groaned.

"We need to move this upstairs," he said even as he turned and took her hand in his.

He led the way, pausing halfway up the stairs to kiss her neck, her shoulders, then her breasts. Even as his tongue circled her nipple, his fingers slipped between her legs and rubbed against her swollen flesh. She was so wet, so hungry, she surged against him. One or two more strokes would be enough, she thought, fighting desperate need.

"This way," he said hoarsely and continued to the second floor.

She had a brief impression of high ceilings, skylights, and a king-size bed. The only light came from the hallway, but it was enough. She saw Zach reach for the button on the front of her slacks. When that was free, he tugged down the zipper.

Below she wore bikini briefs which he quickly stripped off, leaving her naked.

"Beautiful," he murmured, even as he gently pushed her into a sitting position.

Before she'd quite settled on the bed, he'd dropped to his knees and pressed his mouth to the soft skin on the inside of her legs.

Everything was moving so fast, she thought hazily. She barely knew Zach. He was her client. This was all—

Heaven, she told herself as his wet kisses moved higher. Stupid, maybe, but heaven. Need pulsed in time with her rapid heartbeat. She ached down to the very fiber of her being.

She lay back on the bed and rested her heels on the edge of the mattress. The position left her exposed and vulnerable, and him in no doubt of what she wanted.

She didn't have to wait long for him to agree to her suggestion. Warm fingers gently slid into slick folds of hungry flesh. He brushed perilously close to that one magical spot, without touching it directly. She shuddered. A whisper of breath was her only warning, then his mouth claimed her in a deep kiss that made every cell in her body scream.

He brushed his tongue against her tight center, stroking it rhythmically. Over and around, he teased, he promised, he made her gasp, then not breathe at all. She gave in to the journey because she had no choice. When he slipped a single finger inside her to stroke her from that side as well, she gasped his name. When he moved his tongue faster, she fought for control. When he inserted a second finger, she lost it.

Her orgasm crashed over her with an unexpected intensity. Pleasure filled her to the top and spilled over the sides. Every inch of her body participated, bathing in heat and release. She lost track of time, she lost control, she lost everything except the ongoing pleasure that transported her, shattered her, then returned her safe and sound to the universe of her origin.

Zach slowly lowered her feet to the floor, then kissed the top of her thigh. She risked opening her eyes. He was smiling, the pleased smile of a lover who has pleasured his partner.

Coming first made her feel vulnerable. Coming second hadn't been an option.

"That was really good for me," he said.

His words eased some of her nervousness. She smiled back. "Imagine how it was for me."

"Why don't you tell me?"

"Amazing."

"Amazing works."

He rose and pulled off his socks, then quickly unfastened his belt, then his trousers. Seconds later he was naked. Katie shifted back on the bed, all the while watching him. She liked his body, the swirls of dark hair on his chest and the narrow pattern that seemed to lead the eye directly to his groin.

He was hard, ready, and big enough to please. Despite her ten-point-three on the orgasm scale, just looking at his arousal made her insides clench in anticipation.

He opened the nightstand drawer and drew out a condom.

After he slipped it on, he moved onto the bed. She opened her arms, then drew him close. His erection brushed against her leg as her thigh slipped between his. He shifted so she was draped over him.

One of his hands traced patterns across her back while the other cupped her breast. The second his thumb brushed against her nipple, she felt an answer quiver between her legs. She rocked her wetness against his leg.

"Ready again?" he asked. "I can wait if you need me to."

"Manful, but unnecessary."

She expected him to move into place, but instead he put his hands on her hips and urged her to straddle him. Katie didn't hesitate. She moved over him, then reached between them to guide him inside.

His thickness stretched her deliciously. As she came down so he filled her fully, he reached for both breasts and began to gently squeeze her nipples. The combination, her sliding up and down and his attention to her breasts, was too much. She felt the first rippling clench deep inside.

Zach caught his breath. Having Katie's slick heat surround him was one thing, but feeling her climax was another. The thick contractions gripped him tightly from base to tip and about squeezed the control right out of him.

"I can't stop," she gasped as another contraction shuddered through her. "Oh, Zach!"

She rode him, moving faster and faster. Every third or fourth stroke brought another release. The increased pace shattered his control. The swaying of her breasts, the pleasure on her face, the scent of her body all conspired to make him want more.

He dropped his hands to her hips and dug in his fingers. Plunging faster and deeper, he claimed her and his orgasm, burying himself in her and exploding into pleasure.

Katie awoke sometime after midnight. There was no second of confusion, no wondering where she was. She knew the exact location and even why she was currently naked. In this case, clarity was *not* a blessing.

She'd had sex with Zach Stryker. Zach—the man who had promised to do anything he could to get her to change her mind about Mia's engagement. Zach, who was her newest client for the biggest contract she'd ever had, her sister's divorce lawyer, and a potential in-law. The man who was determined to break her sister's heart.

She supposed that in the scheme of things, this was probably not the smartest thing she'd ever done. Nope, it probably wasn't even going to make the top ten.

She turned her head and saw Zach sleeping next to her. He'd been a great lover, and a stellar host. He'd offered her one of his T-shirts to sleep in, plus a brand-new toothbrush, and had taken her order for breakfast. A girl could get used to this sort of treatment.

Make that . . . "A woman." A mature woman who handled sexual relationships with the ease of handling a tricky scheduling conflict. A sophisticated woman who understood the rules of the game and occasionally bent them for her own benefit. Someone savvy. Someone together.

Someone not Katie.

Feeling anything but sophisticated and mature, Katie did the only thing that made sense under the circumstances.

She ran.

12

A light rain fell as Brenna walked through the north vineyard where the Cab grapes were grown. Mostly Cabernet Sauvignon, with a little Cab Franc for blending. Now, in early April, there were only small signs of life. She spotted a few tiny buds that would soon bring forth green leaves and heavy grapes.

She drew in a deep breath, inhaling the scent of damp earth. Come late summer the fragrance of the grapes would be nearly as intoxicating as the wine itself. Today there was only the gray of the sky and the brown of the earth, but in time the landscape would be an artist's palette of colors. Blue and green and gold and purple. She closed her eyes, imagining what it would be, then opened them again. To her, even the barren plainness was beautiful.

For the first time in several weeks, she felt as if she could breathe. As if she, like the vines, was coming back to life.

Carefully, so as not to accidentally kick a plant, she bent down and examined the fastenings that held the vine in place. She touched the small tubing that provided life-giving water. Her fingers curled into her palms as she ached for all she'd missed these years. All she'd lost. All Jeff had taken away.

She knew that in time she would accept his leaving, her stupidity, and the other woman. But she would never, ever forgive him for wanting to lay claim to the land, the vines and the dream she'd given up for him. *Rage* didn't describe what she felt, nor did *fury*. She didn't just want Jeff to back off, she wanted him destroyed. Any thoughts she'd had about being reasonable had ended the second he'd threatened Marcelli Wines.

She straightened and raised her face to the rain. Cool drops trickled down her face like tears. Yet this moisture healed. It brought life—to the vines and to her.

She'd given herself heart, body, and soul to her husband and in the end he'd had no use for the gifts. Obviously her body was hers once again, and while she had no need for her heart—love was not going to be in her future, ever—she desperately had to find her soul if she was ever to reclaim the person she used to be.

"You're a Marcelli to your bones. You always come back to the vines."

She turned toward the familiar voice and saw Grandpa Lorenzo walking toward her. He wore a heavy jacket and a cap on his white hair. Sometime while she hadn't been paying attention, he'd become an old man. Time had bent his back and gnarled his hands. Still, when he stood close to her, she felt safe, just as she had when she'd been a little girl.

"You're right about the vines," she said, staring out at them. "I can't escape them."

"Not even when you try. I heard about your husband. That he tried to claim some of this for himself. That will never happen. This is only for family."

"I know, Grandpa." His words made her feel guilty, as if Jeff's greedy grasping were her fault. "I should never have married him."

"No. We all thought he was a different kind of man."

Brenna wasn't so sure anyone had thought anything except relief that she had married right on schedule. Even at eighteen she'd felt the pressure to marry young and produce a son. She thought of how the current circumstances would have affected a child.

"At least we were smart enough not to have babies," she said. "Better that they not go through this. Plus Jeff would have been tied to the family forever."

She expected a word of agreement, but instead Grandpa Lorenzo sighed heavily. "I would have forgiven many sins for a grandson."

Anger flared inside of her. "You need to get over your gender bias, Grandpa. It's the new millennium. Women are just as capable as men, and they're finally getting a chance to prove it."

The old man looked at her. "They may be capable, but are they as loyal? You left. You went away and the vines were forgotten."

"That's not fair," she protested. "You *wanted* me to get married. All my life I'd been told my duty was to have a husband and a family. I did what I was supposed to do, and now you're blaming me for leaving?"

He ignored the question. "What are you going to do now?" Grandpa Lorenzo asked.

"Get a job." She turned to him. "I want to work here."

He nodded. "I think there's an opening in the gift shop."

She stepped back as if he'd slapped her. Tears sprang to her eyes, but she blinked them away. He would be expecting weakness. She had to be strong to prove herself.

"Except for you, no one knows more about the vines than I do," she said.

"You *knew*. Nine years ago. What do you remember?"

She thought about her years in an office job she hated, and how at night, when she wasn't at her second job, she'd studied. She'd used money they'd needed for things like food to buy textbooks from the UC Davis Viticulture and Enology Department. She'd continued her education, even when Jeff had fumed at her, not understanding why it was so important to her.

"I remember everything," she told him.

Her grandfather looked at her. "What's to keep you from running off with the next man who asks?"

The unfairness of the question fueled her temper. He wanted it both ways—great-grandsons and a promise never to leave.

"Let's just say I've learned my lesson," she told him. "I'm not interested in being stupid a second time."

He studied her, staring into her eyes for several seconds before turning away. "There might be something. Come into my office in the morning and we'll talk."

She nodded without speaking because her throat had tightened and she didn't think she could form words. When he left, she stayed where she was, raising her face to the light rain, letting the cool drops wash away her tears.

Finally, when the cold seeped into her bones, she forced herself to head back to the house. As she turned in that direction, she caught sight of a distant hillside, also covered with dormant vines. But this land wasn't part of the Marcelli legacy. Instead it belonged to Wild Sea Vineyards.

Marcelli wines had an excellent reputation for quality. They consistently received high scores and won medals.

But Wild Sea Vineyards was an international success that dwarfed its neighbor. The two wineries had been founded together, by best friends as close as brothers. Until sixty years before, when there had been a falling out between the Marcelli and Giovanni family.

Wild Sea had grown big enough to dominate the valley. One by one small family wineries faded into bankruptcy or were swallowed up by larger labels—not just here, but in Napa and Sonoma. The days of the "gentleman vintner" were numbered.

Did her grandfather know? Had he recognized the changes coming?

She told herself that in time they would speak of it. Or she would talk, he would listen, then they would argue. It had always been that way with her grandfather.

Brenna walked toward the hacienda. She and her sisters had never paid attention to the feud, which, sixty years after it happened, still influenced Lorenzo Marcelli's every action. They'd listened to the grown-ups talk and had rolled their eyes. But her grandparents had taken it seriously, as had her parents. So when she'd turned sixteen and had fallen in love with Nicholas Giovanni, she hadn't told a soul.

A lifetime ago, she reminded herself. Back when she had been young and idealistic, and had thought that love would last forever.

Zach made notes on the file in front of him, but it was difficult to concentrate with the beat of loud music swirling around him. He glanced at the ceiling, toward David's bedroom. His son was home for a few days, recovering from finals, and he'd invited a few friends over to help him celebrate temporary freedom. While Zach enjoyed having his son around, even for a short time, the teenagers and their loud music made him feel old.

He glanced at his watch, then at the phone. He hadn't seen Katie or spoken with her since she'd disappeared from his bed three mornings before.

Sneaking out before dawn was usually his job, he thought ruefully. As a rule, he preferred to be the guest rather than host so he could end the date when he was ready. That hadn't happened with Katie, and when he'd awakened to find her side of the bed cold and not a trace of her in the house, he'd had a moment of compassion for all the women he'd treated in the same way.

"Payback's a bitch," he murmured.

He knew she'd enjoyed their time in bed, as had he. He guessed the physical connection had left her as rattled as it had left him. So they both needed time to regroup. Not a problem. He could wait her out.

But the cool confidence of his thoughts didn't keep him from glancing back at the phone and wondering why the hell she hadn't called him.

He returned his attention to his notes. He was involved in a particularly tricky case between a software multimillionaire and his high-school sweetheart turned soon-to-be ex-wife. This time he represented the husband who had found out that the love of his life hadn't just been screwing the pool boy. She'd also had a torrid affair with the maid and the maid's husband.

"To each his own," he muttered as he checked a few minor points of law.

Sometime later David turned off the music. Zach barely noticed. However, he did look up when he heard footsteps on the hardwood floor. The kids trooped toward the front door. A couple paused to yell out thanks for allowing them to visit.

"No problem," Zach told them.

David came downstairs last, a pretty redhead walking with him. They were deep in conversation.

Zach made a few more notes in the margin. He and David were going to go grab an early dinner, then take in a movie. Mia had some plans with a club on campus, so he and David were just going to be a couple of wild guys on the town.

Real wild, Zach thought with a grin. Dinner and a movie, home before ten.

A soft giggle caught his attention. He glanced up and saw David still talking to the redhead. She leaned against the wall by the front door. One hand toyed with a long strand of hair, the other rested on his son's chest. David stood pretty damned close and looked cozy enough to make Zach feel as if he were spying.

Zach swore. What the hell was his kid up to?

He slammed the law book shut and they both jumped. David glanced at him over his shoulder, then opened the front door. "I'm going to walk Julie to her car, Dad. Be right back."

Zach watched him go. This wasn't his business, he told himself. Except David was supposed to be engaged—something Zach was still trying to change—and if there was another young woman in the picture, then there were even more reasons the marriage shouldn't take place.

Indecision held him in his seat for nearly fifteen seconds, then Zach rose and crossed to the front window. Julie had already climbed into her car. The door was open and David had crouched next to her.

They were talking, Zach could see that much, but he

had no idea about what. Nor was he sure what happened when David leaned forward slightly. Shit. Had he kissed her? Was David cheating on Mia? Was his problem solved? Or was David going to take after his grandfather and be a cheating spouse? The possibility of the latter made Zach's stomach clench.

Annoyed with both David for acting like an ass and himself for witnessing it, Zach returned to his seat. David strolled back into the house a minute or so later and slumped down on the sofa across from Zach's seat.

"How's work going?" his son asked, jerking his head at the pages on the table.

"Slow, but I'm getting there."

"I don't think I'd want to be a lawyer. Too much boring reading."

"There's a lot of that." Zach couldn't decide if he should say anything or not. If he pushed, David could dig in his heels. Maybe a more neutral topic would be safer.

"Have you given any thought to what you *would* like to do?"

David shrugged. He wore a UCLA sweatshirt and jeans. As usual, his hair was too long. At least the kid had never been into earrings or tattoos. He thought briefly of Francesca in her fake tattoos and shuddered. Going around dressed up like that was a strange occupation for a woman in her late twenties.

No. It was a strange occupation for anyone.

"What classes do you like?" Zach asked. "I was never interested in math, but your mother's father was an engineer. You might have inherited some aptitude from him."

"It's okay." He shifted in the sofa, stretching out. His head practically rested on the arm of the sofa. "Biology has been kinda interesting, but I hate the lab. I dunno."

Zach picked up a pen and turned it over in his hands. "You still have a lot of time to decide." He glanced back at David. "Is Mia pressuring you to pick something?"

"What?" David straightened. "No. Not really."

"Okay. I just wondered. Katie said Mia has known what she wanted from school for years."

"Mia's like that."

"What about Julie?"

David grinned. "She's like me. She doesn't have a clue."

"She seems nice."

David glanced out the window. "She is. We're friends. We were just talking about some stuff." He cleared his throat. "You know, I've been thinking."

Zach wondered if he should pursue the "Julie" line of conversation, then decided to let it go rather than tip his hand. "About what?"

"About school and stuff. I've been thinking that I might want to transfer to a different school in a year or two."

It took Zach a couple of seconds to realize what he'd heard. "You want to leave UCLA?"

Leave? But that was the only college David had ever wanted to attend. They'd been going to football games and basketball games together for years. Now David went with his friends more than his father, but he still went.

"I don't understand," Zach said. "Don't you like your classes?"

"They're okay."

"I know you've made friends. What's the problem?"

David looked as if he'd just tasted liver. "Why does there have to be a problem? I'm doing great. I really like UCLA. I don't want to leave, I just—" He studied the floor. "Mia is going to be graduating next year, and she really has her heart set on going to Georgetown for her master's."

David wanted to change his life for one girl while possibly screwing another? Damn it all to hell.

Zach told himself that exploding at his son would only end the conversation and put them on opposite sides of the issue, but it was hard to keep from shouting in frustration.

Instead he forced himself to sound calm as he said, "Why doesn't Mia get her master's at UCLA? If it took her two years, you'd both finish at the same time."

David looked uncomfortable. "We've, um, you know, talked about that. The thing is, she wants to go into the State Department and being in Washington will make that easier. She'll meet people, get an internship, that sort of thing. We had dinner with some guy she met last summer. He works there now and he's gonna help her."

David shrugged again. His hair fell across his forehead, hiding his expression. "Mia really wants to do this."

Zach drew in a deep breath. "Mia's fortunate to have such a clear view of her future," he said, trying for light, and not sure he was succeeding. "What do you want?"

David grinned. "It sort of seems like under the circumstances that not having a major is a good thing, huh?"

Zach mentally grabbed on to his self-control with both hands. "If you're talking about transferring at the end of your sophomore year, you'll have to declare a major to be accepted, won't you?"

"I guess. I could just take poli sci, like Mia. It might be fun."

"Fun? David, we're talking about your future. What do you want to do with your life? While I'm not suggesting you pick a career that's boring, I would think you'd want to put a little more thought into a major than the fact that it's what your girlfriend is studying."

David's head snapped up. "You said it didn't matter that I didn't have a major."

"It doesn't. Not now. But it will matter soon. It will matter a lot if you switch schools. What if what you want to study isn't available at Georgetown? I don't object to you transferring, if it's in your best interest. But simply to follow Mia?"

"We're getting married. I can't marry her and live on the other side of the country."

Something snapped. Zach heard the audible sound as his frustration and concern exploded into temper.

"Dammit, David, this entire situation is crazy. You're barely eighteen years old. You don't have a clue as to what you want for your future, so why are you so fired up to get married? If you and Mia are so hot to be together, then move in with her. Sharing an apartment for a few months will take the bloom off the rose. You'll both figure out that there's more to love than sex."

David flushed, but he didn't look away. Instead he slid forward in his seat and jerked out his chin. "I thought you'd be proud of me wanting to marry her instead of just living together. Isn't marriage the right thing to do?"

"Sure. If you're ready. If you're sure. You and Julie looked chummy. Want to tell me what's going on there?"

"Nothing." But David didn't look at him as he spoke. "We're just friends."

"Is that why you kissed her?"

David glared at him. "You were spying on me."

"I was concerned." And apparently right.

His son stood. "This isn't your business."

"You made it my business when you said you wanted to get married. You're so in love with Mia that you're going to marry her and transfer across the country, yet four months before the wedding you're kissing some other girl?"

"It's not like that. I love Mia."

"You don't know what love is." Zach stood to face his son. "Mia is your first girlfriend, David. You don't have a job. Marriage requires commitment and responsibility. It requires *fidelity*. What do you know about working out problems, organizing a budget, paying bills, while working and going to school? You're overwhelmed by your current schedule. What happens when it gets worse?"

"We'll be fine. We'll learn together."

Zach played his trump card. "And if I refuse to pay for your college?"

David stiffened. "I didn't think you'd do that, but I can't stop you." He glared at his father. "You don't understand. You'll never understand. I love her. You've never loved anyone in your whole life, so you can't know what that feels like. You get involved for a few weeks, then you walk away. To you marriage is just something that ends in divorce, but it doesn't have to be like that. I know you think Mia and I are going to fail, but you're wrong."

His voice rose until he was practically shouting. David's strength and determination marked his first foray into manhood. It was a hell of a time for his kid to start growing up.

"I know exactly what love is. What I don't have is your rosy view of the future. You can say what you want about me, but know this. I love you and I have always been there for you. Whatever it took, whatever it cost, I was there. And I'll be damned if I'll stand by and watch you screw up your life."

David blinked several times as if holding back tears. "It won't be like that. Why can't you see?"

"Because I've been there. I was seventeen when I married your mother. I know what it's like to be your age and drowning in responsibility. It sucks big time." He clenched his fists as he remembered the daily hell of wondering how much he could screw up the fragile life he'd been given to care for. Being David's father in those early years had been terrifying.

"I would have given anything to walk away from it all, but I couldn't," Zach continued. "First you're married, then she turns up pregnant and everything changes. I don't want that for you."

The second the words were out, he wanted to retract them. But it was too late. David took a step back. He bumped into the wingback chair and moved around it. His gaze never left his father's face.

The anguish in his son's eyes made Zach want to throw himself in front of a truck. "David, I'm sorry. I didn't mean that the way it came out."

Tears spilled down David's face. "You did," he said, his voice harsh. "You did."

"No."

Zach moved toward him, but David held out a hand. "Stay away from me."

"David!"

"No. I didn't realize I'd made your life a living hell. You should have told me before that I was such a pain in the ass. I would have stayed out of your way." He angrily brushed his hands across his face. "Don't worry. I won't bother you anymore."

"David, wait."

But his son was already bolting for the door. Zach hurried after him, but before he could catch up with him, David was gone. The front door slammed shut. Seconds later he heard the sound of his son's car starting. Zach ran outside anyway, just in time to see David driving away. He stood there for a long time before he realized it was raining and that he needed to go back inside.

13

$\backsim$

K *atie picked up* the phone, then set it down. She picked it up again, dialed three numbers and hung up, then buried her head in her hands. This was much worse than the time she'd invited Steve Klausen to the Backwards Dance in high school and he'd made her wait for an answer while he found out if he had to work that night. One would think that at her age she would have learned maturity, poise, and grace. Unfortunately, one would be wrong.

"It's just a business call," she told herself, trying to sound both firm and in control. "I have information to share with a client. It is, in fact, my *obligation* to keep my client updated on what is going on."

Which was nearly the truth, but not completely. The missing factor was, of course, that she and Zach had made love last week. They'd gotten naked, done the wild thing, then she'd crept out in the middle of the night without even leaving a note.

That could have been recoverable if they'd spoken since. But they hadn't. She should have called, but she'd been scared and embarrassed and definitely out of her comfort zone. She'd wanted him to make the first move and when he hadn't, she'd felt . . . icky.

Now she felt awkward and confused about calling him at work. Normally she never sweated getting in touch with a client, but Zach was the first one she'd ever slept with, so the rules of engagement weren't all that clear.

She dropped her hands to her desk and leaned back in her chair. She was going to have to get over this and start acting like a sensible person. Baring that, she was simply going to have to suck it up and call Zach because she had to move forward with the fund-raiser.

And she would like to take this moment to remind herself that she had only herself to blame. She could have said no. She could have walked away while still fully dressed and then not have had to worry about postcoital etiquette. This uncomfortable, slightly embarrassed, definitely weird sensation in her midsection was something to remember the next time a tempting client walked into her life and tried to get past first base.

Determined to be brave and professional, she picked up the phone and dialed Zach's office number. Dora picked up on the first ring and immediately put Katie through.

"Stryker," Zach said in a deep, masculine voice that made her go weak at the knees—never mind that she was sitting down.

"Hi, Zach, it's Katie. I'm calling with some good news about the fund-raiser."

"Okay."

She hesitated. His response didn't have the enthusiasm level she'd been hoping for. Nor did he seem to be in a rush to gush enthusiastically about their night together. Had he forgotten already? Or was he so used to one-night stands that this one didn't matter?

The silence stretching between them was its own response, so she ignored the feeling of being a complete fool and retreated to the safety of business.

"As you know, the, ah, invitations went out two weeks ago. Already we've had positive responses from more than fifty percent of those invited." She consulted her notes. "Of the five hundred we invited to the party-within-a-party, three hundred have said yes. Not only will the rooms be delightfully teeming with guests, but if all goes according to plan, we're on target to beat last year's charitable proceeds by at least twenty-five percent."

She paused and waited for the applause. Or at least a "well done." Instead she heard silence.

"Zach?"

"That's really great, Katie. You're doing a fine job."

A fine job? The man had seen her naked, made her scream with pleasure, and "a fine job" was the best he could do?

"I'm sorry," she said. "Did I call at a bad time?"

"I'm afraid so. I'm in the middle of prepping for court."

She stiffened as if he'd slapped her. The implication of his words being that *his* work was far more important than hers.

Bitter regret burned on her tongue. His rejection couldn't have been more plain. She swore silently as she realized that once again she'd risked believing the best about Zach only to have the worst proved to her.

She'd thought he was a real person. She'd thought they were establishing a connection. She thought their night together had mattered. Damn if she hadn't been wrong on every count.

"I won't keep you, then," she said, forcing her voice into a bright, cheerful "you don't matter because I'm doing fine" tone. "I'm very excited by the positive response to the party and wanted to let you know."

"I appreciate it." He cleared his throat. "Don't feel you have to give me regular updates. Until I hear otherwise, I'm going to assume everything is going great."

In other words—Don't call me, I'll call you.

Her eyes burned, her chest hurt, and she wanted to curl up in a ball and sob. Instead she clutched the phone more tightly.

"Not a problem. Good-bye, Zach."

She hung up without waiting for him to respond.

It took several minutes for her ragged breathing to return to normal. A few tears escaped, but she congratulated herself on only needing two tissues. He wasn't worth more than that.

When Katie had gathered at least a facade of control, she placed her hands on her desk and told herself she'd been lucky.

Zach wasn't for her. He never had been, but she kept forgetting that. Jumping into bed with a man she wasn't emotionally involved with had never been her style. For reasons she didn't understand, she'd slept with Zach, and now she was paying the price.

It hurt. It hurt bad. But in time the pain would ease and she would be grateful not to be taken in by a good-looking guy in a six-hundred-dollar suit. Yes, he was funny and smart and fun to be with. And a good father. Oh, and a great kisser and dynamite in bed. But he didn't care about her. She was a means to an end. One in a long line of women he'd conquered. He used women, then tossed them aside.

If she felt confused and out of sorts, well, so what? She would get over it. People healed from broken hearts all the time. *Not* that her heart was broken. The fact that he was more than a pretty face and that she hadn't responded like that to a man since . . . okay, since never . . . was interesting but not significant. She would get over him in a flash because she had nothing to get over. Nothing had happened. She'd learned a cheap lesson, and now she was going to move on.

Zach drove slowly through the UCLA campus and circled up toward the dorms. It had been three days and he still hadn't heard from David.

He'd called dozens of times, left at least ten messages, and not had one of them returned. Zach was done waiting. He would find his son and make him understand that he had never been anything but the best part of Zach's life.

Careless words, he thought as he parked and climbed out of his car. How many relationships were destroyed by careless words?

He entered the dorm building and spotted several kids hunched over a video game. A couple looked familiar. Zach walked toward them. One of the boys looked up, frowned slightly, then smiled.

"Mr. Stryker?"

"That's right." Who was this kid? Jackson? Jason? Oh, yeah. "Justin, I'm looking for David."

"He's playing pool. Just back there."

Zach nodded. "I know the way. Thanks."

He walked down the back hallway to the rec room. Three pool tables sat in the center of the huge room. There were vending machines along one wall and ratty sofas along the other. All three tables were in use. One had a group of girls, another had guys in sports jerseys playing, while the third had only a young couple at one end.

The girl laughed and turned. As she moved, the overhead light glinted off her long red hair. Zach stopped just inside the room. There was no mistaking Julie, nor his son. David smiled, then slipped his arm around the girl and pulled her close. She welcomed him with an easy familiarity that made Zach's gut tighten. They kissed, slowly and deeply, losing themselves in the passion.

Victory, he thought. The engagement would end and life would go back to normal.

He waited to feel relieved. Happy. But there was nothing except for a hollow emptiness and disappointment in his son's behavior. He didn't care how many girls David slept with, but he hadn't been raised to cheat.

Zach backed up and returned to the hallway. He wanted to talk to David, but not under these circumstances.

As for Julie—and Mia—Zach didn't know what the hell he was going to do. There was no way the marriage could take place—not with David sniffing after someone else. But what was he going to say and to whom? He didn't want to be the one to tell Mia what was going on. That was David's responsibility.

"A hell of a mess," he muttered as he walked back to his car. And he didn't have a clue as to what he was going to do about it.

The hacienda kitchen was empty for once. Francesca glanced around in surprise, then headed for the refrigerator. She was about to drive to Los Angeles for one of her experiments and wouldn't have time to eat once she arrived. Not if she wanted to be in place by the time people were leaving work and hurrying home.

She dumped some leftover pasta into a bowl and stuck the bowl into the microwave. While her food heated, she bent over and studied the tattoos on her ankles. While she planned to carry an umbrella, the rain might still splash on her legs. Unfortunately in the fake-tattoo world, water was not her friend.

Still, she would have to take a chance. She'd pulled on a relatively short skirt and pumps, leaving her legs bare. A long vine-with-roses tattoo wrapped around one ankle, while a butterfly hovered on the other. She'd put another butterfly on the back of her thigh, just at her hemline, so anyone watching her walk would catch glimpses of the design. With luck, she would get some great reactions today.

The microwave beeped. She drew out her bowl and fished a clean fork from the drawer by the dishwasher. Then she headed for the kitchen table. Unexpectedly a door slammed in the house.

Francesca put down her bowl and headed for the noise. A subtle tension seemed to thicken the air, making her heart rate increase.

As she made her way down the hall, she could hear voices coming from the library. Although the door was closed, muffled words became more distinct as she approached.

" 'Tis God's punishment," quiet Grammy M said with a force Francesca had never heard from her. "It was wrong thirty years ago and it's still wrong."

"God has no reason to punish this family," Grandpa Lorenzo roared. Something heavy, probably a book, slammed on the desk. "We've been good Catholics for generations."

"Sometimes that isn't enough to please the Almighty," Grammy M said.

Francesca's father spoke next.

"This is an old argument that doesn't change anything." His voice sounded frustrated. "Do you think there's a day that goes by that Colleen and I don't regret what we did? Do you think there's a day we don't think of him?"

Francesca froze. She didn't want to hear any more, but she couldn't seem to tear herself away. She heard the sound of crying and would guess her mother had given in to tears. Grandma Tessa said something, but was too quiet to be audible.

"I should have been stronger. I should have run away rather than agree."

Francesca heard her mother's words and cringed.

"We're all to blame," Grammy M said, her voice heavy with pain. "We all carry the burden."

Francesca took a step back, then another. She didn't know what her family was talking about, but she didn't like it. She grabbed her purse and hurried toward her truck. Once she was inside, she turned on the engine and cranked up the stereo as loud as it would go. Maybe the pounding beat would drive everything she'd just heard from her head.

Katie paced through her small house. Normally she found the space cozy rather than confining, but not tonight. Even more frustrating, she could no longer fool herself about the nature of her discontent. Restlessness when combined with excess ice-cream consumption could only have one cause: heartache.

She thought about pounding her head against the wall, if only to experience the relief when she stopped, but how would she explain the bruising?

Obviously her little crush on Zach had become something more when she hadn't been looking. While she knew she wasn't in love with him, she was willing to admit to some slight . . . infatuation.

It was the naked thing. If she hadn't had sex with him, she would be fine. She drew in a deep breath. Okay. She'd learned her lesson. She was a mature, adult woman who empowered herself and her life and . . . was there any ice cream left?

Rather than risk the last pint of fudge brownie, she made her way to the bedroom and glanced at her tennis shoes tucked in a corner. Maybe she should go to the gym. A fast-paced aerobics class or some strength training would give her a strong moral backbone, not to mention acting as a counterbalance to all those ice-cream calories she'd consumed. Of course, she didn't actually *have* a gym membership. Maybe she could join a gym. Or clean out her closet. That always comforted her. There was something about perfect orderliness that made her life seem complete.

Rather than face actual sweat at a gym, she moved toward her closet, only to have someone ring her doorbell. She glanced at her watch and frowned. It was seven in the evening, midweek. To the best of her knowledge, her family members were all accounted for. So who would come calling?

The answer to that question stepped across her threshold when she opened the door. He was tall, dark, and very dangerous. He also made her palms sweat, her breath quicken, and her hormones begin a quick salsa step through her midsection.

"Zach," she said unnecessarily, because it wasn't as if they both didn't know who he was. But she couldn't think

of anything better to mutter. Not when she was still sting-
ing from his dismissal earlier in the week.

He leaned against the wall, looking both appealing and
far too good-looking for her mental health.

"I figured one of us had to be mature, and I got tired of
waiting for it to be you," he said.

"What?" Outrage pushed aside confusion. "When was I
not mature?"

"When you ducked out the morning after. No note,
nothing. A guy would think you were just using him for
sex."

She genuinely didn't know what to say. "If I was, it
would serve you right. How many times have you just
walked away in the past?"

He shrugged. "Every time. It's what I do. But we're not
here to talk about me."

"Why not? It's your favorite topic."

He raised his eyebrows. "You have a temper."

"I called and you blew me off."

"You called about the party and that's what we talked
about."

Good point. "Yeah, well, if you'd taken fifteen seconds
to listen, I might have gotten to something else."

"I'm in trouble for not reading your mind?"

She ground her teeth together. "Why exactly are you
here?"

The corners of his mouth twitched. "I thought I'd let
you apologize for leaving so rudely."

She couldn't believe it. "I . . . You . . . But you . . ." She
glared at him. "If I thought I could get away with it, I'd
strangle you right here."

"No, you wouldn't. Because I'm sorry, too."

"Too?"

"Sure. I'm accepting your apology. That's the kind of guy I am."

She hadn't apologized. At least she didn't think she had. Her head was starting to spin and she couldn't be sure of anything.

She led the way to the living room and sat on her floral-print sofa, then waited until he took the club chair opposite. Her thoughts slowly collected and organized. "I should have left a note," she said cautiously.

"Agreed," he said with just enough cheer to make her hair hurt. "And I . . ." His voice trailed off and his humor faded. "I'm sorry about the phone call. I had some things on my mind. David mostly."

She instantly went on alert. "What happened?"

"We had a fight. He stalked out of the house and I haven't been able to talk to him since. When you called, I was caught up in a hellish divorce case and worrying about him."

That she could understand. Zach was the kind of father who worried.

"Okay. We've both apologized," she said. "Want me to open a bottle of Marcelli private reserve as a peace offering?"

"That sounds great."

She rose and started toward the kitchen. "Are you hungry?" she asked before she could stop herself. Dear God, she was turning into her grandmothers.

"No."

She collected a bottle of Marcelli Cabernet, an opener, and two glasses, then returned to the living room.

Zach had settled back in the seat, looking male and completely out of place in a house of floral prints, candles, and too many pillows. He half rose when she entered the room. She waved him back to his seat.

"Here, I'll let you wrestle with the cork," she said, handing him the bottle.

He studied the label. "Must be nice to have an in with the owner."

"A family perk."

While he opened the wine, she seated herself across from him. He poured, then handed her a glass, took one for himself, and held it out toward hers.

"To our complicated relationship," he said.

She touched the rim of her glass to his and nodded.

"Your place is really nice," he said.

She glanced around at the dollhouse-size proportions of her house, at the feminine furnishings and the pastel colors. "I doubt it's much to your liking."

"Agreed, but it suits you."

He set his glass on the coffee table between them.

He'd obviously come straight from the office. He still wore his suit slacks and a white shirt. The jacket was gone, as was the tie. Stubble darkened his jaw and his eyes looked weary.

Zach reached for his wine, then dropped his hand to his lap. "I've been his father for eighteen years. You'd think I'd do a better job of parenting."

She frowned. "I was just thinking I happen to know you're a terrific father." It was one of the things she liked about him, when he wasn't making her want to kill him.

"Not lately." He grimaced. "I was scared to death when he was born, but excited and happy. He was so damn small. Ainsley was useless. She barely got out of bed for the first two weeks, then claimed to always be too tired to take care of him. She didn't want to try breast-feeding. So it was up to me to do the bottle thing. My mom helped out when she had time."

Katie couldn't imagine a woman turning her back on her newborn . . . or any child, for that matter.

"Weren't you still in college?" she asked.

"Yeah. And working. Money from my trust fund really helped with things like rent and medical insurance, but it didn't cover everything."

He glanced at her. "None of that mattered. David was worth it."

She leaned toward him. "Then why are you beating yourself up? You obviously love your son. You've made countless sacrifices, you've always tried to do the right thing. That's what matters. Grammy M is always telling us that we can only do our best. No one can expect more. The rest is in God's hands."

"It's not that simple." He straightened slightly and reached for the wine. "A couple of days ago David told me he wanted to talk about transferring to a different college."

"I thought he really enjoyed UCLA. Why would he want to do that?"

Then she knew, but before she could say anything, Zach spoke.

"Nothing against your sister, Katie. She's a great girl with a lot of potential. She knows what she wants in life, and while I respect that, I think it's wrong for David to have to give up his dreams to follow hers."

Katie didn't know what to say. Mia's plans had been set for years. But David was two years behind Katie, and when she graduated, the choices would be either not being together or one of them giving up what he or she wanted. Katie knew her sister had never been very good at compromising her own plans.

"They're so damn young," he muttered. "Why can't he

see that? Why can't he see that he's potentially screwing up his entire life?" He drank some wine and looked at her. "Unfortunately, that's what I said to him. I pointed out that I knew exactly what came from taking on responsibility too early. He thinks I blame him for screwing up *my* life."

"Ouch," she said sympathetically. "That can't have gone over well."

"You're right. The hell of it is, I didn't mean it that way. I don't regret David or anything that has happened because of him." He shrugged. "With the possible exception of marrying Ainsley. But he didn't stick around to hear that. Instead he took off and I haven't heard from him since."

Suddenly the dark lines and exhaustion made sense. "You've been worried about him," she said, making it a statement rather than a question.

He nodded. "I'm not worried that something happened to him, but I hate us not being in contact." He returned his wineglass to the coffee table. "He's just a kid."

"So they'll grow up together. My parents did. They fell in love in high school and they're happy."

"We can't all live in Fantasy Land."

"It beats your constant pessimism. You could be wrong about this, you know. They may be blissfully happy for the next seventy years."

His mouth twisted. "Right. Or they could just screw up their lives in four months and have seventy years of regret."

She'd been basking in the warmth of having him confide in her, but as usual, Zach's cynical attitude chilled the happy right out of her.

"Not every marriage ends in disaster. Yes, a lot of marriages fail, yes, a lot of young marriages don't make it, but maybe, for once, you could give your son and my sister the benefit of the doubt."

"Why? If you see a car coming, don't you step out of the road rather than get hit?"

She gritted her teeth. "You're assuming. You don't know anything for sure."

"I know David's seeing someone else."

Katie stiffened, then sucked in a breath. "What?"

Zach swore and reached for his wine. "Forget I said that."

She leaned toward him. "I can't. What do you mean he's seeing someone else?"

"I don't know. There's this girl. Julie. She's in one of his classes. She was at the house with a bunch of his friends celebrating the semester break. They looked cozy. Later I saw them kissing."

Cozy? Right. Zach was a smart, smarmy lawyer who would do anything to win his case. She'd wondered why he'd stopped by and now she knew. He would do *anything* to end the engagement.

"Why don't you just hire some digital photography studio to doctor naked pictures of David in bed with the entire cheerleading squad?" she demanded. "Wouldn't that be easier? It's much more a sure thing."

His gaze narrowed. "You think I'm lying?"

"You bet. You told me once you'd do anything to keep David and Mia from getting married and you'd do anything to convince me. I figure this is just part of the show."

He stood and glared at her. "I'm not lying. I haven't lied about anything. I told you David and I had a fight. He didn't call me back, so I went to see him at his dorm."

Katie stood and glared right back. "Let me guess. You found them in bed together. Like I believe that."

"I found them in the rec room. They were kissing and it looked damned friendly to me." He raked his fingers through his hair. "Do you think I wanted it to end like this? I like Mia. If David were older and more together, I'd be grateful he'd picked her. I don't want her hurt."

Zach's sincerity and his concern about her sister made Katie wonder if he might be telling the truth. And if he was . . . then what?

"What did he say when you confronted him?" she asked.

"I didn't. I left and drove around. Eventually I ended up here."

She didn't know what to think or what to believe. If Zach were any other man . . . if he didn't love his son quite so much . . . if he hadn't told her he would do anything to stop the wedding . . .

"What are you going to do?" she asked.

"I don't know. I thought you might have some ideas."

She looked at him and tried to read the truth in his blue eyes. "You won't tell her?"

"She'd think what you do. That it's just a ploy."

"Would you blame her?"

"No, and I don't blame you, either."

He reached out his hand toward her, then shoved it in his pocket.

"I'm gonna head home," he told her.

She watched him walk to the door and let himself out. When she was alone, she sank back onto the sofa and drew her knees to her chest.

Just when she thought things couldn't get more complicated, they took a turn for downright confusing. Was

David cheating on Mia? If Zach was lying, then he was a worse weasel than she'd thought and she should get herself sanitized after having intimate contact with him. If he was telling the truth, then he was even better than she could have hoped and letting him walk out of her life made her fourteen kinds of stupid.

The worst of it was she didn't know if sleeping with her had been a spontaneous response to passion, or just one more part of his master plan.

The trick was separating fact from fiction. So where was a crystal ball when she really needed one?

14

$\backsim$

Mia sat on the floor in David's dorm room and watched him pace the small space from the desk to the door.

"I can't even remember how it started," David admitted, then crossed to the opposite bed and flopped down on his back. "Then we were just arguing."

Mia had a feeling that David remembered exactly how the fight with his dad had started, but for some reason he didn't want to tell her. The fact that he was keeping it a secret bothered her. It wasn't as if she was going to go all hysterical and start screaming or something. That so wasn't her style. She also wasn't pleased that David had taken nearly a week to tell her what was wrong.

She'd known instantly there was a problem, but he'd denied it for the first three days and had refused to talk about it for the next three.

"He said that he didn't want me screwing up my life the way his life had been screwed up," David admitted miserably.

Mia crossed to kneel next to the narrow bed. She placed one hand on his chest. "You know what he was trying to say. He's worried that we're getting married too young. He wasn't telling you that you'd ruined his life. David, your dad loves you. Everyone can see that. He's happy when you're with him and he's proud of you."

"I know." He turned his head toward her. Tears glistened in his eyes, but he blinked them away. "It hurt right then, you know. But I'm okay with it now. The thing is I kinda thought he was coming around. About the wedding."

"But he's not," Mia said flatly, wondering why she hadn't figured that out before. Now that David said the words, she realized it was so incredibly obvious.

For a second she thought about getting mad. It was totally insulting in a way. But she knew in her heart David's dad wasn't mad that David wanted to marry *her*—he would have gone ballistic about David marrying anyone.

"What happened when you talked to him later?" she asked.

David sat up and cleared his throat. "What time is it? Are you hungry?"

Mia stared at him. "You haven't talked to him, have you?"

David wouldn't meet her gaze. "I've been busy."

She rolled her eyes. "Has he tried to talk to you?"

"I think he might have called. I don't remember."

Translation—Zach had been trying to get in touch with his son for days. Mia felt frustration bubbling to the surface.

"If you keep acting like a kid, your dad is going to treat you like one. If you want to show him you're ready to get married, then act like a grown-up. After a big fight you can't just ignore the whole thing. You have to own up to what happened. At least call and say you're okay."

David's blue eyes flashed with determination. "I don't

care if he thinks I'm a kid. I'm over eighteen and he can't tell me what to do."

Mia clenched her teeth. If she allowed herself to say even one word, she would scream. David's "he can't tell me what to do" statement made him sound about four years old. So much for making her point.

He looked at her. "I don't need him to approve."

He sounded defiant enough, but Mia wasn't sure she believed him. David and his father had always been close and going against him would be very difficult. Besides, even though it made her feel disloyal to admit it, David wasn't exactly a poster child for the mature young adult. She loved him, but she wasn't blind to his flaws.

"The wedding is a long way off," she said. "He might come around."

David nodded but didn't look convinced. He flopped back on the bed and stared at the ceiling. "It's weird not to talk to him for this long. We've always talked." A smile tugged at the corner of his mouth. "Even when he was mad at me when I was a kid, he talked. Sometimes when he went on and on about something I'd screwed up on, I used to wish he'd just spank me so we could get it over with. But he never did. Not even once. But he talked for hours."

Mia sat back on her heels and let the love in David's voice chase away her doubts. One of the things she adored about her fiancé was his ability to love with his whole heart.

"He was always good to me," David went on, turning his head to look at her. "After my mom left, there wasn't much money. Dad was in law school and she'd taken the rest of his trust fund. So we struggled. But he made sure there were lots of good times. He traded his car in for a truck with a shell on the back. We'd take it up to the mountains or to the beach and go camping for the weekend. Just us guys."

"Sounds like fun," she said and shifted into a sitting position. Her palm came down on something hard and pointed. "Ouch."

"What?" David hung over the side of the bed.

"I don't know." She raised her hand, then ran her fingers through the shag throw rug David and his roommate had bought at the beginning of the school year. Something metal bounced when she hit it.

Mia picked up a small gold hoop. "It's an earring."

David reached for it, but she held it out of reach.

"Give it here," he told her.

"Not until you explain it," she teased.

He pushed his hair out of his eyes. "Mia, get real. Brian has a new girlfriend every ten days. I have no idea which one of them dropped an earring in here."

She tossed the piece of jewelry onto Brian's bed. "You'd better not be messing around on me, mister. If you do, I'll chop your legs off at the knees."

She laughed and David grinned. Then he looked away. For a split second Mia felt something cold clutch at her midsection. Then she dismissed the feeling and joined David on his narrow mattress, where he drew her close and told her how much he loved her.

"Everything's going to be okay with my dad," he promised.

"I believe you," she told him, because it was easier than speaking the truth.

"Other people have milk with their cookies," Brenna said as she picked up another chocolate chip cookie from the plate.

Francesca waved her glass. "They're philistines."

Considering the amount of wine the three sisters had already consumed that evening, Francesca's ability to pronounce a three-syllable word was impressive. Katie herself had passed coherent about thirty minutes ago and was now functioning in that pleasant state of being buzzed. The world might be spinning, but as she didn't have to go anywhere, what did it matter?

The sisters sprawled across the two double beds in the room that Brenna and Francesca had shared while they'd both lived at the hacienda. Since moving back home after staying with Francesca, Brenna had started packing up memorabilia from high school, but had yet to tackle the excessively pink wallpaper both had loved as teenagers, along with the gaggingly sweet bedspreads, also pink, with flowers, hearts, and swirls of ribbon.

Brenna sat crossed-legged at the foot of the bed, a tray of cookies next to her. Katie sat on the same bed, with her back against the headboard, while Francesca lay in a rather undignified sprawl on the second bed, one arm hanging toward the floor, swinging her half-full wineglass.

"You always had your own room," Brenna said, turning to glare accusingly at Katie. "I always thought that was unfair."

Katie laughed. "It's been nearly ten years. You need to let that go."

"Not even on a bet."

Francesca raised her head. Her straight, thick hair hung down, shielding most of her face. "I thought you liked that we shared a room."

"I did. I just wanted one of my own, too." She grinned. "Now that my lifelong dream has come true, I'll be decorating it in red velvet and black satin."

Katie shook her head. Had the wine affected her hearing?

Francesca looked equally confused. "Because you're going for the sleazy look?"

"No. Because I'm the seductive one."

"Seductive . . ." Katie's mouth dropped open. "You didn't!"

Brenna laughed. "Oh, but I did and it's *so* embarrassing."

She unfolded her legs, then set down her wineglass and slid off the bed. From underneath she pulled a shallow, open box. Inside were three bottles.

Katie saw them and winced. Years ago, after a long, boring weekend spent listening to their parents and grandparents plan the detailed wording of wine bottle labels, Katie, Francesca, and Brenna had decided to create their own. They'd taken three unlabeled bottles from the storeroom and had carefully glued on pictures of themselves in full dress-up clothing. On the back they'd applied hand-lettered labels, detailing the glory that was each of them.

Katie took the first bottle Brenna held out, glanced at the picture of an eleven-year-old Francesca, and passed it across to her sister. Francesca groaned.

"The Sassy One," she read, then gulped more wine. "Francesca Marcelli tosses her long hair in a gesture that marks her as not just the pretty one, but also the Sassy One. Bold, inventive, with just a hint of irrelevance—" She paused. "I think that's supposed to be *irreverence*. . . . she is the essence of blossoming illocution."

Katie laughed as she took the next bottle and recognized a photo of herself. She was dressed in yards of tulle and lace. One of the more elaborate costumes she'd made all those years ago.

"The Sparkling One," she read. "Katie Marcelli is a carbonated combination of wit and charm. She dazzles, she sparkles, she shines. Like the champagne she embodies, she is only ever special, iridescent, and valued." Katie glanced up. "I'm iridescent?" She looked at her arm, then held it to the light. "I must have outgrown that."

Brenna giggled. "At least you get to be glowing colors. I'm just a slut."

Francesca turned onto her stomach. "Read on, O Seductive One."

Brenna sighed. "Brenna Marcelli's sultriness proves that she is the Seductive One. Dark, sweet, and slightly mysterious, she is a gleaming testament to all young women on the verge of lush ripeness."

Brenna glanced at her sisters. "I used to gleam."

"You used to hate boys," Katie reminded her. "What happened?"

"Hormones. I turned eleven and suddenly they were really interesting." She set down her bottle. "Too bad Mia is so much younger. She was still a baby when we made these. I wonder what she would have been."

"The Smart One," Francesca said.

"The One Most Likely to Take Over the World," Katie said.

Brenna smiled and climbed back on the bed. "So, Francesca, I was thinking we'd show Katie's bottle to Zach the next time he comes over. What do you think?"

"Brilliant idea."

Katie shook her head. "No way. I don't need to be humiliated in front of him again. I've already had that pleasure, remember? The first time he came to the house."

"But you recovered," Francesca pointed out. "And you seem to be spending a lot of time together."

Katie felt heat on her cheeks. She told herself it was the wine, but she knew she was lying. "I'm working with the man."

"Uh-huh." Brenna picked up the bottle of Cabernet and topped up her glass. "I wonder if there's more to it than that."

Francesca took the bottle. "Me, too. All those late-night conversations could be leading to something interesting. He's good-looking, smart."

"For a divorce lawyer, he has a lot of heart," Brenna added. "He cares about his son."

More than either of them knew, Katie thought uneasily. "We work together. That means we have to keep things professional."

"And here I was hoping you were going to tell us you've already seen him naked," Brenna said.

"In your dreams," Francesca told her. "As if Katie would sleep with him."

It had to be the wine, Katie thought as her mouth opened and words formed. Because she'd certainly planned to keep this particular piece of information to herself.

"Actually I didn't get a whole lot of sleep."

There was a moment of silence, then both her sisters started screaming and laughing. Brenna recovered first.

"No way! You did *not* do it with your client, our baby sister's future father-in-law, and my divorce lawyer."

Katie grabbed the wine and drained the last few ounces into her glass. "You make it sound like group sex."

Francesca nearly choked. "When? Where? Start at the beginning and talk slowly."

"I went over to his place for a tasting dinner."

"And you were the entrée?" Brenna asked.

Francesca threw a pillow at her. "That's disgusting."

"You haven't had sex in years, so your opinion doesn't count," Brenna told her.

"We actually had the tasting dinner," Katie said, ignoring them both. "We were talking, and then we were kissing, and then we were upstairs."

"And?" Brenna prompted.

"It was very nice."

"It should have been a whole lot better than nice," Francesca grumbled. "You slept with David's *father.*"

"Don't make him sound old. He's all of thirty-five," Brenna said. "I'm guessing all the important bits are still functioning just fine."

"They are," Katie said primly.

Brenna collapsed on the bed and rested her feet on Katie's lap. "I'm going to miss sex. Not that I was having it all that much with my soon-to-be ex."

"Why not?" Francesca asked.

Brenna shrugged. "He was busy, or gone. Or screwing the bimbo. I don't know. In the past few months we just never did it. I guess the flame had been dying out for a while, but I was too busy working all the time to notice."

"Don't think about him," Katie urged. "You'll only upset yourself."

"You're right. I'll think about sex instead. Having it, or not having it. I suppose the good news is that giving up sex with Jeff won't be a huge hardship."

Katie nearly dropped her glass. "Excuse me?"

Brenna sat up enough to take a sip of her wine. "Dr. Jeff might be an up-and-coming cardiologist, but he doesn't know dick about a woman's sexual wants and desires."

Francesca struggled into a sitting position. She shifted so that her legs hung over the bed and stared at her sister. "Brenna? What are you saying? How exactly would you know he wasn't good in bed?"

Katie was also playing mental catch-up. She got there

before her sister. "You had sex with someone other than Jeff?"

Brenna blinked several times. "Uh-huh."

Katie couldn't believe it. She thought she knew everything about her sisters' lives. Apparently she was wrong. "Did you have an affair?"

Brenna dropped her head back onto the bed. "Of course not. I wouldn't cheat on Jeff. Only he did that. This was before."

Francesca nearly fell off the bed. "You weren't a virgin when you got married?"

Brenna stared at her sister. "What century are you in? You were the only bridal virgin *I* knew."

Francesca reached for her wine and took a gulp, then turned her attention to Katie. "Did you and Greg, well, you know?"

Katie laughed. "Yes, we had sex, and I regret every drop of bodily fluid exchanged."

"I can't blame you," Brenna said. "Who wants to be with a man who prefers death to marriage?"

"That's not why he went into the army," Francesca protested.

"Then why?" Brenna asked.

Francesca shrugged.

Katie tried to laugh, but she couldn't. After all this time her lie should feel like the truth, but it didn't. Maybe it never would. That was the thing about lies—they tended to live on forever.

"Okay," Brenna said, reaching for another bottle and the corkscrew. "Your turn, Francesca. 'Fess up. Did you have any secret lovers?"

"Of course not," she said primly. "I was a virgin when I married Todd."

Brenna hooted. "Figures. The family beauty is the only one who waited to get laid."

"I wanted my first time to be with my husband."

"Talk about pressure," Brenna muttered.

"I wanted the memory," Francesca said.

"Fair enough," Brenna said.

"But I regretted it," Francesca announced.

Katie felt her mouth drop open. Brenna pulled the cork out of the bottle and nearly dumped the contents onto the bed.

"Being a virgin on your wedding night?" Brenna asked.

"Well, not exactly regretted it, but I do wish I'd slept with Nic Giovanni."

Katie burst out laughing. "Nic? Our neighbor? Heir to the hated Wild Sea Vineyard? Francesca, I'm shocked."

Francesca rolled her eyes. "Come on, Katie. Nic was incredibly hot. That tall, dark, brooding thing he had going on was irresistible. Plus he rode a motorcycle and dated lots of girls who put out. I always knew he would be the perfect guy to lose my virginity to. He would make a girl's first time perfect."

Katie held out her glass to Brenna, then nodded. "Okay, I'll confess to Nic Giovanni fantasies, too. I ran into him once when he was home from college one summer. We were in town and he stopped to talk to me. I thought maybe he'd ask me out, but he didn't." She sighed at the memory. "I probably would have been willing to give it up for him."

"My sisters are sluts," Brenna announced.

Francesca grabbed the wine bottle. "I refuse to believe you didn't have Nic fantasies, too."

"I had several," Brenna said. "But, as you said, we all fantasized about him. Who else do you wish you'd slept with."

Francesca named a couple of guys Katie remembered

from high school. Back then she'd been more into romance than sex, so while she could list a bunch of guys she would have liked to have dated, she wasn't sure she could claim a willingness to have sex with them.

"You need to just go out there and do it," Brenna told Francesca. "It's been too long. Important parts of your body are atrophying."

Francesca rolled her eyes. "I'm fine."

"You're living like a nun."

Katie had to agree. "Francesca, you've taken the whole 'be independent' thing way too far. Refusing to marry again is fine, but giving up on doing the wild thing is just plain stupid."

Francesca raised her eyebrows. "I can't believe you of all people would say that to me. What happened to waiting for your handsome prince."

Brenna grinned. "She's still waiting, but in the meantime she's not adverse to a little hide the salami."

Katie laughed. "Hide the salami? That's disgusting."

"Easy for you to be all superior and picky," Brenna grumbled. "You just got laid."

"Good point." Katie sipped her wine. "I remembered what I'd been missing." She turned her attention back to Francesca. "Which is my point. I'm not suggesting you fall in love or anything, but give some guy a chance."

Francesca didn't look convinced. "Just some guy? Should I randomly pick one off the street?"

"Absolutely!" Brenna leaned toward her. "I want you to have sex with the next single, reasonably good-looking guy you run across, and I'm not pouring you any more wine until you agree."

"You're kidding."

Brenna looked at Katie. "Are you with me on this?"

"A hundred percent. Francesca needs a man."

Francesca groaned. "Fine. I've probably been out of the game for too long. I'll look around and—"

Brenna cut her off with a shake of her head. "The next single guy. That's the rule. Or no more Marcelli reserve in your glass."

Francesca sighed. "All right. I'll do it. But the consequences are your responsibility."

The three sisters leaned forward and clinked glasses.

When Katie straightened, she rested against the footboard. All this talk of young love and lust made her think of Mia and David, and what Zach had told her. The more she considered what he'd said, the more she came to believe him. But should she tell her sisters what Zach saw between David and that other girl? If she did, they would want to tell Mia, and did *she* want that?

She didn't have an answer, and until she did, she decided she would keep quiet.

"All those lost opportunities," Brenna said mournfully. "Our secret lives."

"Mom and Dad have secrets."

Francesca's unexpected comment silenced Brenna. She and Katie looked at each other, then at their sister.

Francesca swallowed uncomfortably. "I didn't know if I should say anything. I tried to forget what I overheard, but it's been bothering me."

"What?" Brenna asked. "Is it the winery? Is there something wrong with the vineyards?"

Francesca shook her hair off her shoulders. "There's more to life than grapes, Brenna. No, it was something else." She explained how she had come home unexpectedly and overheard their parents and grandparents talking in the library.

"Grammy M said the family is being punished by God," she finished. "Dad said not a day goes by that he doesn't think about *him.*"

"What *him?*" Katie asked. "What on earth are they talking about?"

"I don't know."

"It could be the feud," Brenna said. "Maybe thirty years ago something bad happened with Wild Sea Vineyard and the Giovanni family."

Katie thought about the family history. "How is that possible? The feud started in the late forties, right after the Second World War. Dad wasn't even born then."

"That's right," Francesca said. "Plus Grammy M was the one saying we were being punished, and she didn't become a part of the family until Mom and Dad got married—which was what? Twenty-nine years ago?"

"But you said they said thirty years ago," Brenna reminded Francesca. "Whatever it was happened thirty years ago."

"What is it?" Katie asked. "What could anyone have done? There hasn't even been the hint of a scandal. No whispers or rumors. I always thought we were boringly normal." She turned to Francesca. "Could you have misunderstood?"

"I don't know. Maybe."

Katie looked at Brenna, who shrugged. They both seemed to be waiting for her to make a decision. She thought about the fund-raiser and the upcoming wedding. Not to mention the thousands of beads yet to be attached on Mia's gown, and the mysterious redhead, and Katie's confusing relationship with Zach.

"Let's give it a few weeks and see if anything happens," she said. "If not, we'll bring it up at a family dinner."

"Works for me," Francesca said.

"Maybe the one celebrating my divorce from Jeff," Brenna said. "Or the one where we tell the family how we convinced him to back off on the winery."

Katie was surprised. "You've heard from him about that? The last I knew was that he was determined to pursue the inheritance angle, despite there not being one."

Brenna and Francesca exchanged looks. Katie recognized the combination of guilt and excitement immediately. "All right, you two. What are you up to?"

"Nothing," Francesca said, careful to avert her gaze.

Katie zeroed in on Brenna. "Spill it, now. Every word. Start at the beginning."

Brenna sighed. "It's no big deal. Jeff called to tell me that if I backed off on getting repaid for putting him through school, he'd let go of the inheritance. I told him to go screw himself. If that requires him cutting off certain body parts in the process, I don't care."

"We're going to get back at him," Francesca announced, then covered her mouth and looked horrified.

Katie groaned. "You're what?"

"Nothing." Brenna held up the bottle. "More wine?"

"No. I want the truth. What are you planning?"

"We're trapping the bastard at his own game," Brenna said gleefully. "Francesca's going to meet with him. Play the mourning sister-in-law who completely understands why he left his bitchy wife."

Katie was confused. "Why?"

Francesca leaned toward her. "He's slime. I'm going to dress sexy, see if he comes on to me, and tape the whole thing."

"Why would he come on to you?"

The twins exchanged a look. Brenna shrugged. "Jeff got

drunk once and admitted that he'd always had a thing for Francesca. I didn't think anything about it, except then I saw he was always kind of watching her."

"I didn't know," Francesca admitted, "until Brenna told me."

"But now she can use it against him. She'll tape the conversation. When he's trapped himself, we'll threaten to send the tape to the bimbo. Either Jeff gets off the winery or his new girlfriend finds out he's a real sleaze."

Katie couldn't believe it. "That's illegal. Zach can't know about this."

"Of course not. Although I think he'll be impressed when I tell him."

Katie looked at her sisters. "You can't be serious. This is wrong. It's tacky and horrible and puts you on Jeff's level."

Brenna's gaze narrowed. "That bastard is not getting one square inch of this winery, and by God he's going to pay me what he owes me. Quit spoiling the fun, Katie."

Katie held up her free hand. "Okay, I'll admit that Jeff needs his comeuppance, but this is not the way to do it."

"Do you have a better plan?"

"No, but have you thought this through? Won't Jeff coming on to Francesca be another knife in your back? I love you and I want Jeff punished, but not if you're going to get more hurt in the process. I refuse to rub salt in your wounds."

"You don't know what you're talking about. This idea is brilliant and if you can't see that, we don't need you."

Katie took another drink of wine, but her buzz was gone and in its place was a sense of something important having just been lost.

• • •

"You have a visitor," Dora said through the speakerphone. "It's your son."

Zach dropped his pen and rose. "Send him right in," he said, then headed for the door himself.

It had been nearly two weeks since their fight. His son had finally left a message that he was fine, but he'd said that he needed time to think about what had happened and would be in touch later. Apparently later was now.

David opened the door and stepped into the office. He wore baggy jeans and a worn sweatshirt. As usual, his blond hair needed cutting. He looked tall, lanky, and sheepish.

"Hey, Dad."

"Hey, yourself."

They stood about three feet apart, both looking at the other, both hesitating. Finally Zach moved toward David and held out his arms. His son stepped into his embrace.

The ache around Zach's heart eased. Tension fled his body as his world righted itself. Maybe he'd screwed up a time or two, but all in all, David was the best part of his life.

He moved back enough to grasp David's upper arms. "I'm sorry," he said sincerely. "I didn't mean to hurt you or to imply that you were anything but a joy for me. You were never in the way. Given the chance, I wouldn't change anything. I love you. I hope you know that."

David nodded. He ducked his head, sniffed, then swallowed. "Yeah, Dad. I know. I was kind of a jerk. You know? You got frustrated and I got mad and it seemed easier to split rather than figure out how to make it work. I'm sorry, too."

"Apology accepted."

Zach released him and they both headed for the sofas.

David sprawled across one while Zach took the other.

"How's school?" Zach asked.

"Good. The new quarter started. I got a letter saying I need to be thinking about declaring a major. Especially if I want to go into one of the impacted majors."

"What are those?"

"The really popular ones. Classes fill up fast and it's hard to get a good schedule. At least, that's what the letter said."

"Any more thoughts on what area interests you?" Zach asked the question carefully, wanting to appear interested without being pushy.

David slouched lower in the sofa. "Not really."

He hesitated before asking, "How are things with Mia?"

"Good." He looked at Zach and grinned. "Hell if I know why, but we can't finish getting registered for our wedding gifts. Every time we go to pick out china or something, we have a big fight. I guess we're gonna have to use paper plates."

"I guess so."

Zach wanted to say a lot more, but he didn't. Bringing up Julie when he'd just made up with his son was a dumb plan. Eventually they'd have to talk about her and the importance of fidelity, but not yet.

His son's humor faded. "Look, Dad. I know you're worried about me and I appreciate that. But you've got to give me some space here. I need a chance to grow up. If that means making a mistake, then I'll have to deal with it. But let me screw up before you start yelling at me."

"I agree." Zach took a deep breath. "Here's the thing, David. I'm your father and I want to do everything in my power to protect you from the world. It's like when you were first learning to walk. I went around the house and made sure there was nothing that could hurt you."

"I'm not learning to walk, Dad. I've been walking for a long time."

"I know. But the instinct is damn strong. So I have to bite my tongue to keep from telling you what I think will keep you from getting hurt. Sometimes I forgot that's not my job anymore."

"You can tell me," David said. "Just so long as you don't expect me to listen."

His son grinned. Zach laughed. "As you get older, you're supposed to think I'm smarter."

"That's never gonna happen, Dad. You need to let it go."

15

As Zach drove along the road leading to the hacienda, he could see changes from his last visit. The leaves on the vines were bigger and darker green. At some point the grapes would begin to form. Later they would be picked and, through some process, be turned into wine. That pretty much exhausted his knowledge on the topic. Maybe he should ask Katie for a few of the details, the next time he saw her—assuming she didn't kick him in the head first.

The actual seeing would be in a matter of minutes, he reminded himself. She was supposed to be at the hacienda. For reasons of physical safety, he'd considered messengering the papers to Brenna instead of delivering them by hand, but he refused to be chased off by a woman. Especially not one he found charming, sexy, and a worthy adversary. Besides, he'd seen her naked.

The latter thought made him smile . . . and want. The memory of her anger, not to mention her accusations that he'd made up the story about David kissing Julie, tempered his pleasure. He understood why she didn't trust him, but he didn't like it.

Zach pulled his car to the side of the hacienda, then

stepped out into the warm spring afternoon. Brenna met him at the front door. For once she didn't look as if she'd been blindsided.

"Hi," she said, sounding surprisingly cheerful. "I swear I'm going to start driving down to L.A. to get my own papers. I feel bad about making you come all this way." She took a step back to let him in the house.

"I don't mind," he said, following her inside. "Grandma Tessa invited me to dinner. How could I resist?"

"Her pasta has that effect on people." She grabbed his arm and pulled him into the sitting room, then closed the door to the foyer. After glancing around the small space, as if checking to see that they were alone, she spoke.

"Here's the thing. Francesca and I have come up with a plan."

"I get nervous when clients have plans."

"No. This is a really good one. Remember I told you about Jeff's call? That he said he'd back off on wanting a piece of the winery if I backed off on repayment for putting him through school?"

"Sure, but his lawyer denies Jeff ever made that call. It would be your word against his."

"The man's a sleaze and his word can't be trusted. Which is why we have to get him another way."

She quickly outlined a plan of setting up Francesca to "chat" with Jeff in a bar. "He's always had a thing for her. So we're hoping he'll get drunk, say more than he should, and we'll have him on tape."

Zach was willing to give her points for creativity, if nothing else.

"Katie doesn't want us to do it," Brenna continued. "She says it's tacky and probably illegal and that I'll get hurt, but I think it's brilliant."

"She's right about the illegal part. As your lawyer I have to tell you that it's not something you should do. The law frowns on that sort of thing. There's also the can of worms you could be opening. Do you really want to hear Jeff coming on to your sister? Is that going to make you feel any better?"

Brenna shook her head. "You sound like Katie, which is both weird and unattractive. But I know what you mean. What she meant. Do I want to know exactly *how* horrible Jeff is?"

"I'd think about it."

"Fair enough. But assuming I want to go forward with it, do you think it will work?"

"As your lawyer—"

She rolled her eyes. "Zach, be a regular guy for once. It's not like I don't know you slept with my sister."

He took a step back and bumped into the sofa. He hadn't blushed since he was about fourteen, but he would almost swear he felt heat climbing his neck.

"She didn't"—he swallowed—"Katie—"

"Spilled the beans. Details and all. We were trés impressed." Brenna laughed. "Stop looking so horrified. I'm teasing. She said you guys did it and that was all. Despite the large quantities of wine we had all consumed, she kept to generalities. Neither Francesca nor myself would be able to pick you out naked in a lineup."

"Great." He might never have had a sibling, but if he had, he doubted he would have shared *this* much of his life with him or her.

"Now that I can blackmail you in front of my grandmothers, answer the question. Do you think my plan to use Francesca against Jeff will work?"

"Brenna, I can't commit—"

"Yes or no?"

He grinned.

She clapped her hands together. "I knew it!" She gave him a quick kiss on the cheek. "You're the best. Now go be tortured by my grandmothers. I'm going to call Francesca and tell her it's on."

Brenna hurried out of the sitting room. Zach followed more slowly. While he applauded her ingenuity, he hoped her plan didn't jump up and bite her in the ass.

He headed for the kitchen, then stopped when he spotted Katie in the living room. He entered through the arched doorway and found her sitting on the floor. Stacks of beaded lace flowers stood in piles all around her. As he watched, she counted out groups of ten and placed them next to those already counted. With each group of ten, she made a note on the pad of paper resting on her right thigh.

He glanced around the room. Bags of lace flowers stood by the rust-colored leather sofa. Small containers of beads cluttered together on the glass-and-wood coffee table.

Plans for the wedding, and the dress, were moving forward. He'd expected to have it stopped by now. But David and Mia hadn't broken up, and the wedding date crept closer.

A lace wedding gown lay draped over the loveseat. He frowned, not realizing Katie had already started sewing the dress.

"Hi," he said as he approached. "They let me in the house. Want to run and grab the pepper spray?"

She turned toward him. For a second her expression didn't change, and he wondered if she was still mad.

"I don't think I'd go for anything that boring," she said. "Instead I'd attack you with pruning shears."

"Sounds painful."

"At the risk of being rude, why are you here?"

He sat down. "I have some papers for Brenna." He frowned as he realized not only had he left them in the car, but they hadn't talked about them. "Grandma Tessa found out I was driving up and invited me to stay for dinner." He leaned forward. "I'm in love with her cooking."

"We all are."

"Still mad?" he asked.

"Not at you. David's not one of my favorite people."

"He's a kid."

"He's cheating on my sister."

"Maybe it was just one of those things—cold feet, a last hurrah."

She shook her head. "That hardly makes it all right. He's cheating or just cheated that one time. Neither is acceptable."

"So you believe me?" He wouldn't have guessed that was possible.

"I finally realized you wouldn't lie. You're way too upfront for that. Why slip in a side door when you're willing to blow up the main entrance?"

"An interesting metaphor choice."

"I'm an interesting woman."

"Yes, you are. Interesting, beautiful, exciting. Desirable."

She grinned. "Zach, this is my grandfather's house. You can't possibly have sexual thoughts under this roof. If you do, your pride and joy will shrivel up to the size of a walnut."

"That would be tragic for all of us."

"I'm not going to say yes. You already think too highly of yourself."

He smiled. "I'm not the one who was screaming that night."

She ducked her head. "A gentleman would never bring that up."

"I thought my bringing it up was the entire point."

Her mouth twitched. "You're evil."

"I'm tempting. There's a difference."

He straightened and decided to give them both a break. Mostly because this *was* her grandfather's house and he didn't want to risk his dick.

He pointed at the piles of lace stacked around the room. "What are you doing?"

"I'm trying to figure out where we are, numbers-wise, with the lace flowers. Everyone is complaining about being tired of beading, but we still have a long way to go."

"When did you start sewing the dress?" he asked.

She frowned. "I haven't. I'm thinking I'll get it started next week. I made an under-dress first."

He pointed at the finished gown draped over the love seat. "What's that?"

She followed the direction of his finger, winced slightly, then ducked her head to focus her attention back on the lace flowers. "Inspiration. It's an old dress Grammy M made. I wanted to study some of her workmanship." She made two more piles of ten, then returned her attention to him. "So how are things with you?"

Maybe it was a trick of the afternoon light, but he would swear he could see flecks of gold in her brown eyes. She wore a sweater that hugged her curves, and tight black jeans. The combination made it difficult to follow the conversation.

"Great," he said when his brain finally kicked in. "David and I had a long heart-to-heart. Things are better now."

"I'm glad," she said sincerely, then finished her counting with a sigh. "Just like I thought. We're not keeping on schedule. I guess everyone has so much going on." She grinned. "I don't suppose now that you and David are speaking that you'd be willing to bead a flower or two?"

"Not a chance."

She glanced at the doorway, then at him. "Any more news on Julie?"

"No. I haven't seen her around, but I don't see much of David."

"I want to talk to Mia about it, but I don't know how without telling her what you saw."

"I'm having the same problem with him. I was thinking—"

Before he could continue, he heard voices in the hallway. Both grandmothers swept into the room. He rose automatically, then wished he hadn't when he found himself hugged, kissed, and cheek-pinched. Grandma Tessa might not be twenty anymore, but she had a grip that could snap metal.

"You're too skinny," Grandma Tessa said, poking a finger at his midsection. "Working too hard, eh? Not getting proper meals. Katie, why aren't you cooking dinner for Zach? He's family. We have to take care of him."

Rather than answer, Katie only smiled, but Zach saw her lips moving and suspected whatever she was saying would cause her grandmother to dive for her rosary.

Grammy M clapped her hands together when she spied the wedding dress draped over the love seat.

"Oh, Katie, did you show this lovely gown to Zachary? Lookin' at it still brings a tear to my eye." She brushed her hands over the lace. "Hours we spent on this, but it was no trouble a'tall. We knew our Katie would be a beautiful bride."

Grandma Tessa muttered something in Italian. She turned her dark gaze on Zach. "I've been good all these years, never cursing that boy's name, but I've been tempted."

Katie stood up and grabbed the dress from Grammy M. "I got this out to study how beautifully you put it together, Grammy M. Not because I was feeling nostalgic. As for the curses, Grandma Tessa, don't bother. All Greg is guilty of is changing his mind. That's still allowed, right?"

Grandma Tessa didn't look swayed by her argument. Zach studied the dress in question with renewed interest. So this had been made for Katie, much the same way she now painstakingly sewed a dress for Mia. With luck it would be unworn as well.

Grammy M sighed. "What will you be thinkin', Zachary?"

Suddenly all the attention in the room telescoped on him. *Trapped* didn't begin to describe the sensation. He could see many minefields and lots of pits, but few escape routes. He went for the truth.

"The dress is beautiful and the guy who walked out on Katie was an idiot."

Tension eased between the women as the Grands exchanged smiles. Grandma Tessa winked broadly at Katie and not-so-subtly said they needed to leave "the young people to themselves."

Katie watched them go, then turned to him. "Nice save," she said, then sighed. "They make me crazy."

"First of all, I was telling the truth. Second of all, you adore them."

She smiled. "True enough. But that doesn't mean I don't have fantasies about being an orphan."

"My father, Antonio Marcelli, was a second son," Grandpa Lorenzo told Zach that night at dinner. "He could have worked the land in Italy, but he would never have been in charge. Sometimes a second son is content, but sometimes a fire burns in here." He thumped his chest with a fist. "For my father, the fire grew until he had to leave all he had ever known and travel far away. He came here and found this place. It was 1923."

Zach listened, fascinated as Grandpa Lorenzo detailed the history of Marcelli Wines.

"This was virgin land," Grandpa Lorenzo continued. "He broke the land himself, with a little help. Then he planted the vines he had brought with him from Italy." A smile tugged at the corner of his thin mouth. "He might have gone into France for a sample or two before coming here." Then he chuckled and touched a finger to his lips to show that was a family secret.

Zach figured it would have to be. Stealing clippings from a vineyard had to be a serious offense.

"At the time he had a good friend. Salvatore Giovanni. He, too, was a second son. Their land is next to ours, stretching out in the opposite direction. Together the two men tended their crops and waited for God to work his magic. In time they sent for wives, and a dynasty was born."

Zach frowned. The name Salvatore Giovanni sounded familiar, but he couldn't place it. Brenna, sitting next to him, leaned close.

"The Giovannis own Wild Sea Vineyards. We're mortal enemies now. Don't ask."

He wondered how many times Grandpa Lorenzo told the story of the founding of the winery. The family would know every word by heart, yet he suspected they didn't mind hearing the tale again. In time, when Lorenzo was gone, Katie's father, Marco, would do the telling. And so it would continue through the generations. Perhaps the story would change, perhaps it would stay true to history. Regardless, the heart of the adventure would remain, reminding this family of who they were and where they had come from. He envied them that.

"You're going to have to protect all this," Lorenzo said, staring directly at Zach.

Zach straightened. "Me?"

"Against that jackal. Brenna's husband. We won't give him anything!"

Brenna leaned back in her chair and grinned. "Not to worry, Grandpa. Francesca and I have a plan."

The old man looked interested.

Zach didn't think Brenna should share the details with her parents and grandparents, but before he could make that suggestion, Katie tossed her napkin on the table.

"You can't be serious about this," she said. "Brenna, it's awful. You're going to be swimming in regrets."

"I believe your exact words were *tacky* and *illegal*," Brenna said. "But who cares, as long as it works?"

"What are you two talking about?" Marco asked. "Katie?"

She sighed and quickly filled him in on the basics of the plan.

Grandpa Lorenzo looked thoughtful, but Grandma Tessa appeared to have bitten into a lemon.

"Jeff said that about our Francesca?" She reached into her pocket and pulled out her rosary.

Brenna brushed off her comment. "So what? Now we can use this."

"Katie, dear, what're you objectin' to?" Grammy M asked.

Katie sighed. "It's illegal for one thing. And it's just plain wrong. This puts the whole family on Jeff's level. Let him be slime by himself. But the worst of it is, I think Brenna's going to get hurt more. She can't *want* to hear that Jeff is interested in her twin. I refuse to be party to cutting open another vein and watching her bleed."

"We're going to have to agree to disagree about this," Colleen said. "Let's change the subject."

Katie nodded gratefully. She didn't want to fight with her family. It was never a pleasant experience.

Her mother glanced at her father. "We have some exciting news. Marco and I are buying Mia and David a house."

"What?" Brenna asked. "Why?"

"To help them. They're young and just getting started."

"They don't need your money," Zach said flatly.

Katie mentally winced. He wouldn't like the implication that he couldn't take care of his son.

Her mother turned to him. "Oh, Zach, please don't take this the wrong way. There's a small house that just came up for sale. It's on the edge of the property, so they'll have privacy but still be close. We know David and Mia have been having difficulties working out their plans for next year, after Mia graduates."

Her father touched his wife's hand. "UC Santa Barbara would be a good compromise for them."

"You're buying them a house?" Brenna said. "You didn't buy Francesca and Todd a house. You didn't buy me and Jeff anything. You said we were on our own."

Marco frowned. "This is different, Brenna."

"How?" Francesca asked.

Katie understood her sisters might think the situation was unfair, but that wasn't what bothered her. "Have you discussed this with Mia? She's really set on going to Georgetown."

"Mia will do what's right for the family," her grandfather announced. "She's a good girl. She'll listen."

"Then you don't know your granddaughter," Katie told him. "This is crazy. You can't plan her life, or David's. They have the right to decide where they want to go to school and where they want to live."

Her mother didn't look pleased with her stand. "We're being more than generous."

"You've got that right," Brenna muttered.

"You're being high-handed and dictatorial," Katie said. "This is crazy, Mom. Why are you planning Mia's life without even asking if this is what she wants? Which I happen to know it isn't."

"You don't know anything," her grandfather said loudly.

"Lorenzo has a point," Grammy M said.

Katie turned on her. "You're in this, too? Is it a conspiracy? Don't any of you care about Mia?"

"The family," her grandfather began.

"Screw the family," Katie said loudly, then could have kicked herself.

There was a collective gasp as everyone turned to stare at her. Only Zach looked sympathetic.

Her grandfather pushed to his feet. "What did you say?" he demanded, his voice booming.

She was shaking inside. Shaking, but determined. She tossed her napkin on the table and jumped to her feet.

"You heard me. You're thinking of what *you* want, not what's right for Mia. Don't any of you care about her?"

"You mock the family. You disrespect all of us."

"I don't," she told him. "I care about everyone. But I respect that each of us has the right to choose."

"Either you support the family or you don't," Grandpa Lorenzo told her.

"I refuse to offer blind support to something I know is wrong. Mia is my sister and I love her. I'll stand against all of you before I let you force her to do something that will break her spirit."

Her grandfather began muttering in Italian. She knew what that meant.

She glanced around the table. "It's always been this way with the family. There's no room for personal opinion. There's only ever one right way. One philosophy that fits. Grandpa's. Sometimes that doesn't work. You can't force feelings. You can't make someone want what you want. It's wrong."

"This has been decided." Her grandfather glared at her. "You're not a part of us. You're no longer a Marcelli."

Katie felt as if she'd been slapped.

"Pop, that's enough," Marco said. "Katie's entitled to her opinion." He glanced at his daughter. "Even if it's wrong."

Katie turned to him. "You're getting to be just like him. You used to encourage us to think for ourselves."

"That's where he went wrong," her grandfather said. "You should listen and do what you're told."

"Lorenzo!" her mother said. "Stop it. Katie will come around."

"No, I won't," Katie said. She looked at Brenna. "While I'm being thrown out, I'm going to tell you one last time that you're wrong about what you're doing to Jeff. You may get what you want, but in the end you'll regret it. And when you're curled up and hurting, I'll be there because I love you, even when you're an idiot." She turned back to her parents. "Don't make Mia choose, because if she accepts that house, you'll have lost her forever."

"Get out!" her grandfather roared. "Never come back. You are not my granddaughter. You're not anyone I want to know."

Pain sliced through her. No one stood against him. Not one spoke up for her. She swallowed, then left the room.

Zach watched her go.

Marco faced his father. "That was unnecessary."

"She needs to learn."

"She already knows plenty," Zach said as he stood. "She's loyal, loving, and a whole lot more caring than any of you deserve."

He tossed his napkin on the floor and headed toward the kitchen. From there he walked outside and found Katie seated on the bottom step.

He crouched next to her. "You okay?"

She shook her head.

He pulled her arms away from her knees, and she raised her chin. In the light from the porch he could see the dampness on her cheeks.

"He threw me out," she said, her voice cracking slightly. "He's never done that to me before. To Brenna and Francesca when they were teenagers, but I was always the good granddaughter."

"He doesn't mean it."

"He does right now. Later he'll calm down, but it may take a while. Besides, do you see anyone but you out here? They've all turned their backs on me. They're wrong about Mia."

Tears spilled from her eyes. Zach sat next to her on the step and held open his arms.

She hesitated, then leaned against him. He held her close. "They'll come around. You were right. They'll figure it out eventually."

"Not for a long time. No one will call me. They won't leave messages, they won't check on me. I'll be alone. It's like being dead."

He wanted to tell her that she was confident and capable, but knew that wasn't what she wanted to hear. Instead he stroked her back and said it would be all right.

"When?" she asked.

"By Thursday."

She laughed, then sniffed. "Promise?"

"No. I can't promise that."

She straightened. "I know. I appreciate you trying to make me feel better."

"Is it working?"

"Some." She glanced past him to the house. "They'll talk about it among themselves. The Grands usually support me, but they want Mia and David to move close, so this time they won't. Obviously my folks want that, too. Brenna and Francesca are already mad because of Jeff. Mia . . . I don't know what she'll think."

"That you defended her."

Katie looked at him. "It's probably not enough to get her to stand against the family."

"Why don't you go back inside and talk to them?"

"I can't. My grandfather said I wasn't a part of the family. I'm not welcome back until that changes."

More tears spilled onto her face. Zach brushed them away, then kissed her cheek.

"Want to ride home with me?"

"I can't leave my car."

"Then I'll follow you home. I want to make sure you get there safely."

She nodded and stood. "At least I didn't bother unpacking my car." She pulled her keys out of her pocket, then looked at him. "You're missing dessert."

"I'd rather be with you."

"That's really sweet." She wiped the back of her hand over her cheeks. "I guess this whole scene kind of proves your point about relationships. Maybe you have the right idea about walking away before things get messy."

"You don't mean that."

"I know. I just hate this."

He didn't know how to help, so he put his arm around her and led her to her car. "Come on, Katie. Let's get you home."

16

*K*atie drove back to L.A. with the comforting glow of Zach's headlights in her rearview mirror. By the 405 freeway she'd convinced herself that her Grandfather wouldn't take more than three weeks to get over being mad. The longest one of his rages had ever lasted had been a month. So by the time the fund-raiser was over, her life would be within a week of getting back to normal.

Great. The good news was she would be so busy over the next couple of weeks that she wouldn't even miss talking to her mother or her sisters. Unfortunately, she didn't believe a word of it.

She cried through the next ten miles, then got herself under control by the time they reached her exit. She'd expected Zach to keep going down toward the beach, but he surprised her by following her into her driveway, then stepping out of his car and walking up the drive.

He might be tough, mean, and determined, but he was also kind. He cupped her face.

"How you doing?" he asked.

"Okay."

"Liar."

She smiled. "I'll survive."

"Would you like me to stay?"

Stay?

He pulled her close. "I'm talking about holding you, Katie, not trying to get in your pants."

She raised her head and looked at him. "What if I want you there?"

He sighed heavily. "All right, but only because you're begging me."

She laughed. "You make me crazy."

"Then my work here is done."

Surprisingly, he did hold her for a long time. Secure in Zach's arms, Katie sprawled across her bed and cried her heart out. When she was finally finished, she blew her nose and looked at him.

"You were probably hoping for something more romantic," she said.

"No. Just to be here with you."

"Great line."

"Not a line."

She stared at his dark eyes and knew that she wouldn't mind getting lost in them. When everyone she loved had turned their backs on her, he'd come through. Funny how he was the last one she would have expected that from. Sometimes he was a real bastard and sometimes he was the world's nicest guy.

"Thank you," she said. "For everything."

"You're welcome."

They looked at each other. She waited for him to make his move and when he didn't, she realized he wanted her to be sure. That if she'd changed her mind about wanting to make love, he wouldn't complain. He *would* just hold her.

The thought nearly sent her into another crying jag, but instead of giving into tears, she moved close and kissed him.

His lips were warm, his arms strong as they came around her. Within the tender confines of his embrace she forgot her family, her pain, her loneliness—everything except being with Zach. His tenderness reached inside and gently nudged her romantic heart into wakefulness. His touch excited her body. The combination made her slip closer and press herself against him.

While she'd initiated the kissing, he quickly took over. His head angled as he licked her bottom lip. She parted for him, wanting him to excite her, pleasure her, heal her. He placed a hand on her side and gently urged her onto her back. Her long hair spread out on the pillow, and he toyed with several strands.

"How you doing?" he asked quietly.

She opened her eyes and looked at his face. Concern darkened his irises, passion thickened his voice.

"Good."

He stroked her cheek. "Despite my reputation, I don't travel with protection. Any condoms in this girly place?"

She smiled. "An unopened box in my nightstand."

"I like a woman who plans ahead."

"I'm very organized."

"I know."

He leaned close and pressed his mouth to hers. She wrapped her arms around him, surrendering to the sensations that flooded her. He moved his hand from her face to her stomach where his long fingers rested lightly on her sweater. His tongue slipped into her mouth and brushed against hers.

He kissed her deeply, thoroughly, erotically, until she couldn't breathe. Slow kisses went on forever and made her bones melt. Teasing kisses that made her squirm. Passionate kisses that sucked the will right out of her and left her wanting to beg. Kisses that made her feel she'd never been kissed before. Not like this.

Slowly he moved his hand, sliding up her belly, along her rib cage, and between her breasts. She found herself touching him back. Tracing the width of his shoulders and the powerful muscles in his back.

Zach stroked her arms, returned to her stomach, then repeated the circuit. Up and over, between her breasts to her shoulder, her arm, crossing her stomach, slipping close to the apex of her thighs without actually slipping between them.

She found it difficult to keep breathing. Her skin seemed tight, and if her breasts swelled any more, she was going to spill out of her bra. She wanted to start screaming instructions. And then something amazing began to happen. The anticipation took on a life of its own.

Because she knew that eventually he *would* touch her in every place she wanted to be touched. As their kiss went on and his hands continued to move, she thought about him touching her breasts or between her legs and the tension grew.

When he reached for the hem of her sweater, she nearly moaned in relief. He tugged off the garment and tossed it onto the floor, then flicked open the front hook on her bra. The lace sprang free, leaving her breasts exposed to the evening air. For a second her heart stopped. She froze in anticipation. Then he touched just the tip of one finger to her hard, tight nipple.

The sensation was exquisite. She almost bit her tongue as fire shot through her. Before she could fully comprehend the feeling, he gently pinched her nipple between his thumb and forefinger. She gasped. Then his mouth was on her other breast, and she had her fingers in his hair urging him on.

"Don't stop," she breathed, surrendering to the wanting.

He continued to caress her until she alternately clung to the bedspread, then to him. Tension increased, impossible tension that had only one cure.

When he finally lifted his head, she wanted to cry out in protest. Fortunately he went right to work on unfastening her jeans. While she kicked off her shoes, he pulled down the zipper. Jeans, panties, and socks came off in one easy push that left her naked.

She made a halfhearted gesture toward his shirt, as if maybe she would undress him. Bless the man, he never gave her a chance. Instead he slipped between her knees and kissed her stomach. Muscles tightened in anticipation. He stroked the length of her legs, then bent low and licked the inside of her knees.

He'd done this before, she thought, already finding it difficult to think. He'd done it and done it well.

She tried to sigh, but the sound came out more like a purr. This time, when he moved slowly and deliberately, she abandoned herself to the reality that was his fingers, his mouth, and his tongue. She didn't urge, didn't plead, didn't do anything but let him seduce her into sensual mindlessness that made every cell in her body stand up and applaud.

He rubbed her thighs, moving closer and closer to her waiting heat, but not quite touching her there. He licked and nibbled and sucked on her skin, moving north, always moving north, but again, not touching *there*.

She arched her hips slightly in invitation, her legs parted, but he ignored her. The man had his own pace and he would not be rushed.

She soon found that pace suited her just fine. Slowly, and slowly, inching up until she could feel his hot breath on the apex of her thighs. Need, want, and desire collided. She trembled and he hadn't even touched her intimately. Not yet. But soon. Very soon.

Finally he slipped his fingers along the seam of her outer lips and gently drew them apart. The cool air contrasted with her hot skin. He put his mouth on her and gave her an openmouthed kiss that sent a scream of satisfaction racing through her body.

Katie stiffened and melted all at the same time. He licked the length of her, then found nature's magic place and reintroduced himself.

Quick flicks and slow sucking robbed her of free will and left her gasping. He inserted one finger inside of her, touching her from below. His finger and his tongue circled in perfect harmony, once, twice . . . and she was lost.

The release caught her off guard, sending her flying. She found herself coming endlessly as her body shuddered, sending waves of pleasure crashing through her. Zach read her mind, or maybe just her body, continuing to touch her perfectly until there was nothing left but a gentle hum of contentment.

When it was over, he kissed his way up her body, first her stomach, then her breasts. Finally his head was level with hers. She had a feeling she looked as wiped-out and two-dimensional as a badly drawn stick figure. Zach had that expression of male superiority that claimed he'd just pleased his woman. Frankly, Katie thought he'd earned it.

"Wow," she whispered because she didn't have the breath left to talk any louder. "That was really—"

Words failed her. She gestured with her hand, flicking her wrist and then touching his cheek. He smiled.

"*Wow* works," he said.

She stared at his face, at the lines by his eyes, and the firm set of his jaw. For the rest of her life, whatever happened, she would remember this moment, this night, this time with him. Even if she had to face him over breakfast at family Christmases for the next forty years, she couldn't find it in herself to be sorry.

She reached for his shirt, but found she didn't have the strength to do much more than lay there.

"Maybe you'd like to get naked," she murmured.

"Maybe I would."

He stood. While he unfastened his shirt, she reached in her nightstand for the promised box of condoms.

"Jumbo size?" he joked as he unfastened his trousers.

"Super colossal."

He pulled off his trousers, then his socks. Finally his briefs joined the pile.

She studied his naked body. He had long legs, narrow hips and an impatient erection that seemed to demand her attention. He looked as good as she remembered.

She shifted onto her knees and moved to the edge of the bed. Once there, she wrapped one arm around him, drawing him close, and slipped her other arm between them so she could touch his hardness. He responded by cupping her rear and squeezing.

Something about touching him made her start to tremble. When he kissed her, she found herself frantic. He responded in kind, sucking on her tongue, cupping her breasts and teasing her nipples.

She released his penis and ran her hands up and down his chest. The contrast of cool hair and hot skin delighted her. She slipped lower to cup him, then parted her legs, wanting him inside.

"Not so fast, young lady," he whispered.

She rolled onto one hip, then onto her back while he opened the box of condoms and pulled out a plastic packet. He ripped it open and slipped on the protection, then moved between her knees.

He deliberately pushed her knees farther apart so that he could see all of her. She looked at him looking at her. A shiver rippled through her. Being with Zach was more intimate than being with anyone else. There weren't any secrets between them, no masks or disguises.

When he rubbed a finger against her dampness, he shifted his gaze so he could watch her reaction. She bit her lower lip and groaned. He moved again. She wanted to close her eyes, but she wanted to watch, too. She'd never watched before. At least not so obviously.

He continued to touch her, stroking faster and faster until she started breathing heavily and straining toward him. Tendrils of excitement moved through her; tension increased. She could feel herself getting wetter, swelling, needing.

Faster and faster, rubbing over and around. She pulsed her hips in time with his movements. Then she felt something thick and hard pushing into her. Even as he continued to touch her, he filled her.

She couldn't believe the sensations he created within

her. He withdrew and plunged into her again. Her release was just out of reach. She pulsed faster, her breath coming in gasps.

"Zach!"

She didn't know what she wanted from him. Maybe that he wouldn't stop. Maybe that this would go on forever.

Zach watched the passion flare in Katie's eyes. He could feel the tiny shudders building inside of her. Every part of him screamed out to simply bury himself inside of her and have his way, but he couldn't. Not yet. Not when she was so close.

So he gritted his teeth and thought about the baseball card collection he'd had when he was a kid. If he'd kept it, it would have been worth a fortune. Except then he started thinking about Katie in a baseball jersey and nothing else, and her perched on a counter while he plunged his hard, throbbing c—

Math. Times tables. Seven times seven was—

She gasped. He felt the hard knot of nerves pulse, and suddenly she contracted around him. He groaned as she milked him, making her sweet, slick body impossible to resist. He continued to touch her until the shudders stopped, then he leaned forward and dropped his hands to the bed.

In and out he pumped, feeling the pressure build and build. Her eyes locked with his. Her legs came up around his hips. Suddenly her hands were on his ass, her nails digging in as she pulled him deeper and deeper. Her head arched back and the contractions began again. This time she screamed.

It was as if her entire body conspired to send him over the edge. The pressure was unbearable and the point of no return was a heartbeat away. He squeezed back as hard as he could, waiting until the last of her contractions faded. Only then did he give in to the rush of release that exploded out of him like a bullet.

When rational thought returned, he wrapped his arms around her and shifted them both onto their sides. Katie stared at him wide-eyed and flushed.

"I'm guessing you didn't learn that in law school," she whispered.

He laughed. "I did. It was extra credit."

"Where did you study? There weren't any classes like that at UCLA."

"Sure there were. You just have to know what they're called."

She smiled.

Zach kissed the tip of her nose, pulled back the covers, and waited for her to slip under them before sliding next to her. When they were settled, he turned out the lamp on the nightstand.

Katie rested her head on his shoulder. "I guess it's your turn to sneak away in the night," she said teasingly. "I promise not to take offense."

"I have a seven A.M. meeting. My leaving won't be about you."

She sighed. "You say the sweetest things."

He pulled her close. "I mean them."

"I'm glad."

While her breathing slowed, he stared into the darkness. He *did* mean them. In this case, if he didn't have an early meeting, he would be content to stay in her bed and wake up with her. He could imagine a long time spent in the shower while they discovered just how limber each of them could be, followed by breakfast at her small, painted table. Surrounded by plants and candles and too many pillows, he would listen to her plans for the day and talk about his own schedule.

The concept of domestic bliss usually sent him screaming for the hills, but not this time. This time he didn't want to walk away, and for the life of him, he couldn't say why.

Katie watched the clock slowly ticking off the hour. She stared at the lining for Mia's wedding gown that she'd spent most of yesterday sewing together, then back at the clock.

"Where are you?" she asked aloud, more than a little annoyed that her baby sister couldn't be bothered to show up on time for the very first fitting of her wedding gown.

Katie paced the width of her small living room. She had a thousand and one details to take care of for the fund-raiser. There were phone calls to make, details to confirm, prizes to be picked up, and inventories to go over.

"I don't need this," she muttered and headed for her phone. She punched in her sister's number, then clenched her teeth when she heard the familiar message.

"Hi! It's me, and if you don't know who 'me' is, then you probably have the wrong number. Leave a message."

"Mia, it's Katie. I can't believe you didn't show up for the very first fitting of your wedding dress." She tightened her grip on the phone. "Dammit, Mia, I was defending you and your right to have your own life. I understand the rest of the family not talking to me, but you have no right to be mad at me."

There was so much more she wanted to say, but what was the point? She was being given the cold shoulder. Only time would fix things. She hung up and reached for her ever-present briefcase. With the countdown to the fund-raiser beginning, she had plenty of work to keep her occupied.

17

*B*renna *pulled her hair* into a ponytail and secured it with an old elastic band she'd found in her jacket pocket. She was having a bad hair day—probably because she hadn't bothered to shower that morning. Actually she hadn't done much more than wash her face, brush her teeth, and put on clean underwear.

She looked like hell, which suited her mood because she felt like hell. Whoever said change was good was either an idiot or had never been through a divorce. She alternated between blinding rage and numbing depression—not that she liked either state. She wanted to feel normal again.

She wanted not to be fighting with Katie.

She still felt badly about what had happened last week. While she didn't agree with her sister's stand, she understood *why* Katie was worried about her. In truth, she kind of liked her concern, which meant not talking to her was really stupid. But calling meant admitting Katie might be right, and Brenna hardly wanted to have *that* conversation.

The truth was, she missed her sister, and now that Francesca had contacted Jeff and arranged to meet him,

Brenna *was* having second thoughts. Did she really *want* her ex-husband to come on to her twin?

Rather than dwell on the mess that was her life, Brenna raised her face toward the sun and breathed in the sweet spring air. It was May—a busy month at the vineyard. Training had begun a week ago in the southernmost fields.

Speaking of which . . . she squatted down to examine the vines more closely, then fingered the sturdy plant. Already green leaves covered all the new growth and much of the old. Tiny clusters of flowers danced in the afternoon breeze. Green tendrils found their way toward the sun.

"Not for long," she said, tugging on one tendril, then pulling it free of the stem.

Training the vines was both an art and a science. Each plant produced an excess of leaves, flowers, and new growth. Skilled workers came through and stripped off what wasn't needed, leaving the most healthy and strong growth to produce the best grapes. If too much was removed, the harvest would be small and disappointing. Not enough removed, and the grapes wouldn't grow and ripen as well as they could. Sun and air needed to flow through the vineyard, rolling across like a wave from the sea.

Brenna straightened and arched her aching back. They were well into their first week of training, and she had the sore muscles to prove it. The ache was like an old friend— almost forgotten, but still a bit of a lingering memory. She knew that Grandpa Lorenzo had insisted on the manual labor to test her determination. Brenna wasn't worried; she refused to fail.

She touched another leaf. Here in the southern part of central California, frost wasn't an issue, but it could cause damage in their northern vineyards. Every day she spoke to the managers there as she slowly returned to the rhythm of the vineyards.

She headed toward the property line. For the past couple of weeks she walked a different portion of the land to refamiliarize herself with what had once been her entire world. When she allowed herself to consider all she'd lost by marrying Jeff, she wanted to raise her fists to the sky and demand justice. Unfortunately she had no one to blame but herself. She had chosen what seemed like the safe path because any other was out of the question. Unfortunately she'd chosen a selfish man who had taken advantage of her devotion and left her with nothing to show for giving away her very soul.

She reached the edge of the property and checked on the railings. The posts sat securely in the ground. She was about to return to the east fields when she saw someone walking toward her. Someone on the *other* side of the fence. The evil, Wild Sea Vineyard side.

She wanted to run for cover for a number of reasons, one of which being that she was dressed like a day hire, the second being the fact that she'd gained five pounds in the past six or seven weeks. The combination of self-pity and the Grands' cooking had done nothing good for her hips and thighs.

The third and perhaps most important reason was that he was the last person on the planet she wanted to see when she wasn't at her best.

But there was no way she could escape. Not without seeming like an idiot. Brenna figured she'd done enough of that in the past nine years without continuing the pattern. So she squared her shoulders, took a breath for luck, and turned to face the man her grandfather thought of as the devil incarnate.

Nicholas Giovanni. Nic to his friends.

At one time Brenna had known him well enough to call him Nic. She'd called him a lot of other things, too, depending on her mood and the circumstances. Sometimes he'd laughed, sometimes they'd fought, and sometimes they'd simply lost themselves in sensual lovemaking that had left them both breathless.

The sun was in her eyes, making it difficult to see details. She saw a tall, powerful silhouette walking toward her. The man from her past had always dominated the landscape. Too arrogant, too handsome, too many things. It was pathetic to think that at the ripe old age of twenty-seven there had only been two men in her life. She really needed to get out more.

She hadn't seen Nic in nine years, and she didn't doubt time had been kind to him. Sure enough, as he approached, she saw that he looked good enough to be served with marinara and some fresh focaccia bread.

The passing years had added a few lines around his dark brown eyes, which only made them more appealing when they crinkled as he smiled that easy smile that had once kept her up nights. Stubble darkened his jaw, making him look dangerous and incredibly sexy. His clothes were as worn as hers, but somehow they looked better on him. Wasn't that always the way?

"I heard you were back," he announced when he came to a stop by the fence that separated their property.

That was it—five words and a welcoming smile. As if he wasn't angry. As if the past didn't matter. And then she realized it probably didn't. Based on Jeff's treatment of her, she hadn't made an impact on him, and they'd been married for years. Why would she have been more than an uninteresting blip on Nic's radar screen?

"I'm working the vines," she said, because saying *why* she was back was simply too depressing. Besides, while there might be acres between houses, this was still a small community. She didn't doubt that word of her divorce had spread quickly. Except if she *didn't* say she was getting a divorce, he might think she thought he didn't know and that she was hiding the fact. Which would make her look stupid.

Her mind whirled around a couple more times before she decided to face things head on and blurted, "I'm getting a divorce."

Nic's steady gaze never left her face, which was a good thing, because she could feel every one of those additional five pounds clinging to her thighs like Francesca's padding. Unfortunately her padding didn't unzip and was probably there to stay.

"I heard. I'm sorry."

"Are you?" she asked before she could stop herself.

"Sure. Why wouldn't I be?"

Of course, she thought, wanting to smack herself in the head. After all this time, why would Nic give a damn?

"It's going to be a good year," he said. "We're expecting our largest harvest ever."

"Still in the volume business, Nic?" She mentally winced. Okay, she'd just turned into a bitch queen. Time to tone it down.

His dark eyes narrowed slightly. "We're still in the *wine* business. The market is changing. Elitist boutique wineries are being gobbled up by large, successful companies. Like mine."

Her worry, depression, and ill-temper faded. No need to tone it down. Not if Nic was going to fight back.

"Elitist?" she repeated. "You're proud of the *quantity*

you produce. Here at Marcelli, we worry more about the *quality* of the harvest. There's a reason every reserve we've produced has been a winner at competition."

"In the end it will come down to economic survival. I'm confident of mine. What about you?"

"Oh, you'll survive. Some people will even like what you produce. But you'll never make anything special or significant. What you have is mass produced with so much mechanization that the grapes can go from bud to bottle without being touched by a single hand. Kind of like making a cola drink."

He took a step toward her. Tension crackled in the air. "The Hendersons are throwing in the towel. I bought them out last week."

She hadn't known. Regret filled her. As much as she hated to admit it, Nic was right. The economic climate was changing. Small vineyards were being lost, or bought up.

"Like a circling vulture looking for carrion," she said easily. "Are you going to keep the grapes or replant? You need the Cab Franc for blending," she continued before he could speak. "Of course, their vineyards aren't as tidy as yours. You might actually have to send people in to pick the grapes." She gasped and pressed her hands to her chest. "Whatever will happen to that so important bottom line?"

His dark gaze never left her face. Brenna waited for the snappy comeback. Arguing with Nic left her feeling more energized than she had in weeks. Funny how despite the years they'd been apart, their ability to drive each other crazy hadn't changed.

But instead of taking the bait, he simply shook his head. "I thought you might have mellowed."

"Not even close. You haven't, either."

He shrugged. "Maybe not, but I'm a lot richer."

She didn't doubt that. In the past nine years Nic had taken Wild Sea into the stratosphere. In the same amount of time she'd worked at a series of tedious jobs and a bad marriage. How depressing.

"Rich enough to be a contender," he added.

"For what?"

"All this." He jerked his head toward the Marcelli Vineyards.

"You're crazy. My grandfather would never sell to you."

Nic shrugged. "Maybe not, but word on the street is, he's going to sell to someone."

Brenna stalked into the main offices of the winery and headed for her grandfather's office. She found the old man sitting behind his desk, studying an order form.

"Nic Giovanni says you're going to sell the winery," she announced.

Her grandfather looked up slowly. "What are you doing talking with him?"

"I was walking the fence line, he was doing the same. We met, we talked, he said you were selling. Is it true?"

He had to tell her no, she thought desperately. The winery was the only thing left in her world that mattered. Okay, yes, there was family, but she was talking about work. About losing herself in something she'd always loved.

"You can't," she told him when he didn't speak. "This is a part of all of us."

He shook his head. "Don't listen to everything you hear, Brenna. Nicholas Giovanni is our enemy. He only wants to hurt you."

His phone rang and when he reached for the receiver, Brenna knew he'd said as much as he was going to. She turned and left.

She wanted to take his reassurances to heart. Marcelli Wines was her grandfather's life. He would never abandon all that he'd worked for. And she supposed a case could be made that Nic was the enemy.

Except he'd never cared about the feud. They'd had that in common. And he'd never been vindictive—even when no one could have blamed him.

Nine years ago she'd promised to love him forever. Yet when he'd proposed she'd walked away from him. Within six months she'd been married to Jeff. Was that why Nic had said the winery was for sale?

Surely he wouldn't carry a grudge all this time. Why would her childish actions still matter? She didn't doubt he was more than capable of making up a story about her grandfather selling, just to upset her, but only with good reason. And she couldn't think of a single one.

So somebody was lying. Either Nic or her grandfather. Which left her with two questions: Which one? And why?

"Okay, but what about when the state gets involved, eliminating voters supposedly for legal reasons, but really to make sure the election goes the way the party in power wants?" Carol Rumstead asked. As she spoke, she flipped her long dark hair out of her eyes.

Mia exchanged a look of frustration with her friend Tina. Every time they discussed campaign reform, Carol brought up the exact same issues. It was so incredibly boring.

She was saved from having to make a response by a

quick knock on her front door. She was halfway across the living room when the door opened and David stepped inside.

"Hey," he said, crossing to her and giving her a kiss. "What's going on?"

She accepted the kiss, but barely. "My poli sci study group is having a meeting. I told you."

David frowned. "No, you didn't." He glanced at his watch and frowned. "It's nearly seven. We talked about going to a movie tonight."

"Did we? Gee, I guess I forgot." She glanced over her shoulder at the small group sprawled across her sofa and love seat, then drew him into the kitchen.

"You never forget stuff like that," David said as he leaned against the counter. "Mia, you've been acting strange lately. What's up?"

"I don't know. I guess I'm really busy. Why don't you take someone else to the movies?"

"What? I don't have anyone to go with."

"Really?" Annoyance turned to anger. She folded her arms over her chest. "That's not what I heard. Let me give you a word of advice, David. When you're engaged, it's a really stupid idea to take another girl to a club and then spend the entire night trying to suck out her tonsils. People talk. Word gets around. It gets back to me."

David flushed but didn't retreat. "I don't know what you're talking about. There's no other girl."

"So this Julie person is just a close friend?"

"We hang out."

He was so lying, she couldn't believe it. "Just get out of here. I don't want to talk to you right now."

His face paled. "Mia, no. We have to talk. I love you."

She could feel the warm gold of her engagement ring.

As she turned it and squeezed her hand closed, the small diamond cut into her palm.

"This isn't my definition of love."

He looked at her for a long time, then shook his head. "You're wrong about me. I love you more than you'll ever know."

Nice words, she thought, trying to harden her heart to them. The problem was, even though he'd acted like an ass, she still cared about him. She wanted to forgive him. But wanting and being able to were two different things.

He walked out of the kitchen. Seconds later the front door opened, then closed. Mia dropped her head and told herself to let it go for now. She would take some time and think about what she wanted, then meet with David again. Together they would come to some rational, logical decision.

Which sounded good, but didn't do a thing for the knot in her stomach and the ache in her heart. First Jeff had cheated on Brenna and now David had cheated on her. Were all men lying weasel dogs?

Fifty hours until show time, Katie thought as she walked through the main ballroom of the hotel. The tables were in place, but not set. The tents were up, as were the game booths. She had already toured the gardens, which were in perfect shape. The morning of the party, the gardeners would give the area a once-over, tidying any wayward bushes, sweeping the paths and raking the leaves.

She compared the table layout with the master diagram on her clipboard and carefully counted. Exactly right, she thought when she finished. The decorations were in place, the lighting had been fixed so that no one had to suffer with a spotlight in his or her eyes. The stage had been pushed into the corner and the various bands and musical groups had been confirmed. Check, check, and triple check.

She walked toward the kitchens to go over the food one more time. She pushed open one of the swinging double doors and found most of the kitchen staff gathered around three large workstations. All the head chefs were there, as were their assistants.

Jerome looked up and saw her. "Katie!" he said with delight. "Always compulsively thorough." He pressed his hands to his chest. "Worry shortens the life."

"I worry so my clients don't have to. In my line of work, *compulsively thorough* means 'wildly successful'."

He nodded to one of the other chefs and moved toward her. "All right. I'll volunteer to go through the food with you before you even ask me," he said, taking her arm. "How's that?"

"Very nice of you. Most brilliant chefs are far more temperamental."

"I know. My goodness is a curse. People take advantage of me."

"And then you threaten them with a deboning knife." She glanced back at the crowd of kitchen workers. "What's going on here? You haven't booked another big event, have you? Jerome, there's not room for—"

He plucked a perfect strawberry from a tray and pressed it between her lips.

"Eat," he commanded. "And don't worry. There are no other parties scheduled until Sunday afternoon, and by then you'll be long gone. This tonight"—he motioned to the collection of people gathered around the work tables—"is our menu tasting. We're working on developing some new dishes for the hotel's fine dining room. I like to get opinions from all the staff before making the final decision."

"Okay."

"More than okay. We'll be so inspired by our tasting that for the next forty-eight hours, we'll work feverishly to make your party brilliant."

"It's getting a little deep in here, Jerome, and I'm wearing open-toed shoes."

He laughed, took her free hand in his, and kissed her fingers.

She followed him to the huge refrigerators. He opened several doors, showing her trays of meat waiting to be cut into the right size for grilling on skewers. Two more refrigerators contained the vegetables, as well as fruits for chocolate dipping. Against the far wall, seven-foot dollies held trays to deliver the various courses. In the pantry the chocolates from around the world were waiting to be cut into chunks suitable for melting, while several hundred fondue pots were stacked on more dollies.

"The wine has been pulled from the cellar," he said. "The hard liquor will be delivered in the morning." He cupped her chin, squeezed, then released her. "Fear not, bright angel. Nothing will go wrong. I promise to make your party perfect."

"I appreciate that," she told him. "I do my best to stay calm before big events, but this one is downright huge. I want to make it a success."

"We both have a lot on the line. I won't let you down, my darling girl." He grinned. "Now, is there any way I can convince you to join us for the tasting? I promise you, the food is amazing."

"No, thanks." She tapped her clipboard. "I have four million lists to make."

"Try to get some sleep in the next couple of days. You want to be beautiful for your client."

"I'll do my best. Thanks for everything."

"You're welcome."

She closed the cover on her clipboard and waved good-bye as she headed back for the kitchen. She made her way to her car. There was nothing more to be done tonight. In the morning there was a whole new to-do list, phone calls, and the beginning of the countdown. In the morning it would be less than thirty-six hours until show time.

Francesca entered the popular West Side eatery shortly after seven in the evening. In honor of her meeting with Jeff, she'd pulled out one of the only two nice outfits she owned, a sleeveless summery linen dress with a matching short jacket. Forty-five minutes and a very interesting conversation with a man named Earl at a survivalist-spy store in the San Fernando Valley had steered her toward the lightweight personal recorder she'd tucked into her purse. She'd pinned the tiny, voice-activated remote microphone to the neck of her dress, where it was concealed by the edge of the jacket.

Earl had promised three hours of recording time, given her tips on increasing clarity, and offered to help her put on the microphone. She'd refused the latter.

Now, as she made her way through the crowded bar, she tried to convince herself that this was just another one of her psychology experiments. Her entire purpose was to see how someone responded to her, based on appearance. But instead of dressing in a fat suit, or like the great tattooed lady, she was a slightly vampy version of herself.

She'd suffered through an entire day of rollers to get

her long hair to cascade in thick curls. Makeup accentu-
ated her green eyes, lip liner made her mouth look bigger,
and she'd enhanced her natural assets with a push-up bra.

All a disguise, she thought, trying not to feel sick to her
stomach. What had seemed like a great idea at the time,
was becoming more and more problematic. Had Katie
been right? Should she and Brenna have thought this
through more?

Before she could decide, she spotted Jeff at a table by the
window. He saw her as well, stood and waved. She waved
back and walked through the crowd.

She hadn't seen her brother-in-law since Christmas. He
was still pleasant-looking with sandy-colored hair and
pale blue eyes. The mustache was new, as was the absence
of a wedding band. Only a couple of inches taller than her
own five feet nine, Jeff wasn't a big guy. With her wearing
heels, they were the same height.

"Francesca," he said, sounding delighted. "I'm so
pleased you called."

She forced herself to take the hands he offered and
squeeze them. When he leaned close, she did the same and
let him kiss her cheek. The light contact made her skin
crawl.

"It's been way too long since I've seen you," she said,
sliding into the seat across from him and smiling. "Okay,
you and Brenna are splitting up, but after having you as a
part of the family for nine years, I didn't want to let you
walk away without saying something."

"My feelings exactly."

The waitress appeared. Francesca ordered white wine.
When they were alone, she smiled at Jeff. "How's business?"

"Great. Frantic, but I'm learning more every day. There

are amazing advances in cardiac medicine. The practice is one of the biggest on the West Side. All those lawyers and movie producers. Excellent insurance."

"It's important to get paid," she agreed.

His pale eyebrows rose slightly. "Was that a crack?"

No, but she wouldn't mind thwacking him over the head with a heavy book. "What? Oh, sorry." She smiled. "No. Of course not. You know me—I can't ever be subtle. Besides, I'm still a struggling grad student. I'm impressed by those who can make the big bucks." She leaned toward him. "You worked hard, Jeff. All those years of study and the long hours. You deserve your success."

He relaxed and patted her hand. "Thanks. I'm glad you understand. I figured the entire family would be talking about hiring someone to rub me out."

"My grandfather maybe, but the rest of us understand."

"Really?"

"Sure. I mean, I really love my sister, but she's not the easiest person in the world to get along with." Francesca gave a laugh. "I shared a room with her for eighteen years. I know what I'm talking about."

The waitress appeared with her wine, which was really lucky because Francesca was close to gagging. She'd always liked Jeff, but those feelings had faded. Now she thought he was smarmy and self-important.

She sipped her wine, then stared deeply into his eyes. "Are you doing okay?"

"Sure."

"No. I mean . . . really. I've been worried about you."

Jeff's pale eyes brightened. "So you haven't written me off?"

"Of course not. We've always had a special relationship." She swallowed hard. "Like brother and sister."

She carefully put her hand back on the table, palm down. Jeff covered it with his. She managed not to jerk away.

"More than that," he said.

She wanted to gag. She wanted to throw her drink in his face. Instead she sighed softly.

"So how's your love life?" he asked.

"Pathetic." At least that much was true. "Between school and teaching and studying, I don't get out much. That's why I'm really excited you wanted to see me tonight."

His thumb moved across the back of her hand. "You should come down to L.A. more often. We could hang out."

"I wouldn't want to get in the way."

"You could never do that." He stared at her. "Francesca, you're so beautiful. I might have been married to Brenna, but that didn't stop me from looking."

Oh, man. She could feel his slime oozing across the table. Blech. This was disgusting. She swallowed the need to spit, and smiled instead. "At me? But I'm so skinny and awkward. Brenna was always the Earth Mother. Those damn curves of hers. I wanted what she had."

"You're perfect."

Francesca wished she could fake a blush, but she didn't know how. Instead she straightened and pulled her hand free. "Jeff, I heard you're seeing someone. I'm not the kind of woman who gets involved with taken guys."

"I'm not taken," he said easily.

"But Brenna said there was someone else."

He shrugged. "I date. There's no one special in my life."

She happened to know he was living with the bimbo, but she wasn't about to let him know.

"Oh. Wow. That's . . . interesting."

"Is it?"

She heard the hook snap as he took the bait. "Jeff, come on. Of course it's interesting. After nine years of watching you with my sister, this is exactly what I wanted to hear. You're my fantasy."

For a second she thought she might have gone too far, but after sucking in a breath, Jeff grinned. The idiot.

"You're my fantasy, too," he admitted. "I've been waiting for years for you to tell me you wanted me, too. Come on. Let's go get a hotel room. I want to fuck your brains out for the next three days."

Bingo. Francesca shook her head. "No, thanks. Amazingly enough, I'm going to have to turn down that very romantic offer." She picked up her purse and started to slide out of the booth.

Jeff looked confused. "What are you doing?"

"Leaving. I have what I came for."

"I don't understand."

"Yes, I know." Careful not to disturb the tape recorder in her purse, she pulled a second one out of her pocket. Earl had suggested the duplicate. They had made her feel twice as secure.

She punched the rewind button for a couple of seconds, then shifted to Play. Jeff's voice was tinny but clearly audible.

"I date. There's no one special in my life."

"The woman you live with will probably find that really fascinating," Francesca said. "Although I'm guessing the 'fuck your brains out' remark is going to be the real kicker."

Jeff turned pale. "What the hell are you doing?"

"Playing dirty. Back off on the winery, or the bimbo gets a copy of the tape. Clear enough?"

Jeff swore, then lunged for her. Francesca might have

only made it to a green belt, but she knew enough to side-step him and turn gracefully while he tumbled to the ground. In the process he bumped several patrons who were trying to balance their drinks in the crowded bar area. There were cries of "Watch out!" and "What the hell are you doing?"

While a tall, burly guy who looked very unhappy and very wet grabbed Jeff by his shirt, Francesca made her way to the exit.

She'd given the valet an extra twenty to keep her truck handy. Now she climbed into the cab and headed for the freeway. Ten minutes later she was driving north, back for home. Mission accomplished. The winery was safe, Brenna could go after Jeff for repayment of her effort to put him through school, and Francesca had done her good deed for the week. She was thrilled . . . and fighting the need to throw up.

"I'm sorry," David said miserably.

Mia paced the length of her living room. It was late—after midnight—and they'd been at this for hours.

"It didn't mean anything," he told her for the hundredth time.

Forty-eight hours after denying his relationship with Julie, David had showed up on Mia's doorstep and come clean. Claiming it was little more than prewedding jitters, he'd confessed to hanging out with her, some kissing, and nothing else. Mia had yet to decide if she believed him.

"It meant something to me," Mia told him. "You didn't just cheat, you were sloppy, you publicly humiliated me, and then you lied. In the face of all that, 'I'm sorry' seems feeble."

She continued to pace. As she walked past him, he reached out and grabbed her. "Mia, you've got to forgive me."

"Why?" She glared at him. "Give me one good reason."

"Because you still love me."

She did—because she was a fool. She still loved him and wanted to marry him. She wanted to move to Washington and explore the city with him. She wanted to get her graduate degree, a great job with the State Department, and have David in her life. She had a plan, and he was as much a part of it as anything else.

"Why would I ever trust you again?" she asked.

He hung his head. "I don't know. How do I earn that back?"

How did he? Was it possible? Could something broken and shattered be put whole again?

He stepped close and gathered her against him. "Don't send me away," he begged. "I'm sorry. I love you. I'll do anything."

She believed him. At that moment he would do anything. But what about in a few weeks, or a year? What about the next time things got difficult? Would he work it out or would he run?

"Are you really sure you want to marry me?" she asked.

He stared deeply into her eyes. "I've never been so sure of anything in my life. You're my world, Mia. Only you."

He picked her up and she let him . . . mostly because being in David's arms was where she belonged. Because she loved him. Because it seemed that Marcelli women were destined to make fools of themselves over the men they cared about.

• • •

The phone rang shortly before nine the next morning. Katie munched on toast while she reviewed her to-do list. There were exactly twenty-seven items, which should take her about six hours. That left plenty of time for last-minute things she might have forgotten. She had already had a forty-minute conversation with one of her staff, and a conference call with three others.

"Hello," she said, her attention mostly on her list.

"Katie?"

She froze. There was something horrible about the voice. Familiar, but horrible. Apprehension crawled up her spine, leaving her suddenly very, very cold.

"Yes, this is Katie Marcelli."

"It's Jerome."

Her throat closed. "Jerome? What's wrong? You sound awful."

In the background she could hear voices, then a low groan.

"Katie, I'm so sorry." Jerome sucked in a breath. "I don't know, maybe it was the fish. Something."

Her tight throat made it difficult to talk. "What are you saying?"

He swore softly. "We're all sick. The entire kitchen staff has food poisoning. They've just admitted me into the hospital. All the chefs are here. They're going to keep us at least a couple of days. There's some concern that we've ingested parasites. We should all be fine, but we won't be back to work for nearly a week."

The panic grew and her hands began to sweat. Fish? There wasn't any fish on her menu. "What are you talking about?"

"We had the tasting dinner last night," he said weakly. "Remember? For the new restaurant menu. I'm sorry,

Katie. There's no kitchen staff. At least not at the hotel. They're all here, or at other hospitals."

He continued talking, but she wasn't listening. No kitchen staff? None? She had a party to put on in less than thirty-six hours. Over two thousand really well-dressed people were going to be expecting a fancy meal and fine service and what the hell was she going to do?

18

～

"Zach, you have a call on line three," Dora said. "It's Katie."

"Got it." Zach punched the Off button for the intercom, then picked up the receiver and leaned back in his chair. "Hey, gorgeous," he said with a smile. "Thirty-three hours and counting. Are you nervous?"

He'd expected a laughing response from Katie, or a smart crack. What he got was silence.

"Katie?"

"I'm here. Do you have a second?"

"Sure." Something in her voice made him sit up straight and hold on to the phone a little tighter. "What's up?"

"There's been an unexpected problem," she said, her words more clipped than usual. "Last night the entire hotel kitchen staff had a tasting for the new menu for the hotel's fine dining room." She paused and cleared her throat. "Unfortunately they seemed to have cooked up some bad fish. Most of the kitchen staff is in the hospital, including Jerome."

Zach opened his mouth to respond, but couldn't think of a single thing to say.

"I've already spoken with the hotel manager along with the events manager," she continued. "They're willing to do whatever it takes to honor our contract with them. Outside staff can be brought in. Between that and my own staff, I'm reasonably confident that everything can be worked out in time. However, under the circumstances, I can't guarantee that it will be perfect."

He exhaled heavily. "I don't know what to say."

"Me, either," she admitted. "There's a clause in our contract with the hotel that allows us to pull out at the last minute when they have a disaster like this. They wouldn't be happy with that decision, but they can't stop us. They would return all moneys paid to date. We would have the option of rescheduling there or at another location in the future. I've already contacted a temp agency. I can have a phone bank up in less than two hours. Anyone we can't reach by phone will be visited in person. The hotel will cover that cost. Also, they'll pay for dinner at a nearby restaurant for anyone who slips through the cracks and shows up anyway."

He couldn't believe what he was hearing. "Everyone is sick?"

"Yes. Actually Jerome sounded awful. He's in the emergency room right now, but we're keeping in touch by phone."

Zach swore under his breath. He glanced at his watch. It was nine-fifty. "When did you find out about this?"

"At nine."

"This morning?"

"Of course. I got right to work on the problem."

"No kidding."

Katie had put together a rescue operation with options in less than fifty minutes. Why was he surprised? She gave a hundred and ten percent.

"What do you want to do?" he asked.

"I don't know," she admitted. "I didn't think about that. You're the client."

"The party is as much yours as it is the firm's. We're all in this together. What does your gut say we should do? Can you pull it off?"

"I can get all the elements together," she said slowly. "Will it be what it would have been? I'm not sure. Will anyone know there was a problem?" She hesitated. "Can I get back to you on those odds?"

"That was 'Katie, the owner of Organization Central's' answer. Now give me the 'Katie, the person's' response. What can I do to make this situation easier for you? Do you want to cancel or bluff?"

She sighed. "Oh, Zach, it's a nightmare. I can't believe Jerome and his staff got sick less than two days before the party. It's not fair."

"Agreed. Tell me what you want."

He heard her writing on a piece of paper, then she cleared her throat. "Let's go for it."

He tilted his head to cradle the phone between his ear and his shoulder. "That's my vote, too. No one is going to want the hassle of rescheduling. Plus canceling at this late date may make the firm look flaky. Not exactly the image we want when we're raising money for charity. It's not going to help you, either. Let's move forward and make it work. If there's a problem, I'll take responsibility."

"Because you hired me, right?" She didn't wait for an answer. "If something goes wrong, the responsibility is mine, Zach. I'm the one who agreed to plan the party. While it's not my fault the entire kitchen staff is sick, the buck stops with me."

He figured they could argue that point if it became a problem.

"I have every confidence in you," he said.

"Thanks."

"Is there anything I can do to help?"

She laughed, although the sound was more strangled than humorous. "How are you in the kitchen?"

"I'm a fast learner." He flipped through his calendar. "I'm in court most of today, but I'll clear tomorrow. How's that?"

"Whatever you can give me would be great."

When this was over, they were going to have to lock her up in a nuthouse, Katie thought later that afternoon. Or she would have a heart attack, right there in the middle of the kitchen.

She didn't think her heart had stopped pounding since she'd received Jerome's phone call earlier. There were fourteen thousand details to take care of, not the least of which was the reality of getting a kitchen staff in place in time to prepare the food for the dinner tomorrow.

Her cell phone rang again.

"Yes," she said, automatically reaching for the pad of paper she kept with her at all times.

"Hey."

"Jerome!" The man sounded as if he'd spent most of the day barfing his guts up . . . which he probably had. "Tell me you've got news."

"I have a grill chef for you. Madison. Just Madison. No last name."

"Like Madonna?"

"Exactly. She's great, and she owes me." He gave her a

number. "If she gives you any trouble, just tell her I said to mention Barbados."

Katie scribbled it all down. Great. Code words. She was beginning to feel as if she were living in a very bad spy movie. All she would need next was a herd of elephants trampling through the kitchen.

"Okay," she said. "I've checked the inventory, like you said. Everything is here."

"You've got to get people cutting up the meat and vegetables. It takes time. Then prepare the marinade. Beef in tonight. Chicken in tomorrow. Shrimp goes in an hour before cooking. The vegetables have their own marinade schedule."

She dutifully wrote down everything he said. As the conversation progressed, his voice got weaker and weaker. Finally she took pity on him.

"This is enough for now," she said. "Give me a couple of hours and I'll call you back."

"Okay. We'll have to talk about the chocolate next. You can't just throw it in a pot over an open flame and expect it to be wonderful. I had plans for the chocolate." There was a gagging sound. "I have to go throw up."

The phone disconnected before she could say anything.

Katie tried not to think about Jerome's afternoon activities. As she organized her notes, her phone rang again.

"It's your favorite florist," a voice said cheerily. "The roses were trés ugly, so I want to make some changes. Same cost, but you'll have to approve things. I'm sending a sample over right now. Is that okay?"

Before she could answer, the events manager walked into the kitchen.

"We've set the first table. Want to take a look, Katie?"

She motioned for him to give her a second, then finished her phone call. A quick glance at her watch told her that the booths were being set up and that she'd promised to stop by and check on that. There were also the last-minute prizes to be picked up.

She already had her staff running in forty-seven directions. Taking on the party was one thing, but filling in for the kitchen staff—especially Jerome, who coordinated everything about the food—was another.

"I need a signature for the liquor delivery," a voice called from the doorway.

Katie looked at the uniformed man. "Did anyone go over the inventory with you?"

"No. Were they supposed to?"

She had an overwhelming urge to start pulling out her hair. Instead she said, "Yes. Give me two minutes. I'll be there to go over it with you." Then she looked at her cell phone.

She was out of options and out of time. Under normal circumstances, she wouldn't think twice. But she'd been disowned from the family, and to the best of her knowledge, no one was speaking to her.

Still, she punched the buttons on her cell phone and listened to the ringing.

"Hello."

"Hi, Mom, it's me. I'm in trouble and I really need help."

Zach arrived at the hotel shortly after six the morning of the fund-raiser. He'd tried to get Katie several times the previous evening, but she hadn't been home. By the time he'd realized she was staying at the hotel and that he should try her on her cell, it had been too late. If she was getting any sleep at all, he didn't want to wake her.

He headed for the front desk and got directions to the kitchen. He half expected to find the place deserted, but even before he pushed open the door marked EMPLOYEES ONLY he heard the pounding of loud music and the sound of voices.

He wandered into organized madness. Several people were slicing vegetables. A tall Amazon-like woman in a chef's hat dropped thousands of wooden skewers in a vat of water.

"Zach! Shouldn't you still be asleep?"

He turned toward the voice and was amazed to see Grandma Tessa standing in front of a six-burner stove, stirring a giant pot.

"What are you doing here?" he asked. "I didn't think anyone was speaking to Katie."

She smiled and shrugged. "We were angry, now we're not."

Just like that? "What changed your mind?"

"Katie needed help. Now come say hello properly."

Still considering what she had said, he crossed to her, bracing himself for the hug, kiss, and cheek-pinch greeting she'd turned into an art form. Grandma Tessa didn't disappoint.

As he rubbed the welt she'd left on his skin, he leaned over to get a peek at what was in the pot.

"Ravioli," she announced, then waved at the rest of the kitchen. "All of this is fine, but when Katie told me what had happened, I knew I had to bring pasta. First I cook it in the water, then later, I fry it." She kissed the tips of her fingers. "Delicioso."

He saw dozens of bags of frozen ravioli lined up on the counter behind her. "You didn't just make this last night, did you?"

"No." She laughed. "I keep it frozen, for company. There's marinara sauce, too. Sometimes we have a party."

There was probably enough ravioli to feed an army. "Some party," he said. "Invite me next time."

She grinned. "You're family. You're always invited."

Family. Grandpa Lorenzo had been furious. The rest of them had stood with him. Was all that over because Katie had asked for help?

He continued to walk through the kitchen. The CD playing changed to an old Beatles album. After seeing Grandma Tessa, he wasn't surprised to find Grammy M and Brenna cutting up chocolate.

"Like I need to be near something fattening," Brenna grumbled when she saw him. "I wanted to work on the salad, but no."

He smiled. "Everyone is speaking now?" he asked.

Grammy M nodded, but Brenna frowned.

"I was wrong," she said. "I already apologized to Katie. Tricking Jeff was my own business. I shouldn't have dragged Francesca into it. Or Katie."

Zach thought about Katie's pain and tears. "Did you tell her that? She was really upset."

Brenna raised her eyebrows. "Yes, I did. I've apologized and we're fine now. Sisters fight and then we make up. Oh." She wiped her hands on a dishcloth, then pulled open several drawers until she found the one containing her purse. She dug around, then held up a small audiotape.

"Catch," she said as she threw it to him. "I know, you can't be party to anything illegal. So I'm not telling you what's on that tape. Just keep it safe."

He pocketed the small reel. "Did Francesca get what you needed?"

Brenna nodded. "The good news is Jeff isn't coming after

the winery anymore. That should make your job easier."

"I don't care about easy—I want to win."

"My kind of guy." Brenna nodded in the direction of several giant refrigerators. "The general is over there."

Zach turned and saw Katie talking with some kitchen workers. Before he could get to her, he saw Colleen and Marco mixing up huge batches of marinade and Mia hovering over a jumbo container of rice.

He crossed to Mia. "You're up early."

The teenager yawned. "Actually I haven't been to bed. Once I got Katie's call, I couldn't sleep, so I just came over here." She stirred the pot. "Two thousand people eat a lot of rice."

He watched her add a cup of some kind of spice.

"I didn't know you could cook."

She grinned. "I can't, but how hard could rice be, right? And Madison is helping me, even though she's a grill chef and thinks that cooking rice is way below her." She lowered her voice. "She only works with meat stuff. She told me."

"Okay."

As Madison looked big enough and tough enough to take anyone in the room, Zach figured he wasn't going to argue with her.

"So the whole family's here," he said.

"Yup. Well, except for Grandpa Lorenzo. He's still crabby. And Francesca. Katie left a message for her, but she has yet to turn up."

"Is David coming?"

Mia poured another cup of spices into the simmering rice. "I don't know. I didn't call him. He's really busy with school and stuff."

That didn't sound right, Zach thought. But before he

could pursue the matter, Katie saw him and came over.

She wore jeans and a tank top that had an assortment of interesting stains. A scarf covered her hair, and there wasn't a speck of makeup on her face. She obviously hadn't slept or showered.

Funny, he thought as a strange *twang* bumped up against his heart. She'd never looked more beautiful.

"What are you doing up so early?" she asked.

"I'm here to help."

Her lips curved up in a weary smile. "I'm too desperate to turn you down. Do you want to cut up vegetables or get involved with the chocolate?"

"I'll do veggies."

He took his place in the kitchen. Madison gave him a mean-looking knife and a few minutes of instruction on the proper way to cut up vegetables. He hadn't known there was a wrong way. While John Lennon serenaded them, he worked his way through enough onions to make a football team sob and then started in on eggplants. Amazingly, they were even more weird-looking on the inside.

Katie moved through the kitchen like a general inspecting troops. She stepped in when there was a problem and took continual calls on her cell phone. She never got frustrated, never snapped at anyone, never lost her cool. His admiration clicked up a couple of notches and his attraction . . . well, it had always been fairly high.

At eight-fifteen Dora arrived with breakfast for everyone. "Bagels, cream cheese, coffee, and fruit salad," she called as she walked into the kitchen followed by two of the clerks from the law firm. "I figured you'd all be so busy that you'd forget to eat."

Grateful sighs competed with the music. Zach headed toward his secretary, but Katie beat him to it.

"You're a lifesaver," she said, taking a bag of bagels and passing it around. "We're surrounded by food and there's nothing for breakfast."

"We could have had ravioli," Zach teased.

Katie swatted at him. "That's for tonight. Don't you know all the best parties have grilled delicacies and pasta?"

There was a faint edge of panic to her voice. Zach moved close and put his arm around her. "You're doing great," he breathed in her ear. "The party will go off without a hitch. Just keep telling yourself that by this time tomorrow, it will all be over."

Before she could respond, the main kitchen doors opened again. A tall, overweight dark-haired woman entered. She carried a small paper bag, which she waved around.

"Sorry I'm late," she said. "I didn't check for messages. Sorry, Katie. But I brought my garnish knives. What do you want me to do?"

The CD player chose that moment to switch to a different disk, so the kitchen went silent. Everyone stared at the intruder.

The woman stared back.

"Katie!" she said impatiently. "It's me. I was already dressed for an experiment when I played my messages."

Katie gasped. "Francesca?"

Zach stared. Francesca? Katie's sister? Katie's pretty, *skinny* sister?

"It's a fat suit," Brenna said, coming up and grabbing a bagel. "She can unzip the extra fat. Doesn't that just make you want to slap her?"

Francesca ignored her. "I'm here to do garnishes."

Katie shook her head. "Okay. Great. I don't care what

you look like. You're a lifesaver. We need as many garnishes as you can make. Let me get you a workstation."

Zach watched them walk away. *Francesca?*

Brenna leaned close. "She took this garnish-making class. Frankly, I think she's taken every craft class known to mankind. I mean, the woman can tat lace."

Zach didn't know what that was, but then, he didn't want to. He stared at her unflattering slacks and shirt, and the brunette wig that should have been tossed a couple of years ago, then remembered Francesca showing up covered in tattoos. Why would a normal person do things like that?

"There's something wrong with her," Zach said before he could stop himself.

Brenna handed him a bagel. "You know—I've been thinking that same thing for years."

The first guests arrived shortly before seven. Katie had already spent the previous hour touring the gardens and ballrooms and seeing to final preparations. The serving staff had shown up promptly at four, and the musicians had followed at five-thirty. Now several small combos played in different corners and alcoves, while uniformed servers offered champagne, appetizers, and explained the evening's menu.

Despite her need to check everything one last time, Katie had abandoned her clipboard and briefcase. Instead she kept a mental list, ticking off twinkle lights, the floral arrangements, and individual grills being fired up.

Maybe, just maybe, this was all going to work out. For the first time since nine yesterday morning, she allowed herself to relax a little.

She heard a footstep on the stone path, but before she could turn, someone lightly cupped her bare upper arms and planted a kiss on the back of her neck.

Shivers danced down her spine. She smiled as Zach slipped an arm around her and drew her close.

"I've been looking all over for you," he said, giving her a quick once-over. "For someone who is supposed to be my date, you've been avoiding me."

"Not at all. I told you I had to work."

He smiled. "And I told you I like to watch." He winked. "But that's for later."

He stepped back and looked her over. "You're beautiful. Not that I'm surprised. You do the transition from 'up-wardly-mobile professional' to 'stunning' very well."

"Thank you." She eyed his tailored black tux. "You look very nice yourself. Traditional, yet elegant."

"I try."

She allowed herself to lean against him for a couple of seconds. Weariness dogged her, but she refused to give in. Not until the party was over. Then she could collapse for a few days and attempt to figure out how she'd made it all come together. Assuming it did.

"I've just come from the front of the hotel," he said, drawing her toward one of the bars set up under a large tree. "There are limos lined up around the block."

She touched a hand to her stomach. "I know that's really good, but it doesn't help me not be nervous."

"You're doing great. No one ever needs to know there was any kind of a glitch."

"Uh-huh." She ordered a glass of club soda. "This is when I tell you that Grandma Tessa insisted on *serving* her fried ravioli. She didn't want to trust it to anyone else. Even as we speak she's holding court in one of the tents. Now, if that doesn't make you quiver with fear, you're far stronger than I am."

"She'll be fine."

"I hope so."

He led her toward the main ballroom. "What's the worst that could happen?"

"Don't ask," she told him. "I don't even want to think about it."

They chatted for a few minutes before Zach saw some clients he needed to speak to. Katie excused herself so she could check on the details.

As she headed for the kitchen, she caught sight of herself in one of the ballroom mirrors. Her sleeveless black dress was dressy enough to allow her to fit in, yet not so fancy that she stood out. With the help of seventeen bobby pins and enough hairspray to lacquer a battle cruiser, she'd managed to secure her hair in an upswept style that looked elegant and stayed out of the way. She had applied two layers of concealer to hide the dark circles that came from not having slept in over thirty-six hours.

Across the room she spotted her parents chatting with a TV sitcom star and his wife. Somewhere in the growing crowd Francesca was probably breaking hearts (assuming she'd chosen to dress like herself for once) and Brenna would be tasting the wine Katie had ordered. While Zach had extended an invitation to her entire family, she'd given them strict orders to stay out of the upscale party. No fishing for diamond bracelets.

In the kitchen she found controlled chaos. Rolling carts filled with trays were moved into position. As she watched, members of the serving staff lined up to take them to the various grilling stations. Mia was already manning one of the dessert tents, where she would no doubt charm everyone into dipping with a smile.

She crossed her fingers and gave a little prayer that somehow disaster had been averted.

Three hours later the party seemed to be doing well. Katie cruised through the smaller ballroom and watched CEOs and multimillionaires bob for baubles or try a ring-toss for the chance at a ski trip. She calculated how many prizes were left, then figured there would be enough for an impromptu auction later.

Zach caught up with her by the doorway.

"How are you doing?" he asked.

"Good." She wasn't going to mention the fact that while her shoes were stylish, they hadn't been designed for anything close to comfort. After tonight she would probably walk with a limp for the rest of her life, but at least she knew her ankles looked slender.

"There's something you have to see," he said, taking her arm and leading her out into the garden.

"Should I be nervous?" she asked.

"That's up to you."

He led her toward the bright blue tent illuminated by several spotlights. Her heart sank. "What's she doing?"

Zach laughed. "Being wonderful."

Katie appreciated the kind words, but she wasn't convinced. Sure enough as they entered the tent, she heard Grandma Tessa demanding,

"So, young man, what do you do for a living?"

The "young man" in question had to be pushing fifty and wore a suit that cost close to the GNP of Nebraska. Katie winced.

Her wince turned into a moan when the "young man" answered, "I run a movie studio."

Grandma Tessa's gaze narrowed. Katie braced herself to perform some kind of intervention when her grandmother went off on a tirade on R-rated movies with too much sex and bad language.

Instead she leaned across the counter and smiled. "So tell me. Why aren't there any stars like Sophia Loren anymore? She is such a beauty, even now. These kids today—they're nothing like her."

The studio executive slid onto a stool in front of the counter and nodded earnestly. "I agree. The stars from the old days had something really special."

Grandma Tessa used a pair of tongs to slide several fried raviolis onto a plate, then scooped up marinara sauce into a small bowl. She handed the man both.

"I remember the first time I saw her in a movie. Or Cary Grant. He was really something. Not Italian, of course, but still a very nice-looking man."

Zach drew Katie back out of the tent. "She's been doing that all night," he murmured in her ear. "It doesn't matter if the guests are part of the cleaning staff or billionaires. She has something to say and they love her. It gets better over here."

They walked toward one of the dessert tents. Katie had nearly relaxed when a very loud, very drunk-sounding chorus of "Irish Rover" drifted through the night. She swallowed hard.

"Grammy M's been serving whiskey, hasn't she?" she asked in a whisper, already knowing the answer.

"For at least the last hour." Zach grinned. "Everyone's plastered. They're having a terrific time."

Before she could figure out what she wanted to do, Zach led her away. "There's someone who wants to meet you," he said.

"I'm not sure I can take any more."

Which was true. The combination of no sleep and tremendous stress was catching up with her. Even as they walked down one of the twinkle-light-lit paths, she could feel her brain dissolving.

"Just over here," he said.

They entered one of the private spaces created by trimmed hedges and trees. Several couples sat around a large table. When Zach and Katie appeared, a man stood, then turned to help his very pregnant wife to her feet.

"Hello," the woman said as she waddled over. "You must be Katie. I'm Sara." She patted her stomach. "As you can tell, I wasn't faking the whole baby thing to get out of doing the work."

Katie may have murmured a greeting, but she couldn't remember exactly what. The woman looked pregnant enough to be having an entire basketball team. Were there really only two babies in there?

John shook her head. "Wonderful job," he said. "Simply wonderful. We've heard nothing but compliments."

"It's true," Sara said. "I loved all the grilled food and that fried ravioli. I don't want to think about the calories, but you must get me the recipe. It was divine."

She nodded at her husband, who led Zach away. Sara slipped her arm through Katie's and drew her close. "I was wondering," she said confidentially. "Do you arrange smaller events? John and I would like to host a couple's shower for the babies, and I would very much like you to plan it."

19

The last guest left shortly before two, and the staff had cleared out by two forty-five. Katie sat at a table by the kitchen door and punched numbers into her calculator. The problem was she was almost too tired to see the answer. She squinted, then scribbled down a number.

It looked way too large, so she did the math again. The results didn't change. If her weary eyes were reading things correctly, the fund-raiser had exceeded expectation by more than thirty percent.

"Wow," she said, exhausted but pleased. She had a feeling that the auction for the extra prizes might have been what pushed them over the edge. Well, the auction taking place *after* Grammy M did her best to get everyone drunk hadn't hurt, either.

To cap off the evening, she had fourteen business cards in her small but tasteful satin clutch. She'd been asked about planning everything from a wedding to a restaurant grand opening. Organization Central had arrived in the big league.

She allowed herself a brief fantasy about a larger staff, new quarters, and an on-site day-care center when she realized her feet didn't just hurt, they throbbed. She shifted so she could ease off her shoes. Unfortunately the pain didn't go away, which wasn't a surprise. What she needed was to get to her car and drive home. Once there she could collapse.

Of course, that meant actually walking out of the hotel, not something she wanted to do. But before she could whip herself into a frenzy and try to move, Zach stepped into the ballroom and headed toward her.

"Do you ever plan on leaving?" he asked.

"Sure. Right now." She handed him the paper with her scrawled figures. "If I can still add correctly, the fund-raiser was a success."

"I already know it was. Come on."

He collected her papers, her shoes, and her purse, then pulled her to her feet. She winced and they headed for the door.

"You're too tired to drive," he said. "I'll take you home. We'll deal with getting your car tomorrow."

"Okay," she murmured, because it was too much trouble to argue. "It was really nice of the hotel manager to put up my family for the night."

"I'm sure he's going to regret it. Last I saw, he and Granny M were drinking in the bar. I suspect come morning, he's going to wish he was dead, while Grammy M will chuckle all the way home."

Katie smiled at the visual. "I do have a great family."

"Yes, you do." He glanced at her. "They came through for you."

"I know."

"Were you surprised?"

She thought about the phone call she'd made and that her mother hadn't hesitated. "When I was dialing the number, I would have told you I was terrified. But the second I heard my mother's voice, I knew she'd do anything she could. They're my family." She glanced at Zach. "Like you and David are family."

"Only yours is louder."

They made it to the front of the hotel, where the valet had Zach's car waiting. Katie climbed inside, secured the seat belt, then curled up in the seat and rested her head against the window.

"I think the party was really good," she said sleepily. "I did a good job."

Zach laughed as he started the car. "I agree. I'm happy to write you any recommendation you'd like."

"Okay." She sighed. "I'd never done a job that big before. I was a little scared, but then I got the hang of it. But when Jerome called me, I thought I was going to die. I could see my whole career going up in flames."

"You don't have to worry about that now."

"I guess not."

She didn't know if they continued talking, nor could she remember what was said if they had. One minute they'd been pulling out of the hotel; the next they were turning into her driveway.

Before she could open her door herself (when exactly had door handles gotten so tricky?), Zach came around and helped her out. But instead of letting her walk to the front door, he picked her up and carried her.

The combination of floating and sleepiness made her head spin. Katie wrapped her arms around his neck and breathed in the scent of him. The man was clever enough to have fished her key out of her purse, because the door opened without her having to do anything.

She smiled to herself. She liked that Zach was clever. She liked many things about him. She—

"Thank you," he said as he bumped the front door closed with his hip, then slowly lowered her to the floor.

"What?"

"You said I'm clever."

She blinked. "I didn't actually say all that aloud, did I?"

"I don't know what all you were thinking, but you mentioned that I was clever and that you like that . . . along with other things. Care to talk about specifics?"

She chuckled. "Not even for money."

"But I like it when you compliment me."

"That's because you're the center of your own universe."

"Absolutely. Yet another of my charming features."

"Charming? You?"

"You adore me."

She was saved from having to respond by his kiss. A good thing, because she did adore him. How could she not?

He'd turned out to be a whole lot more than just a pretty face. He wasn't just smart, successful, and a great father. He was also warm and caring. Under that cool sharkskin beat the heart of a genuine nice guy, although Zach would be furious if he knew she thought that.

Whatever else happened, she would always remember how he'd stood up to her family for her, how he'd been there afterward. How he'd cared about her.

The kiss deepened and all rational thought fled. Her exhaustion faded, as if it had never been, leaving behind only growing desire. She curled her fingers against his head, feeling the cool silk of his hair. Their heartbeats seemed to be pounding in a rhythm of sensual desire. Her breasts swelled, and between her legs she felt the telltale ache of liquid need.

All this and he hadn't even made it to first base. She had a feeling that if the man did something wild like touch her bare skin, she might actually start to unravel.

"Katie," he murmured, then licked her lower lip.

He eased lower, nibbling his way to her jawline, then moving toward her ear. He licked the sensitive flesh under her lobe, which made her cling hard and forget how to breathe.

He traced the outside of her ear, which both tickled and delighted, then returned to her mouth, where he entered without warning. He claimed her with deep, passionate kisses that empowered her into responding in kind. She circled his tongue with hers and followed his retreat to claim him.

Somewhere along the way she remembered to breathe again, because when he broke the kiss, she found herself panting.

Tension filled her. Every place they pressed together made her want more. She felt the hardness of his erection and longed to slip her hand between them so she could touch him. She wanted to be naked, in bed, making love. She wanted the night to never end.

"So," he said, cupping her face in his hands and staring at her with his deep, dark blue eyes. "This is where I stop so you can tell me you're too tired?"

She kept her gaze on him. "I'm not wearing any underwear."

Instantly his pupils dilated and his breath caught in his throat.

"Just checking," she said casually, pulling free of his embrace and heading for her bedroom. "Actually I *am* wearing underwear, but I trust you'll know what to do with it."

• • •

Katie rolled over and blinked at the clock. Her eyes focused, but her brain was a little more reluctant to believe. One-thirty?

She glanced at the window, only to see bright sunshine. She'd slept until one-thirty in the afternoon?

She flopped on her back and stared at the ceiling. Considering she didn't get to sleep until close to three, she was actually still pretty tired. But in a good way. In a talk-about-a-couple-of-hours-of-incredible-lovemaking kind of way.

A smile tugged on her mouth. She turned over and placed her hand on the empty side of the bed, where Zach had been. His body heat had long since faded from the sheets, but his scent lingered. She glanced at his pillow and saw a piece of paper there. She grabbed it and quickly read.

"Hey, gorgeous. You needed the rest, so I didn't want to wake you when I snuck out this morning. Call me at the office when you wake up. Thanks for last night. I'm going to have a hell of a time concentrating today. Instead of clients, I'll be thinking about you."

She laughed softly, contentment filling her. Back when she'd first met Zach, she'd thought he was a player. A heartless, egocentric, all-around slimy guy. She couldn't have been more wrong about him.

He was everything she'd ever wanted. He was—

Katie sat up and gasped. Everything she'd ever wanted? As in . . . as in . . . She flopped back on the bed and pulled the covers up over her head. No way. She could not possibly have fallen in love with Zach. It was impossible. It was crazy.

She was the closet romantic who had once kissed a frog

in the hopes of attracting a prince on a white horse. She still had the very first Valentine she'd ever received from a boy. She was hearts and flowers and Zach was anything but.

Except when her entire family had turned their collective back on her, he'd been there for her. She might not agree with his tactics, but he was determined to keep his son from making what he saw as a mistake. He was ruthless, yes, but also giving and kind and holy shit, she had it bad.

All these years of waiting for "the one." The right guy. The man who made her hear bells. Last night she'd heard at least a tinkle or two.

Katie pushed down the covers and studied the note. She had to call him and she certainly wasn't going to say anything. What was there to say? "Hi Zach. Last night was great, by the way, I'm in love with you." Yeah, right. Hardly a well-conceived plan.

She would say nothing, she told herself. She would act completely normal and keep her personal information to herself.

She supposed a case could be made for telling him the truth and giving him the chance to respond in kind. That was probably really mature. Except she wasn't feeling especially grown-up and strong right now.

Four months ago she would have said that Zach Stryker had the emotional attention span of a gnat, that he wasn't interested in anyone but himself, and that she would never fall for a guy like him. She'd been wrong on every count. But was she wrong about him wanting what she wanted? Could the cynical divorce lawyer ever find a way to believe in happily-ever-after, marriage, and kids? Was she more to him than just a flavor of the week, or would he walk away from her the way he'd walked away from everyone else?

Too many questions, she thought, and not an answer in sight.

After sitting up, she pulled on her robe and glanced back at his note. She rubbed her finger over his signature, then reached for the phone.

Dora picked up on the first ring. "Zach Stryker's office."

"Hi, Dora. It's Katie."

"Hi! How are you doing? You won't believe what's happening here. The phones are going crazy. Everybody's calling. They loved the party and the food and your grandmothers. *In Style* magazine wants to get the ravioli recipe for a spread they're doing. The partners are thrilled about the proceeds, and I've been fielding calls from dozens of people who are trying to get in touch with you so you can plan their next event."

Katie's head spun. "I can't believe it."

"You'd better start. I think you're going to need a bigger staff. So, is working for an event planner more interesting than working for a lawyer?"

Katie laughed. "Zach would kill me if I stole you away."

"Just between you and me, I wouldn't leave, but I may hint a bit. Just to keep him humble." Dora chuckled. "Speaking of His Nibs, he's waiting for your call. I'll put you through."

"Thanks."

There was a click, then Zach came on the phone.

"So you're finally up?"

"Sort of. I'm awake, but still tired."

"It'll take you a couple of days to get back to normal." His voice lowered a little. "How are you feeling?"

"Good." She smiled. "Great. I got your note."

"I didn't want to just head out without saying something, but I hated to wake you. We have that history of running out on each other after sex. Oh, wait. Only you did that."

She laughed. "Thanks for the reminder. So you're not a forgive-and-forget kind of guy. That surprises me."

"Oh, I forgive, but I don't forget until I've gotten all the mileage I can out of it."

"How like you."

"Resourceful? I know."

"Impossible was more what I was thinking. How's work?"

He chuckled. "I have no idea. I should have stayed in bed with you. I'm not getting anything done."

His confession made her feel all shivery inside. "Really?"

"Absolutely. You're a distraction."

The same could be said about him. Katie's body still hummed with pleasure, even several hours after the love-making. Zach had done things to her and with her that had left her feeling more like his sexual slave than a bed partner.

"Instead of trying to function on zero sleep, I gave myself and my staff the day off," she said. "As this is my first free weekend in weeks, I'm heading up to the hacienda this afternoon. We're having a beading fest. Want to come along? You don't have to actually bead if you don't want to."

"You read my mind," he teased. "Not about the beading, but about the weekend. I have an official invitation for David and myself. We're coming up first thing in the morning."

"Great. I look forward to seeing you."

"Me, too. And if you look out front, you'll find your car waiting there. The keys are under the mat by your front door."

She clutched the phone more tightly as her heart gave a little *ping* of pleasure. "You went to all that trouble for me?"

"Absolutely. I took the keys when I left this morning and had it delivered. Hey, this is L.A. You can't not have wheels."

Katie sighed. Zach might not have a white stallion, but he was still pretty decent prince material.

"I need to let you get back to work," she said.

"Sure. I can read this file for the third time and see if my powers of concentration have returned, now that I've heard your voice. And Katie?"

"Yeah?"

"Last night was really special for me."

Oddly enough, her eyes began to burn. "For me, too. Not just making love, but the way you looked out for me. It meant a lot."

"I wanted to take care of you. Scary, huh?"

"You bet. I'll see you tomorrow."

David overslept the following morning, which wasn't unusual but, for the first time in years, annoyed Zach. He sat on his son's too-small bed in the dorm room he shared with another freshman and waited while David had his twenty-minute shower. Finally he was ready, with his overnight bag and a backpack full of textbooks.

"I have a lot of homework," David grumbled as he slid into the front seat of Zach's BMW. "I have this project due next week and finals are in three weeks."

Zach pulled out of the parking lot. "I'm sure Mia has the same pressure. You can study together."

David didn't say anything. Instead he stared out the front window, looking sullen.

Zach frowned. "Look, if you don't want to go up to the hacienda, you don't have to." He would be happy to return David to the dorm and continue on his own.

"It's not that," David said, slumping down in his seat. "There's just a lot of stuff going on."

"Want to talk about it?"

David shrugged, which could mean yes, no, or maybe.

"It is school?"

Another shrug.

"Mia?"

"We're fine."

David spoke the right words, but his flat tone said otherwise. Was it the redhead? Were David and Mia fighting?

"Is there a reason Mia didn't want to drive up with us?"

"She left yesterday. After the fund-raiser." His son glanced at him. "So how did it go? Mia said something about everyone getting sick. Were they like throwing up on the dance floor?"

Zach accepted the change of subject for now. When the kid was ready to talk, he would.

"The guests were fine," he said. "Instead it was the kitchen staff barfing their guts out."

He explained the details.

David frowned. "How come no one called *me* to come help? I had some free time."

"I don't know," Zach admitted. "Does Katie have your number? Maybe she thought Mia would let you know."

"I guess."

He didn't say anything more. After a few minutes he leaned forward and clicked on the radio. He pushed the far left station-set button, which filled the car with loud country music. Zach grinned. He and his son were closet fans, although they would rather have their toenails pulled out than admit it.

A rowdy Montgomery Gentry song had them both singing along. When they merged onto the freeway, Zach opened the sunroof and David cranked up the stereo.

There weren't going to be many more times like this, Zach thought as they cruised north. David had his own life, his own interests. Soon he wouldn't come home on breaks. He would have his own life, and Zach would be by himself.

He'd never much thought about life after David grew up. There'd been too much day-to-day insanity to distract him. But now that time was fast approaching, and Zach's life wasn't looking as full as it had. He felt a longing for something more. Something . . . meaningful.

Zach snorted. Right, meaningful. That and a tofu taco would get him enlightenment.

He pushed the ridiculous whisper of restlessness away and concentrated on the drive.

The morning was warm and perfect. The kind of June weather that makes the blue sky look like a computer-enhanced image. He was careful to keep no more than seven miles above the speed limit because getting a ticket would only delay his arrival at the hacienda. Even so he found himself wanting to be there *now*.

He wanted to see the Grands and Colleen and Marco, and even Grandpa Lorenzo. He wanted to look at the vine-yards and examine the changes from the last time he'd been there. But mostly, he wanted to be with Katie.

He'd been unable to get her out of his mind and he couldn't remember the last time he'd been unable to forget a woman. He'd had plenty of sex in the past few years, but nothing that . . . intimate. Being with her was different—

better. She made him laugh. She made him see possibilities and a future. Which should have sent him running for the hills. He was willing to admit it scared the crap out of him. But not enough to leave. So if he didn't walk, what was he going to do?

He and David arrived at the hacienda shortly before noon. When he pulled up next to the three-story house, Mia was waiting on the front porch.

"You're here!" she said as she danced down the steps to the car.

David climbed out. Zach waited for her to fly into his embrace, but instead they only stood staring at each other. In a way, their intensity made the moment seem more intimate than a kiss, and Zach turned away to give them privacy.

He went around to the trunk. David and Mia finished whatever silent Zen thing they'd been doing and joined him.

"Everyone is inside," she said. "Just go on in. They're all talking about the fund-raiser and how much fun it was. Did Grammy M really get everyone drunk?"

"Not everyone," Zach told her. "A few escaped."

"I'm sorry I missed that," she said, then grabbed David's hand. "Come on. Let's go for a walk."

David allowed himself to be led away, leaving Zach to mount the front steps by himself. The door stood open, so he entered and shut it behind him. Once inside, he put down the luggage, then followed the sound of voices to the living room.

All the women of the family sat together sewing. The Grands were there, and Colleen, Francesca (looking normal for once), and Katie. Only Brenna was missing. And Mia, who had gone off with David.

He saw the stack of completed flowers in bags by the coffee table and boxes of beads yet to be attached. Once, not so long ago, he'd seen these women together just like this and had thought they were spiders out to snare his son. Now he realized he'd been wrong. They weren't spiders and this wasn't a web. Instead each fine stitch assembled a part of a safety net.

Had this been another time, had David been older, more ready, more mature, Zach couldn't have asked for better in-laws. He would have considered him and his son incredibly lucky to be a part of this amazing family.

But David wasn't any of those things. As much as he loved his son, Zach saw his faults clearly. The marriage was destined for failure and most of the blame would be David's.

"Ladies," he said easily as he took a seat.

"Zach!" The women greeted him. Katie gave him a quick smile, then ducked her head.

"How was the drive?" Colleen asked. "Did you bring David with you?"

He sat in the chair and stretched out his legs in front of him. "The drive was fine. Yes, David is here. He and Mia went for a walk."

"Are you hungry?" Grandma Tessa asked. "We're having lunch in a hour, but if you need a little something . . ."

He reached over and patted her wrinkled hand. "I can wait. I wouldn't want anything to spoil my appetite."

Francesca picked up Mia's half-finished lace flowers. "Want to help?"

He grinned. "Nope."

"Me, either." She sighed. "Sewing isn't really my thing.

I practically destroyed a sewing machine when I took that quilting class. I keep telling Katie that I constantly prick my finger. I'm getting blood all over the place."

"I can get blood out a whole lot easier than I can bead everything myself," Katie retorted without missing a stitch.

"So is the dress about finished?" he asked, not sure why he wanted to know.

Katie gave him a quick glance. "Don't even bring it up. I'm heading for panic mode."

"The wedding invitations are due any day now," Colleen told Zach. "I think Mia said we had your list of names. We'll be addressing them in the next week or so. In the old days they had to go out six weeks in advance, but now everyone says just a month is enough."

"Where's Brenna?" he asked.

Grandma Tessa frowned. "She said she had to go to Santa Barbara, but didn't say for what. She'll be back in time for lunch."

Katie rose. "It's too beautiful to stay inside. I'm going to follow Mia's lead and take Zach for a walk. We'll be back in an hour." She glanced at him. "If that's all right."

He hadn't been alone with her since Thursday night.

"Great idea," he said, coming to his feet.

"Have fun," Colleen said, not taking her gaze from her beading.

When they were out on the porch, Zach pulled Katie close and lightly kissed her. She responded, holding on to him and sighing.

"It's good to see you," she admitted.

"Same here. I missed you."

They stared at each other. Zach suddenly wanted to say more, although he didn't know what. He also wanted to take her upstairs and make love with her, which wasn't possible. Instead, he took her hand in his and started down the stairs.

"Do you think they'll start speculating about us right away or will they give us a head start?" he asked.

"Five minutes at the most," she said with a laugh. "I'm torn between going for the walk I promised you and sneaking back around to eavesdrop."

"I have a feeling that would embarrass us both. Let's take that walk."

"Okay. Have you seen the tasting room?"

"No."

"Then let's go that way."

As they headed for a path that circled left around the house, Zach tried to figure out why he didn't mind that Katie's sister, mother, and grandmothers were talking about them. He generally didn't like people butting into his private life, but this time it was different. Not that he could say why. For now it was enough just to be with Katie on such a beautiful day.

They strolled past acres of vines, then turned again. A mile or so ahead he saw a beautiful two-story building, surrounded by impressive gardens. Dozens of cars were parked in front and on the side. Obviously the public part of Marcelli Wines.

"Why so quiet?" he asked her.

"I'm still a little tired," she admitted. "And I have a lot on my mind."

"So you're thinking about me?"

She turned toward him and swatted his arm with her free hand. "You are *not* the center of the universe."

"I'm the center of yours."

She rolled her eyes. "You and that ego. It's amazing you have room for anyone else in your life."

He bumped her shoulder with his. "Come on. You're impressed by me. I can tell."

"Not even close."

He chuckled. "Katie, you're amazing at a lot of things, but you're a lousy liar. Besides, you've had a thing for me since the second we met. Don't forget, you told your family I was hot."

She stopped in the center of the path, pulled her hand free, and glared at him.

"Number one, I've told you before—I never used the word *hot*. Number two, you're not all that. Number three, the only reason I mentioned you at all to my family is that they were bugging me about not having a boyfriend. I *pretended* to be attracted to you so they would get off my back and I could have a pleasant weekend. The only flaw in the plan was you showing up ten minutes later."

She planted her hands on her hips and narrowed her gaze. "Is any of this sinking in?"

Temper flared from her brown eyes. Annoyance colored her cheeks. But under that was amusement and affection. He saw it in the way the corner of her mouth twitched slightly.

She was beautiful. Funny. Smart. A hell of a lover. A hell of a woman.

He grinned. "Nope," he said as he put his arm around her. "You adore me. Now let's go to the tasting room and you can buy me a drink."

20

"Try this," Katie said, pouring from another open bottle. "It's a table wine, which means it's a blend. We do a Cabernet Sauvignon–Merlot blend, with a bit of Cab Franc thrown in for interest."

Zach sipped the wine she offered. "I like it. I still like the straight Cabernet Sauvignon best, but this would be good for casual dining."

She laughed. "I'll be sure to tell my grandfather. Considering this little table wine for casual dining sells for about seventy-five dollars a bottle, I'm sure he'll be thrilled with your assessment."

Zach winced. "Okay. So I was wrong."

She leaned toward him. "There is no wrong, just personal preference. Frankly, I'm a white wine drinker, which is blasphemy in this family. When Brenna found out, she threatened to never speak to me again."

Katie smiled as she spoke and her light brown eyes glinted with humor. She wore her hair long and loose. She was so beautiful, he thought suddenly.

He crossed to a large set of arched glass doors. A well-manicured lawn stretched out for about sixty or seventy feet. At the far end two women were on step-ladders decorating a gazebo. White chairs had been set up in rows.

"A wedding?" he asked as Katie came to stand next to him.

"Yes. They're scheduled all through the spring and summer. Upstairs there's a whole suite of rooms for the use of the wedding party. If the reception is held here, it has to be outside, but once we're into June weather isn't usually a problem." She glanced at him. "It's a romantic setting."

He shrugged. "Where are the family weddings held?"

"In the private garden." She dropped her gaze.

He didn't know what she was thinking, but he sensed her uneasiness. The topic of Mia and David's engagement was still a sensitive area of conversation. It was time to come to an understanding.

"They can't get married," he said flatly. "Even if Mia's ready, David isn't. Not by a long shot."

Katie sighed. "I know."

He'd already mentally outlined his verbal strategy, but her quiet response caught him off guard.

"What do you know?"

"That you're right. As much as I didn't want to believe you when you first told me about your concerns, I remembered them. I've been watching Mia and David together. At the beginning they were happy, but something has changed. I don't know if they've been fighting or if she found out about Julie or what. I guess the reason doesn't matter."

"You agree with me?"

She smiled. "Is that all you got out of that?"

"It's the most important part."

"Zach! We're talking about the future happiness of my sister and your son. Isn't that slightly more important than my agreeing with you?"

He considered the question. "It's a close second. Come on."

He opened one of the glass doors and drew her outside.

She leaned against him. "Now what?"

"Now we talk to Mia and David."

"Do you think they'll listen?"

"I don't know. If David gets stubborn, he'll tune it all out. What about Mia?"

Katie shrugged. "She hates to admit when she's made a mistake, but I don't think she'd be willing to get married just to be right. I agree we should talk to them. If we're logical and rational—"

"Oh, so I'll be doing the talking," he said, cutting her off.

She glared at him. "Remind me to toss you in a fermenting vat when we get back to the house."

"You and what army?"

"I can be tough."

He kissed the top of her head. "Sure you can, Katie. Tough and mean."

"I am."

"Uh-huh. So we have a plan?"

"Yes. We'll corner the unsuspecting couple and talk them into submission." She smiled. "I'll go first."

"If you insist."

"Are you okay with this? Us tackling them together?"

"Yes."

Which surprised him. He'd always done everything alone, especially with respect to his son. He had to admit that after eighteen years of being a single parent, it was nice to have someone to share things with.

"So what are the odds of me getting struck by lightning if I sneak into your room tonight?" he asked as they headed back for the house.

Katie raised her eyebrows. "Gee, nearly all of my extended family will be under the same roof with us, including my very crabby grandfather. And let's not forget that I have two grandmothers who take a trip around the beads at the drop of a hat. Lightning is the least of your concerns."

He considered the embarrassment of getting caught— literally with his pants down. "Good point. I'll keep to my side of the house."

She grinned. "I figured you'd say that. So I'll sneak into your room."

They walked into the house twenty minutes later to find the place in an uproar. Grandma Tessa was in tears, Colleen kept saying it would be fine, while Grammy M was pouring a drink. Mia huddled over someone sitting in a chair.

"It's Brenna," Mia said, looking more amused than upset.

"Was she in a car accident?" Katie asked instantly. "Is she all right?"

Mia rolled her eyes. "She went to Santa Barbara to get her hair cut."

Zach waited for the rest of the story. Like in Santa Barbara she'd been attacked or, at the very least, been caught up in a bank robbery, but there was no more information.

"And?" he asked.

Mia shook her head. "That's it. She cut her hair."

"I don't get it."

Katie patted his arm. "I know. Just try to fade into the woodwork. You'll never understand and trying to will just give you a migraine." She glanced at Mia. "They got over you streaking your hair."

"Yeah, but I'm the rebel. Brenna is about to be divorced. How is she supposed to catch a man if she has short hair?"

Katie groaned and stepped toward her relatives. Zach felt as if he'd stepped into an alternative universe. So Brenna had cut her hair? If no one liked it, wouldn't it just grow back?

"Enough," Brenna said, and stood up. Her long hair was gone. In its place was a short style that grazed her chin.

Zach studied her. She had a rounder face than her sisters, and bigger eyes. Somehow the layered cut flattered her features, making her look sexy.

"I like it," he said, before he could stop himself.

Katie and Mia looked at him with something like pity, but the Grands and Colleen turned on him instantly.

"Her crowning glory is gone," Grandma Tessa said as she brushed away her tears.

Grammy M sighed and took a sip of her drink. " 'Twas lovely hair."

Colleen simply muttered something about "Men."

"Hey," Zach said, "as a *man* I think it looks good on her."

Mia moved close. "And you looked so bright, too," she whispered in his ear. "You're in trouble, now."

"She was attractive before and she's still very attractive," he insisted, ignoring the sensation of falling into a pit where he would be trapped forever.

Brenna sighed. "Okay, enough everyone. I agree with Zach. I like it. If I decide I don't like it, I'll grow it out. In the meantime, my hairstyle is off limits. Does everyone understand?"

Grammy M and Colleen nodded. Grandma Tessa sniffed.

Brenna muttered something under her breath, then grabbed his arm and drew him down the hall. "I'm going to have a private conversation with my lawyer," she yelled back. "It will take about ten minutes. That should be enough time for you to recover from the shock and finish getting lunch ready."

They entered the library and she slammed the door shut behind them.

"Family," she said with exasperation. "Sometimes I want to run away and never come back."

"You don't mean that," he said, studying her. There was something different about Brenna today. Something that didn't have anything to do with her new haircut. An energy and a purpose.

"I don't," she admitted, sinking down on one of the leather sofas. "I love them all and would be lost without them. But every now and then they really get on my nerves." She fluffed her newly shorn hair. "This would be one of those times."

He settled on the other sofa. "Fair enough. So did you really want to talk to me about something or did you just need to escape?"

"No. I have an actual thing. When you called to tell me that Jeff's lawyer had been in touch to formally withdraw the question of the winery inheritance, you told me to think about what I want from Jeff."

"Did you come up with a wish list?"

"Yes, but little of it is legal. As I already pushed the limits of the law with the taping stunt, I'm not going to try it again."

"But getting Jeff on tape worked."

Brenna fluffed the ends of her hair and shrugged. "I guess."

"He backed off. Isn't that what you wanted?"

"Sure. It's just . . ." She shrugged again. "Katie was right."

"About?"

"Francesca. I wanted her help and I'm glad to have the tape, but listening to my husband saying he wanted to fuck her brains out didn't exactly make my day."

"I'm sorry."

"It wasn't you doing the talking. I know Francesca would never have anything to do with him, but it still makes me feel weird." She shook her head. "None of which is your problem. My actual point for having this conversation is to tell you I don't have a wish list. All I want from Jeff is repayment for putting him through school. You showed me that chart before, remember?"

He nodded. "The state has a schedule."

"Then that's fine."

"I could probably get you more."

"Thanks, but I've been tacky enough for one divorce. Plus, if I'm out for blood, that means I'm still putting energy into our relationship. The whole situation makes me sad and angry and frustrated, but I want to move on. He doesn't matter anymore. I want to act like that's actually true."

"It's your call," he told her. "I'll do exactly what you say."

She smiled. "Now *see?* If Jeff had acted more like that, our marriage might have worked."

"Don't go wishing for miracles. I'm only agreeable because I work for you."

Her smile broadened. "So the secret is to pay someone to be my husband and then he'll do exactly what I say?"

"Something like that."

After his meeting with Brenna, Zach stepped out of the library and found Katie waiting for him. They'd agreed to try and corner Mia and David before lunch.

"The Grands have already announced lunch is ready," she said. "We'll have to do this after."

"I don't want to wait."

"Because you want what you want when you want it?"

"Something like that." He wanted to get the conversation over. He wanted to know that the engagement was off.

"It's lunch," she reminded him. "How long could it take? Besides, they're already engaged. What's the worst that could happen?"

He didn't have an answer for that, but something in his gut told him time was important. If he waited too long, the situation might be unrecoverable.

She grabbed him by the arm. "Listen to me, Zach. Look into my eyes and listen very carefully. You *have* to wait. You can't take this on during lunch. Not with my family there. For one thing, the loud shrieks will be a distraction. For another, it will get very ugly. Remember what happened when I pissed them off? This is way more important and serious."

"You're right," he said.

She didn't look convinced. "Somehow I don't believe you. Do you promise you'll wait to talk to them privately?"

He bent down and brushed her mouth with his. Brenna walked out of the library just in time to see.

"Get a room," she told them with a grin.

Katie leaned against Zach. "You only need a room if there's tongue."

"Yuck. Don't be talking about that sort of thing with me." Brenna shuddered. "At least not with Zach standing right there. How can I ask any really good questions?"

"I'm leaving," he said, walking toward the dining room. "You'll have to have this conversation behind my back."

"Chicken," Brenna called after him.

Katie watched him go, then looked at her sister. "You doing okay?"

"Yeah. I hesitate to actually admit this, but you were right about taping Jeff. Francesca got what we needed, but I feel weird about it."

"I didn't want that to happen."

"I know. You were trying to protect me, but would I listen?"

"See. If only you'd let me run your life, things would go much smoother."

Brenna raised her eyebrows. "Because your life is so perfect?"

Katie was surprised by the question. "Things are going really well."

"You don't say? So what's up with Zach?"

"I just—" She cleared her throat. "We're—" Deep breath, try again. "Things are fine."

"Uh-huh. So you have no idea where your relationship stands."

"Not one."

"And you're too afraid to ask."

"Exactly."

"Ha! And you want to run *my* life. I think not." Brenna linked arms with her and steered her toward the kitchen. "So he's the one?"

Katie wasn't ready to admit that. "Maybe."

"Bells?"

"A faint ringing sound."

Brenna squeezed her arm. "So long as it's not an alarm."

Lunch with the Marcelli family was a casual, intimate affair. There was less wine than at dinner, more pasta, and enough salad to make an entire colony of herbivores vibrate with ecstasy.

Zach found himself seated on Grandma Tessa's left and Colleen's right, with Katie across from him. While he wanted lunch to end so he could corner Mia and David, he couldn't complain about the view.

After the food had been passed around the table and the Grands determined that everyone had more than enough, conversation turned to the recent fund-raiser.

"We're very proud of you, Katie," Marco told his daughter.

Katie smiled. "Thanks. Weeks of hard work and preparation laid low by a single fish. It's a little scary to think about. But the family came through for me."

Grandma Tessa dismissed her statement with a wave of her hand. "We cooked a little, talked a little, you did the hard work." A sharp elbow jabbed his ribs. "A smart, successful young woman." Grandma Tessa nodded knowingly. "Surprising that no one has snapped her up."

Katie briefly closed her eyes and muttered something under her breath. Zach didn't doubt that the exact words would have Grandma Tessa reaching for her rosary. He held back a smile.

"It is surprising," he agreed.

Katie opened her eyes and glared at him. He could read her thoughts—she wanted to know what the hell he was doing, playing along with her grandmother.

He winked.

"A man shouldn't be alone forever," Grandma Tessa told him. "David is already in college. Your big house gets empty."

Zach raised his eyebrows. "You've told them about my house?" he asked Katie.

She opened her mouth, then closed it. The glare became lethal. "Not a single word."

"But you've been spending so much time there."

"I have not!"

He glanced around the table—everyone was watching with interest. "Oh," he said, sounding as if he'd just figured it all out. "They weren't supposed to know."

"Zach, what are you doing?"

He grinned. "Making you squirm."

He enjoyed teasing her, ruffling her usually perfect self-control. He liked that he could push her buttons. He liked the direction the conversation was going. Hell. He liked *her.*

Something brushed against his leg. "Are you trying to put your foot on my lap?" he asked.

Katie jumped. "I was trying to kick you."

"Katie, darlin', if you're tryin' to get Zach's attention, you should work on your aim," Grammy M said with a wink.

Katie nodded. "My grandmother thinks I should kick you."

"What is with you two?" Mia asked.

Brenna leaned toward her. "You've been so busy with your own happily-ever-after that you've not been paying attention. Your future father-in-law has been making the moves on your sister."

Mia's eyes widened. "Zach? Is that true?"

"I wouldn't say moves."

"What would you say?" she asked.

Zach picked up his wine. "Great lunch."

The Grands grinned, Katie obviously still wanted to kill him, Grandpa Lorenzo was giving him the once-over, and David looked stunned. Apparently Mia wasn't the only one who hadn't noticed the sparks between Katie and himself.

Colleen took pity on them and asked Brenna about a particular vineyard. Grandpa Lorenzo announced his opinion on the subject. Marco spoke with his youngest. Zach watched Katie and realized that sometime when he hadn't been looking, he'd started to care.

Not just about her, he thought as he glanced around the table. All of them. They weren't perfect, but they were good people. He relished the sense of belonging. They accepted him and welcomed him. It felt . . . good.

A faint knocking interrupted the conversation. Colleen excused herself and went to answer the door. She came back holding a large box.

"That was Milly from up at the office. These were delivered and she knew we'd all been waiting." She smiled with delight. "The invitations. Marco, pass me a knife."

She set the box on a spare chair, then took the knife her husband offered and cut through the tape.

Zach glanced at Katie, who shook her head. He knew what she was trying to tell him—not now. Not in front of the family.

"Oh, they're beautiful," Colleen said as she pulled out a stack of embossed heavy card stock. "So lovely and elegant."

She handed an invitation to her husband, who passed it on to Grandma Tessa. Marco walked another one around to Mia. Rather than study the writing or the graphic, Zach watched Mia and David.

His son glanced at the invitation, then at Mia. His eyes darkened and his mouth pulled into a straight line. Mia's identical expression of suffering made Zach's gut clench.

Holy hell. He didn't have to break them up. They'd already done it themselves.

Apparently he wasn't the only one watching them. Grammy M picked up an invitation.

"Is there something wrong, darlin'?" she asked. "You don't seem happy."

"They're lovely," Mia said, shifting in her seat.

"Why not tell them the truth," Zach said.

Mia looked at him. Her eyes widened. "I d-don't know what you mean."

"I think you do. It's time, Mia. The situation is only going to get more complicated. You want to have this conversation *after* three hundred of these have been mailed?"

"Zach," Katie warned. "Please."

He knew she was right; he knew he should wait. But he

couldn't. Not with both David and Mia looking miserable and trapped.

"If you're old enough to get married, you're old enough to admit you've changed your mind about getting married," he told them. "Go ahead and tell the family you're not engaged anymore."

21

M ia ducked her head. David looked as if he wanted to crawl under the table. Grandpa Lorenzo's fist crashed down next to his plate.

"What are you doing?" the old man demanded, his voice rising with every word.

"Making sure this is what David and Mia really want," Zach said.

Grandpa Lorenzo's thick eyebrows drew together. "You're trying to break them up?"

"I didn't have to. They made the decision on their own."

"You what?" Colleen asked, staring at him incredulously.

Katie shook her head. "I warned you," she murmured just before conversation exploded at the table.

"What the hell is going on?" Lorenzo demanded.

"Mia, what is this about?" Marco asked at the same second.

"We should all calm down," Grandma Tessa urged.

"Calm?" Colleen echoed. "The invitations are *here.*"

"When did this happen?" Brenna asked.

"This is no time for shoutin'," Grammy M warned.

Katie reached for her wine, while Zach watched the show.

"You didn't want them to marry?" Colleen asked him, then rose to her feet. "Zach, I don't understand."

Zach stood as well. "I thought the engagement was a mistake from the beginning. Mia is David's first girlfriend. They're both too young to be settling down. David still has two years of college left. Mia wants to go to Georgetown."

He glanced at the kids, who both looked miserable. Grandpa Lorenzo roared for everyone to be silent.

He stared at Zach. "You come into our family. We welcome you with open arms, but you're not what you seem. You're a traitor and a thief."

Zach recognized the beginning of the tirade. He braced himself for a lot of bluster.

"You can't dictate to me," he told the older man. "I worry about my son as much as you worry about your family. Katie had it right before. You pick a side or an opinion and you expect everyone to embrace it, to put it on, no matter how ill-fitting it may be. You have no respect for personal differences. You want what *you* want, not what they want. If they agree with you, they're smart. If they don't, you badger them. That's not leading the family, that's being a bully."

A collective gasp shot from the family.

Color flared on Grandpa Lorenzo's cheeks. He muttered something in Italian, then pushed himself to his feet. "You are not welcome here. You're a snake and we don't tolerate your kind."

"Or the truth," Zach said. "Everyone at this table can see David and Mia are miserable. But you don't care about that. Having more heirs is more important than your own granddaughter's happiness."

"She's a child. What does she know of what is right?"

"If she's a child, Pop," Marco said, "then she's too young to be getting married."

Zach was surprised by the unexpected support.

"Get out!" Lorenzo roared. "Both of you!"

Marco shook his head. "That's always your solution, isn't it? Get rid of the dissenters. Soon you'll be living here all by yourself."

Colleen gripped her husband's hand. "That's right."

"Yeah. You can't talk to my dad that way," David said, coming to his feet. "He's right. You tell Mia and her sisters what to do, but you don't listen to what they want."

Mia clutched his arm. "David's telling the truth, Grandpa. Why can't you see it?"

Lorenzo ignored her and turned his attention to David and frowned. "If you defend your father, then you can go with him."

"Fine. I will." David looked across the table. He shrugged. "Because you're right, Dad. I'm not ready to get married. Neither is Mia. We're not engaged anymore. We broke up yesterday. We just didn't want to tell anyone yet."

There was a second explosion of conversation. Zach ignored all of it. He looked at his son and nodded, proud that David had made a stand.

"You okay with that?" Zach asked.

"Breaking up or making everybody mad?"

"They're mad at me, not you."

David smiled ruefully. "I think that just changed."

Zach didn't care about that. What was important to him was keeping David safe. That's all he'd ever wanted. Now his son had a chance to grow up and find out what he wanted to do with his life, without the added responsibility of a family.

Katie looked at Mia. "That's why you didn't show up for your fitting. You were having second thoughts about the engagement. I figured you were mad at me about the house."

Mia moved close and hugged her. "No way. I knew you just wanted me to be happy."

"Happy?" her grandfather asked. "When you're not getting married?"

Mia rolled her eyes. "Grandpa, you're going to have to get over it."

The older man glared at her.

Zach looked at them all. "I'm sorry," he said loudly, to be heard over the cacophony. "I didn't want anyone to get hurt."

"What do you care for us?" Lorenzo asked. "You care only for yourself."

"You're wrong."

"Get out."

"No, don't," Katie said. "No one's going anywhere and no one is being thrown out of this family ever again."

Zach shook his head. "You're wasting your time. He's not going to change."

Lorenzo pointed to her. "You're to have nothing to do with this man. Ever. He's not welcome here."

"Grandpa—" she began.

Zach cut her off. "Don't bother. It's not worth it."

"You can't just leave," she said.

"Sure I can. It will end the fight sooner."

He headed for the door.

Katie watched him go. Her heart tightened as he walked down the hall, then turned and was lost from view. She couldn't blame him for not wanting to be a part of this right now. He'd never been one for families, and hers could try the patience of a saint. Walking away made sense. He—

She caught her breath. He'd left. That's what Zach did in his relationships, and he'd just walked out on her.

He was gone. The thought repeated itself over and over again. She wanted to run after him, but shock rooted her in place.

She loved him and she'd never told him. How could she blame him for treating her like any other woman when she'd never told him how she felt?

Her grandfather turned on Mia. "What is wrong with you? Once again, like your sisters, you disappoint me. I have no granddaughters."

That was the final straw for Katie. She threw her napkin on the table and stood. "Dammit, that's enough."

The Grands gasped and her grandfather nearly swelled with rage. But her parents moved next to her and nodded at her to continue.

She sucked in a breath and braced herself to face the storm. "Leave Mia alone," she told her grandfather.

"You will not speak to me this way. I am in charge of this family."

"Yeah, maybe. And you know what, Grandpa? You've done a lousy job. You're trying to get what you want, without considering what will make us happy. Can you honestly tell me that Mia marrying someone she doesn't love is your dream for her?"

"One of my granddaughters should marry and produce babies."

"Why? Why should we do that? Because it will make us fulfilled? No. Because it's what *you* want. If you want babies in this house so badly, go adopt them."

"Yeah," Brenna said, coming to stand next to her sister.

He turned his attention on her. "Be careful. Your place here isn't secure."

"Why?" Brenna asked. "You rule by fear, Grandpa, not by love. Is that what you want?"

Katie took her sister's hand and squeezed it, then turned back to her grandfather.

"You should be proud of Mia. She's only eighteen years old, yet she's together enough to know what she does and doesn't want. She's also brave enough to stand up to everyone she loves and say no. Even though it will disappoint her family. I can't believe you would push her into something that is obviously wrong for her. You should celebrate her honesty, because she's telling the truth. And that's the one thing I could never do."

Katie hadn't meant to say that. Somehow the words had slipped out, and suddenly they took on a life of their own. The room went silent as everyone stared at her.

So here it was . . . after all these years. Her chance to come clean. How many times had she wondered if she would? One thing was sure—she'd never pictured it taking exactly this format.

She turned her attention to her parents. "I'm sorry," she said quietly, trying not to think how much she was about to disappoint them with her confession. "I didn't mean to lie, but I didn't have the strength to tell you the truth." She sucked in a breath. "Greg didn't break off our engagement all those years ago. I did."

Her mother gasped. Her father looked as if she'd hit him. But Katie didn't retreat. This was her one chance to get it all said.

"The closer it got to the wedding, the more scared I got. I couldn't sleep or eat, I was having panic attacks, and I knew deep down inside that I didn't want to marry

Greg. I couldn't imagine spending an entire week in his company, let alone a lifetime. But so many things had already been set in motion. The wedding was planned, the invitations had been sent out. I knew if I told you, you'd try to convince me that it was just pre-wedding jitters."

She paused to brush her cheeks. It was only when she touched moisture that she realized she was crying. She didn't take her gaze from her parents.

"So I broke up with Greg without telling anyone. When he said he wanted to go into the military and left the next day, I used that to my advantage. I lied."

Her mother began to cry as well. "Katie, we never wanted you to marry someone you didn't love. You could have told us the truth."

"I wasn't strong enough, and I was afraid you wouldn't love me if you knew what really happened. I didn't go to work in the winery. I didn't get married and have children. I felt like a failure. Mia's not like that. She's brave."

Suddenly Mia was hugging her. Their parents joined them. Katie felt drained, but also strangely light. As if a burden she'd been carrying around for years had suddenly fallen away.

"We love you," her father whispered. "No matter what, Katie. You have to know that."

She nodded because it was too difficult to speak.

He touched Mia's hair. "If you're sure about David, that's okay with me."

"It's not all right with me," her grandfather said. "You're all crazy."

Marco straightened. "You know what, Pop? Get over it. You've been ruling this family with an iron fist ever since your father died. I remember when I was little, I would hear you talking to Mama about him. How he controlled things. How he was a bully. You hated him as much as you loved him, yet you turned out exactly like him."

The room went silent. Katie raised her head and looked at her grandfather. He paled, then sat heavily in his seat.

"That's not true," he murmured. "My father was a hard, cruel man."

Grandma Tessa reached for her husband's hand. "Lorenzo, you're a good father. A good husband."

In a matter of seconds he seemed to age twenty years. Katie's throat got tight as she watched his skin turn gray. His broad shoulders seemed to shrink.

"You all stand against me," he whispered.

"Pop, it's not that dramatic," her father said.

Brenna sniffed. "Yeah, Grandpa. We all really love you, but sometimes you're a giant pain in the ass."

Brenna slapped her hand over her mouth. Katie sucked in a breath. Grandma Tessa reached for her rosary. Grandpa Lorenzo turned his attention to Brenna, and the life returned to his face in the form of blotchy red color.

"What did you say?"

She cleared her throat. "You can be a real pain in the ass."

Katie braced herself for the tirade, but instead she heard an odd sound. Almost a choking. She blinked. Her grandfather's mouth was open. He was . . . laughing.

Laughing?

She and Brenna looked at each other, then at him.

"Pop?" Marco asked cautiously.

Grandpa Lorenzo slapped the table. "I wish I'd told my father that," he said, still chuckling. "Fine. I'm a pain in the ass, but I'm still in charge of this family. You, Mia."

She jumped. "Yes, Grandpa?"

"No more engagements until you're sure. And maybe older."

She swallowed. "Okay."

"Brenna?"

"Uh-huh?"

"Stop calling me names."

"Katie's right. It's time to stop throwing people out of the family."

He frowned. "It's one of the few pleasures I have in my old age."

"Get a hobby."

He grinned and held open his arms. Brenna flew toward him and they embraced. Katie swallowed, knowing she would be next. She felt a little like Dorothy, about to face the great and all powerful Oz.

Sure enough, her grandfather released Brenna and turned his attention on Katie. "What have you to say for yourself?"

Everyone else was being brave, so she supposed she would have to suck it up as well.

"That you better get over being mad at Zach because I'm in love with him."

It had been an hour for announcements and stunned silences, she thought as everyone stared at her.

She shrugged. "It's true. I don't know how he feels about me, but as soon as we're done here, I'm going to go find him and ask. If there's a chance for us, I want to take it."

"You love him?" the old man bellowed.

She nodded. "Completely."

"She hears bells," Brenna offered helpfully.

"That *bastardo*. That—"

"Amazingly nice guy you're thrilled to have in the family."

Katie gasped and spun around when she heard Zach's voice. He stood in the doorway to the dining room, casually leaning against the door frame. She couldn't believe it. Oh, God! How much had he heard?

Brenna recovered first and asked the question for her. "How long have you been standing there?"

"A while. I got halfway to my car when I realized I didn't want to walk away. Not this time." He straightened and started toward Katie. "You stood up for me."

She swallowed and nodded. He'd heard everything? Even her declaration of her feelings? And he hadn't bolted for Montana?

She was hopeful, embarrassed, excited, and terrified.

His blue eyes darkened with an emotion she couldn't read. "You told your whole family that you loved me."

She nodded again.

"Don't you think you should have told me first?"

She bit her lower lip. "I was going to call you on your cell phone as soon as we were finished here."

He touched her cheek. "I had this big plan when I met you, Katie Marcelli. I was going to use you for my own purposes."

"I know."

"I wasn't even subtle about it."

"You're not subtle about many things."

"You weren't what I expected."

She felt some of her confidence returning. "Because I didn't cave to your demands? Because I stood up to you?"

"That and because you tricked me."

"What? When?"

"When you made me fall in love with you. I don't believe in relationships, remember? I don't believe in happily ever after or forever, or even the next morning."

Her throat got all tight, but in a good way. She started shaking. "Zach . . ."

"But I believe in us. You and me." He smiled. "Do you really hear bells when we're together?"

"Yes," she whispered.

"I'm not a knight on a white horse. I'm a hard-assed lawyer. Cynical, stubborn, set in my ways." His expression softened. "But I love you. I want to spend the rest of my life with you."

Katie threw herself at him. Zach caught her and pulled her close. "I love you, too," she whispered, just before his lips claimed hers.

"This is romantic," Brenna said as she picked up one of the invitations. "You know, we could still use these. We could just scratch out David's and Mia's names and put in Zach's and Katie's."

Just then a tall, pregnant woman walked into the room. "Hi, everyone. What did I miss?"

Brenna stared at her twin and shook her head. "What is wrong with you?"

Francesca held up her hands. "What? I was working."

"This is not about your studies. This is a sickness. You need a twelve-step program."

"I'm ignoring you." Francesca looked at Katie and Zach. "They're kissing."

"They're getting married," Brenna said.

"Wow. That's great. What happened?"

"Dad found out they'd had sex and threatened Zach with a machete."

"You're lying." Francesca grabbed a couple of grapes

from the fruit salad. "Katie, I'm really happy for you."

Katie, still lost in Zach's kiss, waved at her sister.

Brenna grinned at her twin. "You know what this means, don't you? Another dress to bead."

Francesca patted her stomach. "Not in my delicate condition."

POCKET STAR BOOKS
PROUDLY PRESENTS

THE SASSY ONE

SUSAN MALLERY

Coming soon in paperback
from Pocket Star Books

Turn the page for a preview of
The Sassy One . . .

*F*rancesca Marcelli had only been pregnant for twenty minutes and already her back hurt.

"Talk about realistic," she muttered adjusting the straps that held her fake eight-months-pregnant belly in place. The size was daunting enough—she couldn't see her feet or find a comfortable sitting position—but the weight was the real killer. Someone with a twisted sense of humor had decided to simulate what felt like the pressure of a baby elephant. The small of her back screamed out in protest, while unexpected pressure on her bladder made her want to duck into the nearest ladies' room.

"All for a good cause," she reminded herself.

Francesca shifted to ease the throbbing in her back and leaned against the heavy cart she'd maneuvered into the service elevator of the six-story bank building. When the doors opened, she shoved her over-loaded cart into the main hallway. Stacks of boxes wobbled precariously and threatened to tumble onto the carpeted floor.

It was just after five on a Friday afternoon. All around her dozens of businesspeople headed for the main elevators to start their weekend. Francesca pushed up her glasses and paused to smooth down the front of the ugliest maternity dress she'd been able to find. The oversized collar dwarfed her shoulders and made her head look too small. The pinks and roses of the busy floral print sucked all the color from her pale olive skin. She'd brushed powder into her hair to lighten it to a mousy brown. The little make-up she'd put on had been applied to make her look tired, drawn, and unattractive.

She glanced at her watch, then squared her shoulders as she prepared to begin work.

"Show time," she said softly, not that anyone was listening.

Three men from the insurance office at the end of the hall walked past her without even giving her a nod. Francesca continued to push her pile of packages slowly against the flow of foot traffic. Two women in suits gave her a quick, sympathetic smile. A man and a woman, both carrying expensive looking briefcases, followed. The woman looked, the man didn't.

Another corridor branched to the left. Francesca shifted her cart to make the turn. Several boxes went tumbling. A single man walked by without breaking his stride. A college-age girl stopped long enough to help Francesca pick up the boxes, then hurried toward the elevator with a call to "Wait for me!"

Five minutes later, Francesca reached her destination— an office she'd scouted out the previous week, chosen because the company had recently shut down. There she was, pregnant, lost, over-loaded with more than a dozen boxes to be delivered and no one to accept them. Had she been any sort of an actress, she might have been able to force out a tear or two.

The rules stipulated she was not allowed to directly ask

for help. It had to be offered. She would wait for the required thirty minutes, mentally tallying who ignored her, who smiled and who, if anyone, stopped to actually offer assistance.

This was a high powered crowd with expensive tastes and busy lives. She didn't hold out much hope for rescue. In her experience—

"You look lost."

Francesca whirled around to see a tall man standing beside her cart. A tall, *good-looking* man in a dark blue power suit.

"Hi," she said before preparing to launch into her canned speech about needing to deliver packages to a non-existent firm. Except she couldn't remember anything she was supposed to say.

The man waited patiently. He had dark blond hair and sort of tawny colored eyes. There was an intensity to his expression that reminded her of predators watching prey. A shiver rippled through her as she thought of gazelles being brought down for the kill. Unfortunately in her current condition she was more water buffalo than gazelle.

He looked confident, important, and powerful. Not the sort of person who should be stopping to help an unattractive pregnant woman in trouble. Men like him sent assistants to take care of life's unpleasant details.

"Do you speak English?" he asked, enunciating each word clearly.

"What? Oh. Of course." She sucked in a breath, not sure what could be wrong with her. She would blame her sudden mental hiccup on food poisoning, only she hadn't eaten anything that day. "I'm ah—" Francesca cleared her throat. Brain function returned and she launched into her spiel.

"Hi. I'm Francesca. I'm supposed to be delivering these packages here—" She motioned to the closed and locked office door. "But there seems to be a problem."

The man glanced first at the boxes, all carefully addressed to the defunct company, then to the door where a hand-lettered sign said that Malcolm and White Data Tech was no more.

"Bringing these here was the last thing my boss told me to do before he left town," she went on. "If I don't get them delivered, he's going to kill me."

In an effort to look terrified, Francesca thought about how little she had in her checking account and how that pesky electric bill was going to come due soon. Eventually she would reap the rewards of her post graduate education, but until she could actually slap the letters "Ph.D." after her name, she seemed destined to a life of poverty.

"You'll have to risk his fury," the man said calmly. "These boxes aren't going anywhere today. That company closed the door about ten days ago. From what I've heard, the main players skipped town with the last few dollars left, leaving several employees with lots of angry customers and no paychecks. What's your name again?"

"Francesca Marcelli."

He smiled at her. A genuine, happy-to-meet-you smile that made the corners of his eyes crinkle and caused her palms to suddenly start to sweat. This was the most fun she'd had in days.

Her rescuer introduced himself as Sam Reese.

"Let's get you out of this hallway and we'll figure out what we're going to do next."

We? They were a *we*?

Sam took charge of the cart, wheeling it down the hallway with an ease that made her envious. Of course he didn't have to worry about a pregnant belly getting in the way of his actions. She trailed after him, wondering what the next step would be. How far was Sam willing to take things? In situations like this—a non-emergency—people generally stopped at the point of inconvenience.

"Just through there," he said, pointing to a set of double glass doors.

Before Francesca could read the name of the company, one of the doors opened and a huge man stepped into the hallway. She involuntarily came to a stop to stare.

The man had to be at least six foot seven. He was built like a mountain with a massive neck and shoulders broad enough to support a couple of trailer homes. Dark skinned, with penetrating eyes and a firm, unsmiling mouth he looked both dangerous and more than a little scary.

"Sam," the man said, glancing between her rescuer and herself. "Is there a problem?"

"I think there might be." Sam looked back at her. "Ms. Marcelli was trying to make a delivery to Malcolm and White."

"They split last week."

"As I explained to Ms. Marcelli." He motioned to the cart. "Take this inside, Jason. Store it in one of the conference rooms." He turned his attention back to her. "If your employer's expecting payment for a delivery, that isn't going to happen. At least not right now. Come on inside and we'll get this situation straightened out."

Francesca found herself being ushered into a plush office with a gray and burgundy waiting area. An attractive woman in her early forties manned the front desk. She spoke over a headset as they walked by, pausing only to nod at Sam.

"I can search out Malcolm and White," Sam said as they moved down a long corridor decorated with elegant prints and the occasional slim table pushed up against a wall. "I've been looking for an excuse to track them down."

He sounded fierce as he spoke, as if he had a personal beef with the missing businessmen. Francesca trailed after him, torn between wondering why Sam Reese would care if a company in his building closed and trying to figure out what she'd gotten herself into. They passed several large conference rooms, what looked like classrooms, and a few offices containing large desks, computers, and file cabinets. All generic stuff that didn't hint at the kind of business done here.

At the end of the hall, they made a left, then a quick right before stopping in front of an open foyer containing a large desk and computer set-up manned by a well dressed young man wearing a sports coat.

"Jack, this is Ms. Marcelli."

The young man, probably around twenty-five and built like a football player, rose to his feet. "Nice to meet you, ma'am."

Francesca walked to the desk to shake hands. As she did so, her purse slipped down her arm and plopped onto the ground before she could catch it.

"Oops," she said, bending down to pick it up.

As she straightened, all the blood rushed from her head, causing the room to spin and her body to sway. For a split second, she thought she was going down.

Less than a heartbeat later, a strong arm encircled her, holding her in place. "Ms. Marcelli? Are you all right? Is it the baby?"

Baby? What . . . oh, *the baby.*

Francesca shook her head slightly. Her sense of equilibrium returned enough to her to realize she was standing amazingly close to Sam. Close enough to see the surprisingly dark lashes framing his eyes. Speaking of which—she stared more intently—seen from such a close range, his eyes were the most unusual color. Light brown, shot with gold. Otherworldly eyes. Cat eyes.

Cat eyes on a powerful man. She felt both the heat of him and the strength. Somehow she'd always assumed that executives in expensive suits were sort of wimpy under all that designer wool. She had been seriously wrong.

"Ms. Marcelli?"

Tension filled his voice. She shook her head again and tried to shrug free of his hold. When he didn't release her, she gave him a quick smile.

"I'm fine."

"You nearly fainted."

"I know. I haven't eaten today. I do that sometimes. Work distracts me. Then I get low blood sugar."

"That can't be good for the child."

As there was no child, his concern made her feel a little guilty.

"I'm fine," she repeated. "Really."

He slowly removed his arm from around her waist. "Jack, bring Ms. Marcelli some herb tea. There's a selection in the coffee room. Nothing with caffeine. Also, check to see if there are any sandwiches left from the lunch meeting."

Francesca thought about protesting again, but before she could figure out what to say without blowing her cover, she found herself being ushered into an office the size of Utah.

Floor-to-ceiling windows offered a view of Santa Barbara and mountains from one wall and Santa Barbara and a hint of ocean from the other. Tasteful paintings decorated the remaining walls. Two large leather sofas formed a conversational area in a corner. Between them and the desk was enough room to hold a kickboxing class.

Sam settled her on the sofa, then sat next to her. Before she knew what was going on, he had her hand resting in his and his fingers on the inside of her wrist.

"Your pulse is rapid. Would you like me to call your doctor?"

She generally went to student health services whenever she needed a check-up. Somehow she didn't think her friendly chit chat with the nurse practitioner qualified as having a doctor of her own.

Although she *would* have to admit that having her hand cradled by a handsome man held a certain thrill. He was warm, solid, and plenty sexy. Had she looked slightly more appealing than something gacked up by a stray cat, she might have tried smiling, flirting, and witty conversation. Not that she could think of anything witty right at the moment.

"No doctor calling," she insisted, reluctantly drawing her hand free of his. "There's nothing wrong with me. Although I have been taking up too much of your time."

She started to rise. Sam kept her in her seat with nothing more than a steady gaze.

"Have some tea," he said. "You'll feel better."

Both were an order.

Before she could protest, Jack appeared carrying a tray. There was a steaming mug of tea, along with a wrapped deli sandwich.

"We only have turkey left," the young man said apologetically as he set the tray on the glass coffee table.

The small amount of guilt she'd felt before doubled in size. "Look. You're being really nice—both of you. But there's no need to fuss."

The men ignored her. "Get on the computer," Sam told his assistant. "See if you can track down either Malcolm or White. You'll find a file in the usual place." He turned his considerable attention back to her. "You said your boss had left for the day. How do you get in touch with him? I want to let him know that the boxes can't be delivered. I'll also make arrangements for them to be returned to him." His fierce expression softened slightly. "He should never have left you to take care of them yourself."

"I didn't mind," she said weakly, feeling the floor beneath her crumbling into quicksand. In a matter of seconds she was going to sink so deep, no one would ever find her. "And you can't get in touch with him. He's, um, heading for the airport. To, ah, get on a plane."

She mentally winced. Lying had never come easily to her. Heading to the airport to get on a plane? Why else did people go to the airport?

Francesca sighed. Somehow this experiment had gotten out of hand. According to her research, Sam shouldn't have stopped to help her and he should never have taken things this far. The man was messing with her data.

"What airline? What flight?" He pulled a small leather covered notebook from his jacket pocket.

Francesca didn't know what to say. "You won't be able to track him down."

"Try me."

Uh oh. She was in way over her head. She gave Jack a

frantic "rescue me" look which he either didn't get or chose to ignore. Jason, the big and strong, poked his head in the office to inform them that he'd put the boxes in Conference Room 2. Jack disappeared with Jason, closing the door behind them. Leaving her very much alone with a man obviously capable of ruling the universe.

"So, Ms. Marcelli, your boss's flight? His name would help, as well."

"Please call me Francesca," she said and reached for the tea. Her stomach growled, but she refused to touch the sandwich. Not while she was here under false pretenses. "Can you really get in contact with someone on a plane?"

"If I have to. It would be easier to reach him before he left. Is he driving down to Los Angeles, or taking a corporate flight out of Santa Barbara?"

Francesca thought of all the times she'd created situations to find out if strangers would take the trouble to stop and help her. She'd had nice old ladies offer her rides, friendly couples give her directions, even the odd school kid help her find a lost dog. But never had anyone taken things as far as Sam Reese. Nor had any of her other subjects bothered her as much as him, either.

She drew in a deep breath. "You've been great," she said. "Really terrific. I don't know how to thank you."

His tawny gaze settled on her face. She regretted her dull colored hair and over-sized glasses, not to mention the deliberately unflattering make-up. Successful, gorgeous men like him didn't much inhabit her grad school world. Why couldn't she have put on her sexy biker girl disguise today instead of ugly pregnant woman?

Sam waited patiently. As if he had all the time in the world. As if he was used to people being reluctant to give up information.

"If you don't want me to track down your boss, that's your decision," he said. "At least eat something. For the baby, if not for yourself."

She really wished he would stop mentioning the pregnancy. Okay, so in all the years she'd been doing this sort of thing, she'd never once been put in a position of coming clean, but hey, this wasn't her fault. She was being overwhelmed by guilt. Well, guilt and a more-than-mild attraction to a handsome guy.

"I'm not pregnant," she said.

His gaze never left her face. One point for his side. She pulled off her glasses and tossed them on the table. It was a small gesture of vanity, but under the circumstance—wearing the world's ugliest dress, sensible shoes, and an unflattering hair style—it was the best she could do.

"I'm a grad student studying social psychology. I observe how people react under different circumstances. In my work I'm trying to see if social standing, appearance or gender influence behavior."

Sam tucked his notepad back into his jacket pocket. One eyebrow rose slightly. "Will busy people eager to get home on a Friday afternoon stop and help a pregnant woman?"

"Exactly."

His eyes narrowed as he studied her face. She wanted to say something stupid, like she cleaned up real well, but held back.

"What's in the boxes?"

She cleared her throat. "Mixed paper recycling."

"You deliberately chose to address them to a company that had recently closed?"

"Yes."

This time his gaze dropped to her protruding stomach. "And that?"

"A medical condition."

His eyes widened.

She laughed softly. "Just kidding. It's a device to simulate pregnancy. I borrowed it from a maternity store. Women use it to see how clothes will look as the baby gets bigger."

He picked up the glasses and glanced through the lenses. "Clear."

He smiled. A slow, sexy smile that made her long to trade in her black sensible shoes for a pair of red strappy sandals.

"I'm not easy to fool, Francesca," he told her. "You did a hell of job. The fainting was a nice touch."

She shrugged. "Actually that part was real. I haven't eaten all day and that messes with my blood sugar."

He motioned to her protruding belly. "You spend your day like this in the name of scientific research?"

"I don't always dress up with a pregnancy belly. Sometimes I go out in a wheelchair, or tattoos and black leather."

He leaned back against the sofa. "That would stop traffic."

She smiled. "That depends on where I am." She reached for the tea. "There have been dozens of studies done about the affect of appearance on behavior. Do you know that more people will stop to help an attractive person than an unattractive one?"

"Men are visual creatures."

"But it's not just men. Women do it, too. I'm studying—" She stopped and put down her tea. "Sorry. I get on a roll. My studies fascinate me."

"I can see why. Who are you going to be tomorrow? If your costume involves black leather, feel free to stop by."

She laughed. "Actually I'm supposed to be done with the research phase. My project for the summer is to write my dissertation. But the thought of spending all that time at the computer makes my skin crawl so I've been putting it off."

"What do you want me to do with the boxes?"

"Oh. I can take them with me. I need to return the cart, too. I borrowed it from the building maintenance guy."

"So he gets full points for helping out the pregnant lady?"

"Absolutely."

"What about me?"

Sam had a great voice, Francesca thought as a shiver rippled through her. Deep, rich, seductive.

"You get bonus points," she told him.

"Good to know." He angled toward her. "How about I let you keep the points and in return you join me for dinner tonight?"

Under normal circumstances, Francesca never would have accepted the invitation. She didn't know Sam Reese from a rock. Yes, he was plenty appealing, but in the scheme of things, did that really matter?

"Dumb question," she murmured as she maneuvered her truck through the early evening Santa Barbara traffic. It was early June, with the tourist season in full swing. Sidewalks were crowded, restaurants full, and traffic moved at a crawl down State Street.

"Appeal matters."

So did those cat eyes, the tempting smile, and easy conversation. But the real reason she'd said yes was she needed to have sex. After all, a promise was a promise.

Francesca grinned as she thought of Sam's reaction if she'd told him that particular truth. Would he have bolted for safety or started unbuttoning his shirt? She liked to think it would be the latter, but she'd taken a good look at herself when she'd gone home to change and her out-loud shriek hadn't been from pleasure. Nope, the man would have run for his life.

One shower with three shampoos to get the powder out of her hair, a quick change of clothes and a light dusting of make-up later, she was ready to, if not dazzle, then at least intrigue. She figured with as bad she'd looked before, anything would be an improvement.

So she was off to dazzle Sam Reese and see what she could do about keeping her promise . . . the one she'd made to have sex with the next attractive, single man to cross her path.